THE ANNIVERSARY

 RANDOM HOUSE NEW YORK

THE ANNIVERSARY

Rachel Canon

Library of Congress Cataloging-in-Publication Data

Canon, Rachel.
The Anniversary / Rachel Canon.—1st ed.
p.   cm.
ISBN 0-679-43731-2
I. Title.
PS3553.A537J36   1996
813',54—dc20   95-4717

Random House website address: http://www.randomhouse.com/

Manufactured in the United States of America on acid-free paper.
9 8 7 6 5 4 3 2
First Edition

Book design by Lilly Langotsky

FOR ANN

Acknowledgments

As this is my first book, I'm indebted to practically everyone on the planet for inspiration and support in one way or another. I'd particularly like to acknowledge my agent, Molly Friedrich, whose phone call when I was still knee-deep in glass from the Northridge earthquake started everything rocking again, and my editor, Kate Medina, whose steadfast confidence in this book kept me going. I'm also grateful to Sheri Holman and Frances Jalet-Miller, whose insight and ideas were invaluable, and to my friend Barbara Woolhandler, who provided a home away from home in New York.

I owe a great deal to fellow writers Jane Baeumler, Christine Culler, Miriam Ellenbogen Sidanius, and Donas John, who suffered through every word with me at our workshop meetings, as well as to dear friends, David Saindon and Kathleen Scott, who simply suffered with me.

My thoughts on virtual reality were gleaned from myriad sources, including Michael Deering's lecture "Virtual Reality 101" at the 1993 World Science Fiction Convention, and Howard Rheingold's excellent book *Virtual Reality.*

To Lusijah Marx, Maureen Sterling-Reeves and Mary Forst—thanks for the years, the adventures and the unique contributions to my life. To my late friend Ann Parkinson Woolf—this one's for you.

And, finally, I want to acknowledge my extraordinary family. My son and daughter, Roderick and Marcella Casilli; their father, Richard; and my mother, Marvel Canon, who read me poetry before I could walk.

THE ANNIVERSARY

It was a lucky day for the photographer who caught the shot. Melanie wore a bright red muffler that matched her cheeks and set off the flurry of yellow hair that bounced above it. She stood firmly in the middle of the sidewalk on a frozen dirty New York street, blue eyes blazing, arms spread wide. Her words came out in frosty puffs. She was speaking Spanish.

In front of her, a half dozen Puerto Rican youths with nail-studded two-by-fours and other homemade weapons shifted their feet and spat obscenities. Behind her, the sidewalk had cleared except for one old man who stood in the doorway of his small grocery, a shotgun clutched in his arms. The boys had come to teach him a lesson—he and his fat Italian wife, who counted every piece of fruit. And Melanie Lombard, hearing the angry clamor from down the block, had intervened, placing her slight body between age and youth, between have and have-not, between fear and anger.

The first boy called her bluff—he tried to step around her, daring the old man to use his weapon, taunting him with smirks and gestures. Melanie was faster, blocking his path with her small frame and tilting her head to meet his eyes. She was a New York City councilwoman—somebody important, even then—and the boy knew it, but that wouldn't have stopped him. He was a street child, filled with primal wrath and battered defiance; he seethed, ready to explode—then, suddenly, his coiled muscles slackened in confusion. What made him fling his board onto the sidewalk and walk away is still their secret . . . something she whispered to his face . . . in his language . . . something now only he knows.

It played in the *Times* the next day as bravado in black and white. What most people remember, though, is the full-color poster that launched the campaign that made Melanie Lombard the first woman president of the United States. Created fifteen years later by a savvy aide who saw a way to quicken the national pulse with a single image, the poster featured that same photo: Melanie with her red muffler and red cheeks, five feet four inches of blond courage, facing down everybody's fears in the form of Enrico Perez, with his pals threatening in the background. For millions of people, that image spoke to an underlying sense of helplessness; of course, it made Melanie Lombard a superhero.

The poster was particularly effective in the five boroughs where that same Enrico, now a grown-up ACLU attorney, served as her campaign manager. People still associate Melanie with the red muffler, but sometimes they forget its history. I've probably told this story a hundred times.

She wasn't wearing her famous red muffler that day. She had on an expensive tailored suit, befitting her new position. It was a suit I had never seen before, and a far cry from the caliber of clothes we had worn during those years we shared a wardrobe. On television, it appeared a soft beige—before it was splashed with blood; I only glimpsed it clearly for a moment. It's Hank's face that stands out the most on the TV clips. Stark, scarcely human, his shock splits your reason; his pain brands your heart. Melanie is barely seen at all; she falls too quickly. How does the world end? With the zing of a bullet . . . the ring of a telephone.

ONE

Two thoughts from that day remain. One has to do with a blind spot in my perception. But the first is pure sex.

I piece it together this way: sometime around noon, I pushed aside the cold coffee and the stack of unread software proposals, cupped the palms of my hands tightly over my eyes and attempted to convince myself that my life was not about that lusty kind of love that ends up feeling like a heavy rock in your stomach. *Sex distorts things, makes you forget who you are!*—I probably whispered that bit of wisdom to myself several times, making sure the point was absorbed by the more stubborn parts of my body.

I was, of course, trying to rationalize. Just the night before, an impossibly young man named Kent had abruptly broken off our brief relationship. Oh, I knew he'd leave eventually; I was too old for him—he wanted kids for God's sake—but Kent and I had barely gotten started and I recall being very attracted to him. I was experiencing that intense, sixteen-again class of suffering, embarrassing in its shallowness; I just wanted to put it behind me and get on with my work.

And so, on that day, at that particular moment, I was in the midst of performing a simple bit of emotional exorcism—the same process I'd used many times before—when Thought Number Two slipped in through a side synapse, did a wheelie through my right hemisphere and rudely parked itself in the space reserved for "focus." *How do you know there's any more to you than that? Any more than sex?* Now that was definitely an atypical tack for my mind to take, coming from nowhere; I recall feeling confused. What about all those lofty qualities that were supposed to define me? And then the phone rang.

It must have been the impact, the force of the moment, that froze only these memories, caused them to remain while everything else—the horror, shock, outrage that I surely must have felt when I heard the news—is gone. The rest of the day, from that phone call on, is gone too. I'm told that I spilled a cup of coffee over a box of floppy disks; that I threw myself onto a plane and arrived luggageless at Dulles Airport in Washington. I recall none of it. The day Melanie Lombard died—the day my closest friend was assassinated—my brain did a fetal act, curling up like a ball in yesterday's corner.

On some level, of course, I didn't believe it. Although the radio insisted and anchorpeople hung their heads and newspaper headlines stared out at me in indelible hard copy, I valiantly hoped it was all a mistake, some mass perceptual disorder. But if there *is* power in the mind to alter the roller-coaster state of reality, I didn't have it. Melanie was dead; she left the world before she had a chance to change it. As for me, as for all those bold, bigger-than-sex ideas I thought my life was about, they died along with her.

Melanie was supposed to be invincible—she took it for granted and so did I. I imagined her as a core of granite surrounded by a force-field of guardian angels.

I think I started believing in her magic the very first time I saw her, an hour or so after I arrived at Penn, on our first day of college. As I gazed out the window of my fourth-floor dorm room, I noticed a small blond girl lugging a metal trunk across the quad; I watched her stop, look around at the trees, the ivy, the university-perfect lawn. In an instant she was surrounded by helping hands; strong backs hoisted her trunk, friendly upperclassmen pointed her in the direction of the dorm.

Melanie was my new roommate, then my ally, finally my best friend. From the beginning she had that uncanny ability to make things work. When I met her, I was stuck in an emotional cul-de-sac; my parents' divorce only two months before had upset my view of the world. Then Melanie reached out to me, adjusted a few dials, and all of a sudden *I* worked, too.

With the confident eyes of an insider, I watched Melanie ace each college exam, graduate with honors and go on to soar through law school—absorbing information, formulating ideas, building her vision as she grew. It was a vision so big that it took your breath away, and her special talent was getting people to share it with her; she made her "big picture" seem so exciting, you almost forgot how amazingly idealistic it really was.

It was easy to believe in her, because she believed in herself so absolutely. She also believed in everyone else. No one was too small, too insignificant, too ruined; she never gave up on anyone. That alone made people love her.

Wherever Melanie went, she walked boldly—even in the streets of New York, no mugger dared touch her. Over the years, I watched her scale the ranks, staring down the mighty, until finally she achieved the pinnacle of what every little boy could grow up to be.

There are majorities and there are majorities—silent, moral, however you want to tweak it—but Melanie Lombard crossed all lines. Her clear blue eyes met and held the gaze of a diverse humanity, tired of getting the short end of compromise.

It turned out, though, that she was not invincible. In the end, a crazy got her—a crazy *woman*, no less—and Melanie was dead. There's no compromise available when you're dead. Dead is black and white . . . beyond the realm . . . berserk. Melanie Lombard had been president of the United States for exactly three days.

And so when a reporter phoned me this morning, on the first anniversary of her death, I didn't mind being interviewed. A million little girls still mourn Melanie and I can tell them nearly everything about her; I can pass along all the encouragements she would want me to give them. I didn't resent the call, but it started the cyclone inside me all over again.

It's ironic that Kent's face is the only clear picture I have from the day Melanie died, the only image that isn't distorted, surreal. I lean back in my desk chair and close my eyes, studying the memory of his face, hoping, I suppose, that it will help me fit myself properly into that day so I can experience it once and for all; it doesn't work. All I see is Kent, his lips forming words, telling me that I make him feel too much like—what was the word he used?—oh yes, like fluff. When the phone rings again, I'm glad for the interruption.

"It's Mr. Cochran. The elder," Katy announces through the intercom. Melanie's husband, not Melanie's son.

"Hi, Hank," I say. "Media hounding you today too?"

The man who was America's first gentleman for three whole days groans. "I ought to make a recording I can play back: 'Yes, the late president scrupulously replaced the cap on the toothpaste tube. No, she would never have backed down on her key programs. Actually, I have no idea if she's tried to contact me from the other side, I'm out a lot.' "

"Oh Hank, yuk."

"I'm going to get the same questions every year, so I guess I'd better get used to it. Look, Nora, I'm flying out to the West Coast tonight; I need to talk to you."

I offer to pick him up at the airport. "It'll be great to see you" collides in my head with "What's up?" I say neither.

I notice my hand is shaking when I hang up the receiver and it isn't from the pot and a half of coffee I drank this morning. Hank and I are old friends and we get together whenever we can, but he rarely comes to LA. When he does, it's usually with lots of advance notice so he and his son Bennie have time to memorize their lines and put on those stiff masks they wear around each other.

For the rest of the day, I spin. That's what a computer-disk drive does when it malfunctions—spins away tirelessly, reading and writing zilch. Katy, an aspiring actress who plays my secretary between auditions, diverts all calls. Besides being one of the leading causes of male whiplash in West Los Angeles, Katy has this confidential alto voice that makes most men forget instantly why they called—the strategic benefits outweigh the occasional frustrations.

My company, Learning Parallels, develops educational software for computers. We're nowhere near as big as the multipurpose software giants, but so far no one designs better software dedicated solely to education. It's an exciting business, particularly right now, with our industry on the verge of important breakthroughs. My job as executive VP in charge of product development is to make sure Learning Parallels always comes in first.

That means I spend most of my time searching through the work of techie geniuses looking for some innovative twist we can develop into a hit. After twenty-two years on one end or the other of the computer business I'm still astounded by the possibilities, but I need to make sure ingenuity stays within the boundaries of dollar signs—what a public school system, for example, can afford. I can't let my excitement override the analytical strategies I picked up along with my Harvard MBA.

It's not always an easy call. Over the last year, distracted and depressed by Melanie's death, I've been nervous that I might blink and find the company and myself stuck back in the starting gate looking at everyone else's backsides.

On this day especially, self-doubt makes me read everything twice. A proposal from our London office seems very interesting, but I'm having trouble reading between the lines. As far as I know, what it describes isn't quite possible. I page back to the beginning and start over when Katy interrupts me. Danny Court is on the phone.

"Nora, it's the president . . . *of the United States.*"

"Oh?" I say, feigning nonchalance. But in truth, I have never before received a call from this particular president of the United States. I met him twice within the same week, at Melanie's inauguration, and then again at her funeral.

"Hello, Mr. President. What can I do for you?"

"Call me Danny." There's a pause, the sort one refers to as "with child." "Nora, I realize it's unusual for me to call. I just . . . wanted to talk to you today. You know your face is one of my most vivid memories from that dreadful afternoon at Arlington—you, standing next to Henry." His voice conjures up a strong visual in my mind of his TV image: too much sandy hair, those perfectly aging, boy-next-door features.

"To tell you the truth, I don't remember much about the funeral," I admit.

He goes right on as if I haven't spoken. His tone is almost intimate, as if we're old friends. "I didn't really know her well, although we spent a lot of hours together during the campaign. I could count on one hand the number of times I'd talked to her before that. It's my loss and I regret it every day. Melanie was . . . is . . . an impossible act to follow. It would have helped a lot if I had known her better."

I listen to his words, carefully straining to imagine what, in the name of anything, he wants from me. "Well, I knew her very well, Danny, but the things I know wouldn't help you."

He laughs. "I wouldn't be too sure about that, Nora. I asked her once, somewhere in the middle of that amazing campaign . . . you know how she had an incredible ability to walk right out on a limb? A dozen politically adept, scholarly advisers would be clinging to the trunk, but out she'd go, and it would hold her—and it'd work?"

He waits, but I can't say anything. I know too well exactly what he means. It hurts to be reminded of how much was wasted.

"Well, I asked her how she could do that. How she could be so sure. And she told me that whenever she had any doubts she asked Nora."

My stomach contracts as if he'd punched me. "We knew each other a long time," I say. "We had developed an interesting synergy."

"I hope you don't mind my sharing that story with this author—what's his name? Weinhardt. He said he'd heard it more than once already. By the way, I liked him. I think he'll write a good book about her."

"I hope so; I haven't met him yet, but I've read some of his work." My hand, holding the shiny black receiver, is starting to shake again. It's impossible for me to simply talk to this man. You don't just chat with the president of the United States! Not with this one, anyway. *I don't even know him.* "Mr. Pres . . . Danny. Are you trying to tell me something?"

Another long pause. I attempt to picture him sitting behind that huge desk in the Oval Office, but I can't. "To tell you the truth, Nora, I've got a problem. I've been struggling with myself over the commitment I made when I signed on to run with Melanie Lombard, when I accepted the job of vice president. Now it's all in my lap and the kind of politics I've always practiced just isn't working. As no doubt you've noticed." *What does all this have to do with me?* I'm wondering.

"Correction," he says, "it's working the way it always worked . . . which is barely. Melanie would never have stood for the nonsense I've put up with, and her memory deserves better. Certainly the people who elected us deserve better."

I have no idea how to respond. He's right—he didn't really know her. No one could fairly expect him to accomplish what she would have; after all, he's only human. These thoughts flash through my mind but dissolve, thank heaven, before they reach my lips. Of course I know that Melanie was human too, and she was very much a politician. It's just that she—well, she was definitely special.

My silence doesn't seem to bother him; he goes on in the same frank tone. "I'm making some changes that I can't talk about quite yet, but I know you were an important part of Melanie's success from the beginning, and I'd like to line up your support."

Another punch in the stomach. This time the blow bounces up to stick in my throat; I barely manage an answer. "My involvement in politics ended with a bullet, Danny. I . . . I just don't think I have the heart for it."

"I understand how you feel," he says. "I'm not even sure what I'm asking at this point—maybe just for you to think about what you'd do if you were in my place. You don't have to say anything now, but I hope we can talk again."

As soon as I hang up, Katy pokes her head in the door, eyes propped wide with question marks. *No* must be written all over my face, because she looks disappointed and withdraws quickly. I stare for a minute at the walls of my big corner office, watching the dance of sunlight refracted through vertical miniblinds. All of a sudden I feel scared. People say I'm tough, but I've never been the Russian-roulette kind of tough that Melanie was. *Melanie is dead.* And I'm sitting here spinning like a broken disk drive.

It occurs to me that I've been sitting here in a daze for a whole year. Sure, I've gone home each night and come back to work every morning. I've marched on numbly. But I might as well have never moved from this chair. It's as if she took all the meaning with her when she died, and I don't know what to do to bring back the spark.

For the first time in more than a dozen months, I start to cry. I lay my head down on a sheaf of papers and finally let loose with a torrent of life/death/goddamnit/fear and misery tears. So help me, like a baby.

TWO

ank's plane is due in at 8:30 and it's already past eight when I pull out of my driveway. I've been to the gym, showered and changed into a pair of navy blue sweats. My hair is still a little damp, but my spirits have lifted. It's more than the exercise endorphins. Emotionally relieving myself all over my desk this afternoon had the same effect as telling a secret. It left me a little embarrassed, very drained, but a lot lighter. It's a feeling I haven't experienced in a while.

That's because I've always been such a superb keeper of secrets, I remind myself, gunning my Nissan Z up the freeway ramp toward the airport—other people's secrets. The thought carries its own sadness. In my darkest hours I fear that by keeping other people's secrets I helped form them as "secrets," molded, added substance—making me, in some bizarre way, also responsible for them. Nora Whitney, the trusted secret-keeper—part control freak, part voyeur.

I'm sure I haven't any secrets of my own; that's a whiny little complaint tied to the fact that to have secrets you've really got to care about something, and the things I've cared about have a way of disappearing—Melanie, the several men in my life. So the exposure makes me crazy. I remember secrets can be insidious, puffing life up into something it isn't. Secrets can be deadly.

A monster truck blares its horn as I slide in front of it to join the flowing light show. To me, the freeway at night looks like a computer game—sixteen streaming illuminated lines, half white, half red, and an occasional flash of yellow when the lines decide to cross one another. Same kinds of rules and limitations. Same fleeting sense of being in control. Gearshift, joystick, whatever.

And, of course, I can't help remembering:

"I only have one real secret," Melanie had said, sitting cross-legged on the upper bunk of our tiny college dorm room. *"One thing I've never told anybody."*

I step on the gas and whip across into the fast lane. Yeah, Melanie, and it was a nice one. I didn't think much about it at the time, only that it was kind of weird the way she took it so seriously. We'd been roommates for a year. We knew all about each other's first loves, pet peeves and most embarrassing moments. For a major holdback, this secret was a disappointment, but in fact it changed things between us, bonded us in a special way. Perhaps some part of me had already accepted the role I would play, in her life, in mine, even then.

"When I was four years old, my mother told me I would grow up to be the president of the United States. And I believed her." The strange tightness in Melanie's voice kept me from laughing. *"I mean I really believed her. For a long time—until I was twelve—for eight whole years of my childhood, I was absolutely convinced I was a future president. I didn't know it was practically impossible. Then one day . . . well, it was like I just woke up."*

Her blue eyes looked down at me with such perplexity, like a little girl lost in an illusion she didn't understand. A minute later, her face relaxed and she giggled. *"Can you believe that? What a weirdo I was,"* she said. We never talked about it after that. I never told anyone and neither did she—not even Hank.

And years later, when it had begun to happen, I held my breath as well as my tongue. At the convention, with the nomination in the bag, our eyes locked across a cheering crowd. On election night, she took my hand and squeezed it. Melanie's mother was an odd duck, and no psychic. It's just the best damned example of self-fulfilled prophecy I've ever seen.

The traffic into LAX is lighter than usual and I swing around to the United terminal with a minute to spare. It's occurred to me more than once that Melanie's big secret illustrates a primary difference between us. My father must have told me a million times that I was the smartest little girl in the world, could get anything I wanted. I just never knew how to make it come true.

A crowd is milling inside the baggage claim area, and I make a show of rolling down the window and straining to peer through the doors so the uniformed airport gent will know I'm "loading." A timely gesture, for otherwise I might have missed seeing the two men emerge from the double doors, pause, sweep the curb with identical scanner gazes and climb into the Chevrolet Caprice parked about twenty feet in front of me.

I was around Melanie enough during the campaign to recognize that these men have all the mannerisms of the Secret Service, including being impeccably dressed, like governmental twins. What are they doing here? I can't help wondering if my face, car and license plate number have been noted for the record, although they were professional enough not to let a glance pass between them.

Hank is only a few bodies behind the two agents. As he bends to show his luggage tag to the woman at the exit, I notice how his once-thick hair has given way to a clearing on the top of his head. I lean across the seat and wave.

"I have company, as you can see," he says, nodding toward the car in front of us. He tosses his bag in the backseat and slides in beside me.

"Yeah, I spotted them. Secret Service—what are they doing here?"

He hugs me and smiles. "Protecting me, so the story goes. This being the first anniversary of the assassination, the late president's husband merits an official escort—sort of a cautious formality. These guys are pretty low-level; they won't be intrusive."

I can't help shivering. From the day Melanie announced her candidacy, the Secret Service was everywhere—but I never got used to them. The sight of all those regimented men and women moving around according to strict procedures punched big holes in that strongbox where I'd tucked away the notion of vulnerability. Something bad *could* happen—and it did. I start the motor and pull across two lanes, out into the loop. "But there's no particular reason?" I ask Hank. "No threats, no terrorists in town?"

"Not that I've been told. Of course, you know me—I'm more inclined to think they're using this as an excuse to keep tabs on me. It's never as simple as it seems."

"Danny Court called me today," I say, watching in the rearview mirror as the Chevy maneuvers to keep pace with us.

That gets a reaction. Hank looks at me as if I've grown an extra head. "What did Court want?"

"He said he was making some changes that he couldn't talk about yet, that he might need my help and wanted me to think about it. Nothing really specific. It's odd. I mean, I helped Melanie because I knew her so well, but there have to be a zillion people around who are more skilled in politics than I am. I'm not sure what Court could want from me."

Hank frowns, staring at me as if he's trying to read my mind. "Sounds like the president is thinking of trying something heroic. You . . . you wouldn't really want to get mixed up in that sort of thing again, would you?" There's an edge to his voice that makes me uncomfortable. Suddenly I remember that his spur-of-the-moment visit is not at all usual.

"Probably not. I don't know, actually." I glance at him quickly, then back at the street. He looks miserable. "When are you going to tell me why you're here?" I ask.

"Can we stop someplace? I still can't eat airline food."

The Chevy trails a few car lengths behind us. I pull off Sepulveda and take some side streets to a Mexican restaurant I remember. We're greeted by authentic Mexican decor, several Hispanic women pat tortillas right off the lobby, but the hostess is a fortyish redhead with a Brooklyn accent. She seats us at a booth in the corner; her smile is generic, there's not the slightest gleam in her heavily made-up eyes. It always amazes me how few people recognize Hank. *The president's husband, for heaven's sake!* The media played him up as a feminist cult hero, yet only once since Melanie's death has he been recognized in my company. It was at a cocktail party in Beverly Hills. A very young girl—ironically the date of an ex-lover of mine—came bounding up to tell us that her mother still kept his picture magnetized to the refrigerator.

"When do you meet with this writer, David Weinhardt?" Hank asks abruptly, after the waitress has brought us a couple of double margaritas.

"This week sometime. Maybe even tomorrow. I'd have to check my book."

"Well, look," Hank says, staring at me funny. "I don't know how fast he's going to put it together, but eventually he will. It could jeopardize everything Melanie tried to build."

Hank's eyes are a paler blue and less intense than Melanie's. He's a good-looking man, but he usually has this otherworldly air that comes from being incredibly rich, and a scholar—Hank's never had to bother with the nitty-gritty, he's concerned with things on a more lofty level. But not tonight. His tense shoulders and narrowed eyes form a singular focus that's more than a little alarming. I lick the edge of my glass, feeling the need for salt. "What's up?"

"Jacques DeBrin."

Margarita slush splashes over my chin. I haven't heard Jacques's name since I got up the nerve some years back to tell it to my therapist. I dab at my face with a napkin, not wanting to meet Hank's eyes. "That's certainly a jolt into the distant past. Is this writer going to interview her kindergarten teacher too?"

"Jacques DeBrin may have been Melanie's lover."

"Oh, for God's sake, Hank, so what? It was a summer fling, over twenty-five years ago. She was a kid. Long before she ever laid eyes on you. This guy's a reputable journalist. How can he make anything out of that?"

Hank reaches over and takes my hand. My heart goes cold. "Melanie had been seeing Jacques. At least twice a year. The whole time she was in the Senate. Right up until the campaign for president took off."

"That's not possible. No."

"Yes. I'm pretty sure it's true." He looks at me, his eyes sad, then he takes a sip of his margarita, letting the news sink in.

But it isn't sinking in. My body has gone rigid, every part of me is rejecting his words as if they were alien organs. She wouldn't have done this—at least not without telling me. She couldn't have had a secret affair during the whole time she was in the Senate—that would be ten years. Besides, she *knew* about me and Jacques.

Misreading my distress as a reflection of his own, Hank is eager to share the comfort of a pathetic rationale.

"It may be more complicated than it seems. It's impossible for me to believe that Melanie would risk everything for a sexual attraction. There must have been another reason. Information. He must have been a contact."

I'm too numb to say what I'm thinking—*Oh, come on!* Instead, I stare at a large painting hanging behind Hank's head of a group of Navajo women squatting on the ground, working their fingers into red clay. The stark simplicity of their task nearly makes me sick with longing. Finally I manage to ask, "Tell me how you found out about this."

"When this guy Weinhardt first started gathering material for the book about Melanie, I gave him a list of Melanie's friends. I just went through her address book and pulled everyone I could find that she kept in contact with. One of the names was Cynthia Jacobson—I think you knew her as Cynthia Powell—from Penn. She and her husband have a place outside Philadelphia. Melanie used to visit them now and then. To unwind. I only met them once when they came to Washington. We took them to dinner."

The waitress brings Hank a plate of flaming fajitas, and while she adjusts all the condiments before him my mind does a quick scan through our undergraduate years. There was a girl named Cynthia Powell who lived across the hall from us our freshman year. I don't recall seeing her after that first year and I know she and Melanie never became close friends. But I'm not ready to tell Hank that.

Hank piles a little of everything on a tortilla and takes a bite. I stare at the table, trying to force back the cold premonition that's edging out my shock.

"A couple of days ago Weinhardt came to the apartment," he continues. "We'd arranged to go through a box of Melanie's old pictures. In an envelope at the bottom of the box was a snapshot taken that summer the two of you went to Paris. He took one look at it and muttered some comment about the elusive Jacobsons."

"You're losing me."

"The photo was of Melanie and Jacques and you and Dennis Jacobson. 'Jacques's flat' was written on the back. Weinhardt assumed that you were Cynthia Powell Jacobson because Dennis Jacobson, the man with you in the picture, is Cynthia's husband."

Dennis. The American boy Jacques fixed me up with. After twenty-five years I don't remember him very well. But then I didn't pay much attention to him while I was with him.

"It didn't click with me at first," Hank goes on. "I looked at the picture and, sure enough, there was a youthful version of the Dennis Jacobson we'd taken to dinner. Melanie never said that he and his wife were *both* old friends, but it didn't seem that strange. Maybe she introduced them."

The chill continues to work its way from nerve to nerve. I'm a step ahead of him now. It doesn't matter who Cynthia is. There's only one reason why Melanie would keep in touch with Dennis Jacobson—Jacques's American friend—only one possible reason.

"It wasn't until Weinhardt told me about his attempts to interview Cynthia Jacobson that I started to get suspicious. He said he phoned to set up an appointment, but she seemed very upset, wouldn't talk to him. He happened to be going to Philadelphia anyway—his family's there—so he dropped by, thinking maybe she was just nervous, that he could convince her his intentions were honorable. Dennis answered the door, told him in no uncertain terms to go away and leave his wife alone—that they wanted absolutely nothing to do with the book. That's how Weinhardt recognized Dennis in the photo. But he never saw Cynthia, so he just assumed that you were—"

"—that I was Cynthia. And you didn't tell him. But he'll clear that one up soon enough. Why do you think he suspects something about Jacques?"

"I don't think he does. But I could tell it bothered him that Cynthia Jacobson wouldn't let him interview her. It's public knowledge that he's doing the book with my blessing, so why were the Jacobsons behaving like that? What were they so afraid of? If it didn't smell right to me, you can bet it didn't smell right to him.

"It was after he left that I started thinking. Why had Melanie never mentioned knowing Dennis all those years? Then I thought about the weekends she spent at Cynthia's house. But most of all, I kept looking at that picture of the four of you. At her face. At Jacques's face. To make a long story short, I called up Jacobson and tried a bluff. I told him I knew about Melanie and Jacques and was trying to keep it from Weinhardt, to protect her image. He admitted he was their liaison—that they'd used his home as a meeting place."

"Oh, Hank."

He bends to his plate, jerkily spooning the filling into a cold tortilla. I watch him in silence. His face has the look of a man trying to fight his way out of a nightmare and I suppose it's the latest version of the same nightmare he's been carrying with him since the day Melanie died—a dream full of plots and whispers, the echo of his own voice, incredulous, crying that they got away with it, and nobody pays any attention. Melanie's assassin, Jennie Wheeler, was completely insane. Three renowned psychiatrists testified to that fact; there wasn't even a real trial. And the Senate commission that investigated the assassination unanimously proclaimed that Jennie Wheeler had acted alone, but Hank still doesn't believe it.

Now, piled on top of all his pain at losing her, he has to face the age-old curse of cuckoldry. No wonder he's desperately trying to sweep it under some rug, turn Jacques into something else, a spy, anything but a lover. My heart hurts for him, and for a second it's almost enough to make me forget that in all this Melanie betrayed me too.

Hank puts down his napkin and reaches inside his breast pocket, taking out a thick envelope and laying it on the table. "I need to ask you a favor, Nora. I think it's critical for us to find out what's at stake here—what kind of domino effect might occur if Melanie is linked to this . . . Frenchman."

I'm thinking that it's obvious what will happen. Melanie Lombard, the first female US president, aka the perfect woman, aka the brilliant martyr of the new order, will topple from her pedestal.

Hank's eyes are faded blue stone as he pushes the envelope across the table. "Here. It's an airline ticket to London—Paris would be too risky. You and Jacques DeBrin are old friends. Go see him. See if you can find out something powerful enough to convince Weinhardt to let it go. He's writing a biography, not a political exposé."

The thought of standing face-to-face with Jacques after all these years washes over me like an arctic wave. I pick up the envelope, but don't open it. "What makes you think Jacques had access to any sort of confidential information?" I ask. "The key talent of the Jacques De-Brin I knew was picking up girls in Place de la Concorde." *And in airport bars!* I think, but I'm careful to keep the memory off my face.

The words of Hank's response are slow and deliberate. "You mean something besides the fact that my wife fully understood the effect she had on this nation, accepted her role as a sacred responsibility and would never have risked the obvious consequences for anything frivolous?" I simply look at him and say nothing. What can I say? "There is one thing, though," he continues. "I had a friend do some discreet checking; Jacques DeBrin appears to travel in the Middle East quite a lot: Libya, Algeria, Saudi Arabia—just in the past year. Some sort of business." He raises his eyebrows meaningfully.

This last disclosure sends my brain into overload. Flashes of thought collide in my head, split into fragments; nothing makes sense anymore. I put the envelope in my purse. "Let me see if I can work it out."

London. My mind races. Hank knows Learning Parallels has an office there; it's our company's only overseas operating unit, handling distribution in the European market. The small research and development section—my baby—hasn't produced much so far, but there's that proposal I read this afternoon. Yes, I decide. I can go to London. I have a very good reason to go to London.

Dennis Jacobson's home and office phone numbers are written inside the travel packet, so I agree to call and ask him to contact Jacques, see if he can set up a meeting. The two Secret Servicemen are sitting at the far side of the room, nibbling on chips and salsa. They seem to be paying no attention to us. Hank notices me noticing them. "You know, this little escort could have something to do with Jacques," he suggests. "My phone could be tapped. Court might be looking for a way to discredit Melanie, sully the image that makes him pale in comparison."

The idea of President Court wanting to discredit Melanie doesn't seem very likely to me. If she gets dragged down, so will her programs and ideas, and he's already having a hard enough time trying to keep an agenda afloat. My look of disbelief must be obvious. Hank shakes his head. "Okay, I know I sound paranoid, but I don't trust Court . . . and the idea of you helping him out, whatever he wants you to do, makes me nervous. Just to humor me, why don't you call Dennis Jacobson from a public phone."

Hank pays the check and we leave. Within a block, the Chevy has caught up to us. "Tell me something, Hank, why did you pick today—of all days—to make this trip? Why not tomorrow? Or the next day?"

He looks away from me, out the window. "I couldn't trust myself to go to the university; I couldn't stand being in the apartment. Traveling today seemed like the best solution." Abruptly, he turns to face me, forcing a smile. "Besides, I thought it would be fun to make these Secret Service guys run around a bit."

"You're going to see Bennie while you're here, aren't you?" Despite the day's shocks, nothing can relieve me of my inherited task of helping father and son discover at least one thread of commonality.

"If he can fit me in. I have to take the red-eye back tomorrow night and you know how much Ben likes to make any last-minute change in his precious schedule."

"Are you going to tell him about all this?"

Hank looks at me as if I've suggested something perverse. "Why would I want to tell him? Not yet, anyway. Maybe he'll never have to know."

"It might help if you included him—if you didn't treat him like a child."

"I'm sure you're right. As his surrogate mother, you know him better than I do. But I don't think this is the place to start, Nora. Besides, the whole thing makes me sick. Let's find out more first."

I don't feel up to responding to that, so we drive the rest of the way to his hotel in silence. Exactly where do you start? At what point do you hold your breath and jump, praying that the other person is strong enough to hear what you have to say?

I trusted Melanie, but apparently she didn't really trust me.

"I'll call you tomorrow," Hank says, giving me a friendly peck on the cheek.

I wait until he gets inside, watch him give his bag to the bellman and disappear into the posh lobby. He still stands so straight, like some sort of traveling dignitary, but I can tell that now it takes an effort. He seems very tired and, suddenly, older. I can't help thinking how he must have looked the day she first saw him. That was back when my best friend and I shared our first apartment in New York City and she could never wait until morning to tell me anything.

"Nora, wake up—I met the most incredible man at the rally in Central Park this afternoon."

"Melanie . . . it's three o'clock in the morning."

"I just got in. We went to the movies. And we walked. He teaches history at Columbia, Aesthetic type, but funny. Tall, blond and he makes me laugh. His name's Hank and I think I'm in love."

I'm crying again . . . fat tears sliding down my face and soaking into my blue sweatshirt. Fuck you, Melanie. You and all your secrets.

THREE

When the alarm goes off at five-thirty, I jump as if someone just threw a rock through my window. The shattered remains of whatever I was dreaming are knocking around inside my head like a hangover. Groping my way to the kitchen, I switch on the coffee and lean against the counter, positioning my cup to intercept the first drops.

I arose at this ungodly hour to get to a pay phone and have a better chance of catching Dennis Jacobson on East Coast time. And I'm tired—even though I left Hank at his hotel around eleven, it was late when I finally got to sleep.

After pulling a half dozen boxes from the top shelf of my den closet and emptying their contents all over the floor, I finally found what I was looking for. Like hers, my copy of the photo has "Jacques's flat" written on the back in Melanie's hand. In it are four ecstatic young people obviously reveling in the hiatus of freedom between one responsibility and another. Melanie sits on Jacques's lap on a faded couch of indistinguishable color. I'm on the floor, the back of my head resting against her knee and a bottle of beer held high like a torch in my right hand. Dennis is sprawled awkwardly at my side, having dived into the shot a half second before the flash.

I sat here last night staring at Melanie's face, trying to see what

Hank had seen—what clue, hidden in her youthful features, had made him question his wife's fidelity enough to approach Dennis. He's never been the suspicious-husband type, no more than Melanie was the type to play around. She looks, in the photo, exactly as she looked then—not beautiful in the sense that my secretary Katy is, but certainly pretty and typically electric. I've never met anyone ever who gave off as much energy as Melanie Lombard did. Her blue eyes sparked; her complexion glowed as if she had a low-grade fever. She looked, nearly all the time, like the world's most terrific idea.

The dynamics of our little group are obvious in the picture, would be apparent even to someone from another planet who'd never heard of Melanie Lombard. Sitting on Jacques's lap, wearing cut-off blue-jeans, a red sleeveless shirt and scuffed white tennis shoes, Melanie is clearly the center. You can practically see the aura around her, an intense energy that embraces the rest of us, but emanates from her. What Hank saw in that snapshot, I realized last night, was a young woman who could clearly squeeze whatever she wanted from life, from the world, and whose boundaries had little in common with those of average folks.

Around her neck she is wearing the tiny locket Jacques bought her in Montmartre on the day the photo was taken. Fragments of that afternoon drifted back to me . . . how we stood on the hill outside Sacré Coeur and watched the sun set over the city . . . how we got caught in the rain walking back to the metro . . . Jacques's dark hair plastered wet against his achingly handsome face.

In the photograph, Jacques isn't looking at the camera. He's looking at her.

If anything in the picture can still reach out across the years, it's the obvious fact that the man on the couch is utterly in love.

Adding the look on Jacques's face to the glow on Melanie's, even a quarter of a century later, Hank had guessed. Sadly, I couldn't help thinking that if I'd studied the photo more carefully myself—way back when it was new—if I had truly seen that totally enamored, nearly engulfed look on Jacques's face, I would have known better. Then, four years later, wrapped in the warmth of his arms, I wouldn't have been foolish enough to think our embrace could end any differently than it did. I was still hurt and confused when I went to bed.

Jacques DeBrin, a man we had both loved, was another secret Melanie and I shared. The fleeting summer she and Jacques spent together, my even briefer affair with him a few years later—these memories had been absorbed into the body of a friendship that had earned its intimacy long before we met him. And continued to deserve it, or so I'd thought, until the day she died. He was like an old shared treasure, a souvenir of our youth.

But somewhere along the line he came back into her life . . . and she never told me. I think of the countless hours Melanie and I whispered together, confiding all our ups and downs. At what point did she become someone else?

The idea that Jacques could have been passing some sort of confidential information to Melanie—that their relationship might have been political—seems pretty far-fetched to me, but I understand why Hank seeks the comfort of such an explanation. I fell asleep last night caught between a tiny hope that he was right—that the force at work here was not that traitor Love, but some mysterious political tangle of global significance—and a vague, uneasy dread of the very same thing.

Daylight is just beginning to show through my kitchen window. I fill my cup and sit down at the table, propping my bare feet on the opposite chair and picking up the picture once again, trying to remember what Dennis Jacobson was like, before I call to ask him a favor after all these years.

The boy askew on the floor has a pleasant, open face, freckles and brown eyes. Looking at him, I recall a little—his infectious laugh, his caution, the way we sometimes had to wheedle him into doing things, the terror, then triumph, on his face the day Jacques took us hang gliding. Dennis was good, if not memorable, company on those warm summer days and nights. He was studying to be an engineer and Jacques had collected him the same way he collected us. There's only one person in the picture with whom I cannot possibly relate. The girl with the beer-bottle torch. Myself. She seems like a total stranger.

That Nora, I remind myself, was excited, driven, bordered on hyperactive. I wince at the funny haircut, shorter than I'd ever worn it before because I wanted it to be easier to take care of on the trip. Of course my thick dark hair never floated nicely about my head the way Melanie's did; it hung straight around my ears, waiflike, making me look like an underfed Roman senator. Still, there's something appealing, even attractive, about that old self with the younger, smoother features. She looks . . . well, she looks content. Did I ever really feel like that?

I throw on a pair of jeans and a sweatshirt, tuck a few bills in my pocket and head down the street. At Winchell's, I pay for a doughnut with a ten and take all my change in quarters. A few minutes later I'm plunking the quarters into the phone outside the 7-Eleven.

Dennis comes on the line after his secretary announces me; his voice sounds guarded. "Hello, Nora. It's been a long time."

"That it has. How are you, Dennis?"

"Normally, I'm just fine. Look, Nora, I told Henry Cochran to keep us out of this. I don't want that writer bothering my wife. She has nothing to do with it."

"I know that, but apparently you do. If Melanie's relationship with Jacques DeBrin becomes front-page news, you're likely to have a bit part in the story."

There's a soft sound in the phone as if he's just remembered to breathe. "Isn't it enough that she's dead? Why can't they just leave her alone?" His voice is pained. "Melanie Lombard was the only decent thing that's happened to this country in my lifetime. She cared about people, Nora; she inspired other people to care. She stood for real action—things that needed to be done. You know my wife is sick, thinking we might be part of something that could drag down her memory."

"Dennis, is it true what Hank told me? Were Melanie and Jacques meeting for years?"

"Yes, it's true. Hank Cochran said he already knew about it, that he was trying to keep the writer from finding out. He thought maybe their involvement was more than personal, asked me to talk to Jacques, said he might be able to convince Weinhardt to back off if there were important political secrets at stake."

"Do you think there are?"

He sighs. "I think it's a stretch, but how do I know? Melanie and Jacques were always over my head. I just helped them out because they were my friends. I told Cochran that I won't do it. In the off chance there *is* some kind of spy stuff going on, it could get very sticky. I can't know what I don't ask. To tell you the truth, I'm tired of being used by these people."

I think he has a point—at least I stopped using Dennis when that summer was over. He must know, though, that you always pay an admission price when you enter the inner circle of people who are larger than life. It was that way from the beginning.

"Dennis, do you remember that summer when we were in Paris? What'd we do every day?"

He's silent for a minute, thinking. "Pretty much whatever *they* wanted to do," he says.

"Precisely." I pause, hoping he'll catch my meaning, but his response is not at all what I expected.

"Don't ask me if I'd do it again, Nora. You, maybe. I really liked you. Them? Now, I'm not so sure."

It's my turn to be silent. It never occurred to me that the inner circle might not be worth it—to some people anyway. For a second I wonder if I might actually have been attracted to Dennis Jacobson if we'd met under other circumstances, if I hadn't been so dazzled by

Jacques, so infatuated with everything Melanie loved. Oddly enough, I feel closer to Dennis now than when we cuddled together in the back of Jacques's Citroën.

"I just have to ask you to do one thing," I say, "and then neither Hank nor I will bother you again. I don't need to tell you what this kind of news would do to everything Melanie worked for. I'm going to try my best to keep it quiet, but I've got to know what I'm dealing with. I'll be in London on Sunday. Could you contact Jacques, ask him to meet me there?"

"That's all?"

"That's all."

We agree that I'll call him back later, after he contacts Jacques, gets a London address where Jacques and I can meet.

"And tell your wife not to worry," I add. "By the way, her maiden name isn't Powell, is it?"

"No. And she never went to the University of Pennsylvania."

Of course not. Melanie couldn't very well tell her husband she was spending the weekend with her old friend Dennis, so she claimed to know his wife, Cynthia. She pretended that they'd met in college, and she gave Dennis's wife the name of a real girl from our college years, just in case someone bothered to check.

"I kind of guessed that." I start to say good-bye, then stop. I have to ask. "You know, I'm still having trouble figuring out why Melanie never told me she was seeing Jacques. When did they—when did they start meeting again?"

"Well, I was their go-between from the time she became enough of a public figure to need one. That's a lot of years. I can't be sure before that, but I always assumed that they never stopped seeing each other." His voice trails off suddenly, as if he's realized that this could be a real shock to me. "Uh . . . I don't know that for certain."

Never stopped seeing each other? Never! For a second, I have diffi-culty grasping what he is saying. When I do, my mind goes blank and I nearly drop the receiver. It feels as if ice water has been poured over my head, turning it into a vast canyon with the word *never* echoing through it.

Standing at a pay phone in Santa Monica, California, I wish more than anything that Dennis Jacobson would reach through the telephone wires, take me in his arms and hold me. It demands every bit of strength I have to put myself back together.

"I won't keep you any longer," I say, hoping my voice doesn't sound as shaky as I feel. I'm reluctant to break the connection. "About that summer. We *had* fun, didn't we? I never really thanked you for sharing that with me."

"To tell you the truth, I didn't think you even noticed me that much. It took me a while to get over you, you know. I love my wife a lot, but even after we were married I used to follow your progress in the business section. Congratulations, you've done very well."

"Oh, Dennis, thanks . . . and I'm really glad you're happy."

I hang up the phone, still struggling to keep myself in check. Good for him. At least he's been successful in love, which is certainly more than I can say for myself. Fortunately, newspapers don't report the stats of failed relationships unless you're a celebrity.

I can't let myself think about Jacques and Melanie yet, so I walk the few blocks back to my house, nibbling on the doughnut and pondering Dennis's last words. He's right, I *didn't* notice him—not Dennis or any of the other nice guys who came along. In short, they weren't *him.*

This particular problem of mine has been the subject of much therapy over the years; I'm living proof you can stare at something once a week ad infinitum and—presto!—it's still there. In fact, it's gotten worse as I've grown older, because my glands seem to be frozen in time: I always seem to be attracted to very handsome men far too many years my junior.

My former therapist, Dr. Ferris, concluded that I never completely let go of Jacques, that my sexual clock got stuck somewhere around my late twenties—at about the same age Jacques was the last time I saw him; the same age I was the last time I really fell in love. All I know for sure is that I feel more comfortable with younger men and, as luck would have it, they're often attracted to me—something about my particular personality being complementary to the needs of the youthful male. Of course, what starts out ecstatically never lasts. I lose patience with their narrow youth; they inevitably wake with a start and run off to find young, fertile wives. I try to leave first, because I'm tired of being left.

"Did you tell Melanie . . . from the very beginning . . . how you felt about Jacques?" Dr. Ferris once asked.

"Of course I did. She and I talked about everything."

"Really?"

"Sure. We laughed about it. It was a running joke for a couple of years— how I measured all of my dates on a scale of un à dix.*"*

Dr. Ferris didn't crack a smile. *"If you laughed about it, maybe you didn't* really *tell her."*

I unlock the front door and walk into my empty living room. Very astute, Dr. Ferris. Of course, I hedged a bit at first; Jacques had been her lover, after all, not mine. But later, when he came back into my life—my life, not hers—when he became *my* lover, then I told her everything.

Halfway to the kitchen I stop, sinking down on my overstuffed sofa as adrenaline drains from my body in a single rush. I shut my eyes, then open them, scanning the room for a focal point, something to reconnect me to myself, but my living room, I see, is surprisingly impersonal. I've never had an eye for decor, have always told myself I'm too busy, so all the little keepsakes of my life are stuffed away in drawers and boxes, waiting for me to buy the right piece of furniture, find the right niche, to display them. This room could belong to anyone; I'm not really *here* somehow. Without warning, fury explodes inside my head. *I—I hate her!*

The force of the emotion, the idea of it, stuns me. I realize I'm boiling over with anger, erupting like a volcano. It's not because of

Jacques. He was never mine, really. It's because I *trusted* her, she was supposed to be my friend, we had built a rare thing, a lifelong friendship, a special bond. And now I find out it wasn't real! But most of all I'm absolutely furious because I won't be able to shut her out of my life, I can't even try to forget about her. She left me Bennie and Hank, she left me all of those ideals that were supposed to be bigger than both of us: her vision, her whole damn "big picture" permeates my world.

Already I catch myself seeking excuses for her, squirming at the condescending, patronizing possibility that she thought I was too fragile to handle knowing about her and Jacques. But Melanie wasn't that considerate; she would never have catered to what she saw as my weakness. Obviously, she put the same spin on her concept of friendship as she did on her concept of marriage.

Today's business suit hangs on the back of my bedroom door. I've calmed down a bit, but there's no way I can march into the office in this state. I'll take a walk first. Then I think about Bennie; the idea of him sitting through another stilted lunch or dinner with Hank, having no clue as to what's going on, is suddenly unacceptable to me. Damn Melanie—she dumped her family in my lap, and I refuse to let them suffocate under the weight of her secrets. I pick up the phone and dial Bennie's number, knowing I'll get the machine.

"This is Ben Cochran. I may be out; I may be in. But either way, I'm busy. Leave a number and I'll probably call you back."

"Wake up, Bennie. You might as well wake up right now because I'm going to keep calling until you do."

I'm rewarded by the rattle of a receiver and a sleepy voice. "Nora? It's not even seven o'clock."

"Sorry. How about if I make it up to you by springing for coffee at La Pâtisserie? Say in half an hour."

I ring up Katy's voice mail and leave a message that I'll be a little late. Then I call information for the number of Hank's hotel. Unlike his son, he's not a late sleeper so I catch him in the middle of his room-service breakfast. He listens politely to my argument that Bennie has a right to know what may turn out to be a surprising truth about his mother.

"I understand what you're saying, Nora, but I don't think I can bring myself to talk to him about something like this. I wouldn't know how. And, besides, we don't even know for sure."

"You could tell him what you're feeling," I persist. "He's your son."

"It's pretty obvious, isn't it? How would it make him feel? She's his mother."

"You could ask him that."

"No, I can't."

Why am I not surprised? "All right, what if *I* tell him? I'm meeting him for coffee in a few minutes anyway. I think he deserves to know as much as we do." Whether Hank agrees and whether he'll manage to discuss the situation openly with his son when they meet, he neglects to say, and I don't press. At last, punctuated by a couple of sighs, he gives his consent.

"Be my guest, Nora. You're as much his parent as I am."

FOUR

I lean against a post in the parking lot of La Pâtisserie, a steaming cup of coffee in hand, listening for the sound of Bennie's cycle. I feel better already. No matter what happened, Bennie is Bennie—and he's the best gift Melanie ever gave me.

I watch today's sun begin to work its way through the clouds, experiencing an eerie sense of suspension as this morning superimposes itself on scores of other mornings when the coffee and I used to wait on a hard bench in Central Park for a late and panting little Bennie to run across the grass. A dozen years and the not-so-small fact that the world has moved on. For a moment, I allow a tiny delusion that all this craziness is just some novel I'm reading. Real life is the single clear note of a Santa Monica morning. Me standing here in jeans; the smell of coffee; and Bennie always late.

I hear him coming—a politely muffled roar, more of a run-on cough. He pulls into the lot at the far end, putts around the loop and comes to a stop by my post. Hanging from his youthful chin is a flowing gray beard attached to his ears with elastic strips.

"Hey, lady. Sorry I'm late, but the phone rang just as I was leaving. It might have been my Muse. Turns out it was only my father."

"I see you didn't have time to shave."

"You like it? Quick disguise. Some asshole with a camera followed me all over town yesterday." He unwinds his long form from the cycle. "You know, I don't really want any coffee. Let's walk down to the beach?"

Tossing my cup in the bin, I take his arm. "Like a sweet old couple?" I tease, eyeing the phony beard.

Bennie frowns. "Please, Nora. Never *sweet.*"

Typical of any mother, real or surrogate, I watch him as we walk along. Sunlight plays across his face, picking up silver speckles in the silly beard. At twenty, Bennie looks more like Hank than he does his mother, but he has her eyes and it's a compelling combination. Bennie's a prize student at the UCLA film school; he's madly inventive and bursting with youthful impatience. Despite my efforts, the futuristic filmmaker and his historian father may never be comfortable together in real time.

In a voice ripe with exasperation, he describes his conversation with Hank and the inevitable dinner invitation. "He asked me about my *um-project* . . . he puts that childish twist on it, makes it sound like I'm working on a model airplane."

"He's never figured out how to talk to you," I explain, for the millionth time. "That doesn't mean he doesn't want to."

Bennie gives me one of his you-just-don't-get-it looks. "All Henry wants to do is get me across some table for a couple of hours so he can stare at some leftover part of *her* in me. He's not interested in me—he never was. All he ever cared about was Mom." He looks up at the sky, shakes his head slowly. "If Dad were ever to really see *me* . . . hear *me* . . . well, I'm sure he'd be disappointed. He sees what he wants to see, and it has nothing to do with me. It's a dumb game and I'm tired of playing it."

"You might consider that he's still feeling rather vulnerable."

"Yeah, well, he's always vulnerable. That's just part of being Henry. He's vulnerable, soft-spoken, sooo refined. He's rich as God, but he still pulls that simple-professor shtick."

I'd like to blame Bennie's impatience with his father on his youth, but some of what he says is true. Besides, he and Hank have night-and-day contrasts in their approaches to life. Melanie told me once that if Hank were to find the Key-to-All-Knowledge, he'd take it home, wrap it up in a velvet cloth and hide it in the back of his bureau. Then she laughed and said that if Bennie found the Key-to-All-Knowledge, he'd take it out in the street, close his eyes and throw it up in the air, give it away. Hank collects rare books; Bennie made his first film when he was nine.

"Does it bother you when I talk about your mother?" I ask.

"No. You just talk about her. You don't try to re-create her in me. You don't try to mold me and every bit of existing matter into her image."

We reach the beach and sit down on a stone abutment that separates the bike path from the sand. I'm looking for the right words. "Bennie, there's something I need to tell you."

In deference to my sober tone, he pulls off the fake beard and shoves it in his pocket; then he turns to me expectantly and I understand why this would have been so difficult for Hank. In spite of all the confidences this kid and I have shared, I still feel like an empty-souled creature about to debunk Santa Claus.

"There's a man. Melanie and I met him a long time ago. Apparently she . . . she was seeing him . . . until she decided to seek the nomination." I don't say "she was seeing him all your life"—my mouth simply can't form those words. Bennie stares at the sand thoughtfully and says nothing. "Hank told me last night. He found out by a fluke, and we're checking it out. But he's afraid this writer—David Weinhardt—might dig it out, too."

"I'm supposed to meet with Weinhardt next week," Bennie says.

"We don't know much about it yet. Your dad thinks there's a possibility that the relationship was intelligence-related."

Bennie snorts. "Right. He'd *have* to think that, Nora. Or at least he'd work real hard at thinking it. The idea of Mom having an affair would drive Henry bats."

"Yeah, I know. But did you ever think that maybe, just maybe, there's something to all his speculation? Couldn't you give him the slightest benefit of the doubt? I mean—there *are* some odd coincidences. Hank finds out Melanie was seeing somebody, then a couple of days later the president assigns a Secret Service team to follow him around."

Bennie sighs. "Leave it to Dad to play *that* up. The Secret Service kept me company yesterday too, Nora. Larry and George, the same guys that never left my side through that whole tiresome campaign. In fact—" He sits up straight and cranes his neck, looking around; then he grins, raising his hand in a broad wave. "Turn to your right, Nora; about a couple of hundred yards down you'll see George and Larry. They're stuffing something into their mouths and they're impossible to miss." I follow his instructions and, sure enough, I spy two men in suits, holding bulging napkins to their faces. "I hadn't noticed them yet this morning," Bennie says, "but they told me they might hang around another day. I don't really mind. They keep out of the way and they scared the hell out of that photographer yesterday. Want to meet them?"

I shake my head emphatically and he shrugs. "So much for Dad's sinister plots; this is all just standard procedure. Still, illicit sex wasn't exactly Mom's style. Who's the guy?"

"A Frenchman named Jacques DeBrin."

He's quiet for a couple of minutes, rubbing his eyes with the back of his hand. Then he looks at me and his face softens with the hint of a smile. "I guess there are things about my mother that we let ourselves forget."

"What do you mean?"

"When I was a little boy and she was just a councilwoman with an occasional hour of free time, she used to make up stories to tell me. The hero was always this mysterious Frenchman named Jacques."

Something reaches inside my head and squeezes. Bennie and I sit for a moment, memories settling around us.

"So tell me what's going to happen," he says finally. "Am I going to read about this scandal at the checkout stand?"

"If no one uncovers the news before Weinhardt, you'll see it first in hardcover, beautifully written but just as devastating. All the drivel will come later. I promised your dad I'd go talk to Jacques."

"What for?"

"To find out exactly what went on, what might be at stake. Your mother didn't tell bedtime stories to me and Hank. We're still sort of hoping there's another explanation."

Bennie looks exasperated. "Oh come on, Nora, don't tell me you really believe that bit about Madame President and the French connection." He rolls his eyes. "Dad twists everything around so he won't have to look at the truth. Mom did whatever she wanted to do, that's the way she was."

Bingo. He's right about that. Funny how we're always so smart when we're young, so certain, so amazed at the ignorance of our elders. I take a deep breath, trying to refocus, to force myself to remember that the consequences of Melanie's affair becoming public extend way beyond Hank's feelings—and mine. "I *have* to talk to Jacques," I say. "I need to know what was going on and whether anyone else knows about it. Your mother was on her way to doing great things for this country and preserving her memory is important."

It's like Dennis said—Melanie inspired people, she had a way of making people see how they could gain from their own selflessness. She may have been a lousy friend, but she was a great American stateswoman, and if Danny Court or someone else hopes to salvage anything of what she started, her image has to stay intact—which means, like it or not, I'm stuck with her.

"Was my father going to tell me about the lover? Or was he planning to wait until it's in print?"

"I drew the short straw. He knows I'm telling you."

"Your idea, I'm sure. Well, I guess it's easier for both of us this way. I don't think I could stand seeing that sick look come over his face as he choked on the words." Bennie makes a face. "That means dinner tonight will be the same as always. Dad will hem and haw about the classes he's teaching and about my *um-project,* then he'll launch into his favorite subject: his latest conspiracy theory—who was behind the nut that shot Mom. Then there'll be the speech about the million or so weird groups that sneak in and out of every aspect of our lives. I'll bet I could give it to you word for word, right now."

When I don't respond, the sarcasm leaves his face and he stands, looking out to sea with his mother's eyes. His tone softens as it always does when he speaks of her. "You know what it was like for me growing up, Nora. Mom was hardly ever there, but she gave me what she could and she never tried to pretend any different. She was so vivid— when she was there, she was really *there.* And she gave me *you,* and never once made me feel bad when I slipped and called you Mommy. I have no problem with my mother. At least she was straight with me."

"I know, Bennie." I think what he says is essentially true from his young man's viewpoint, but I remember a little boy whose trusting acceptance didn't keep him from missing her, from hurting when she wasn't around.

Bennie and I walk slowly away from the beach. I notice that his Secret Service chaperons head in the opposite direction, probably to get their car. When we arrive at La Pâtisserie, they're already in the parking lot. Bennie climbs on his cycle and putts out of the lot, waving his arm for them to follow.

As I walk back to my house, I find myself feeling sorry for Hank and wondering about the games genetics plays. His own father was such a disaster—how could Hank have been expected to relate to a raucous little boy like Bennie, who'd inherited his mother's spunk?

Hank's mother, Bennie's grandmother, was an insurance heiress, a strong, quiet woman who understood the foibles of her emotions and shrewdly protected her fortune before she married the handsome playboy who had swept her off her feet. When not gambling away his allowance in exotic locales, her husband's favorite pastime was finding ways to get even with his wife. Hank learned at an early age to avoid being used in that regard by giving his father a wide berth.

He was thirteen when his father died—officially, a suicide in a hotel room in Acapulco. However, in view of the father's enormous gambling debts, murder seemed more likely. When Hank's mother succumbed to cancer twenty years later, her fortune was still whole. Hank is probably the only college professor who owns an apartment occupying an entire floor on Central Park West—Melanie's earnings had been pin money. Bennie's carefully structured trust fund provides enough income to pay the bills, but not enough to spoil him.

Bennie knows all this, but it doesn't make him cut his father any slack. Like his mother, he doesn't cater to weakness.

That thought continues to gnaw at me as I unlock the door. No weakness: that was Melanie, all right. She had boundless compassion for the underprivileged, but if you weren't hungry, if you weren't bleeding, if you weren't sick or poor or politically oppressed, then you were expected to give as much as she did. Feed everyone, educate everyone, cure everyone, save the planet. Two hundred percent? Three hundred percent? Is it possible that she might have worn us all out in the end?

I never saw Melanie angry, but her disappointment was withering. For a second, I feel like calling up Danny Court and telling him it's all right to be human, that he can still do good things, accomplish *great* things even—that hers can't be the only way.

Instead I shower quickly and get ready for the office. I'm tying the bow on my beige silk blouse when it hits me suddenly how I got hooked on Melanie's expectations. It wasn't true, what I said to Bennie earlier. His mother did indeed tell me bedtime stories. In fact, it all began with her stories.

I sit on the edge of the bed, blinking rapidly, holding back tears that threaten my just-applied makeup. I went away to college—met Melanie—only a few months after my parents' divorce had left me unsettled about everything I thought I knew. I was ripe for Melanie's stories.

Late at night, after we'd put away the books and crawled into our narrow bunk beds, she on the top, me on the bottom, Melanie spun tales about a different world, a world where everything worked.

All the people in her stories were unfailingly strong. They weren't concerned with petty things; they looked beyond the obvious and created solutions to questions that were bigger than themselves. She told fairy tales, really—fantasies—but they challenged me, made me feel as if I could really matter. And, of course, in the light of day, there was always Melanie herself, living proof of that kernel of possibility in the tales she told.

I suddenly wonder if I'm not, at forty-seven, in the very same mental state I was in when I went away to college confused and angry, viewing humanity in general with a fairly cynical eye. The thought pushes a string of buttons, starts me fuming all over again.

To hell with you, Madame President!

I walk into the den in search of my briefcase. I'm not doing this for her, I assure myself. I've agreed to fly across an ocean to meet with a man who broke my heart. And I've agreed to do it for two reasons: to satisfy my own huge curiosity—all right, *obsession*—and to do whatever I can to preserve a modicum of that bright new world she owes us.

FIVE

he first thing I do when I get to the office is place a phone call to the president of the United States. Mentioning that President Court called me personally only yesterday gets me through three layers of White House bureaucracy, and I'm able to leave my name and number with a secretary who actually sits in the vicinity of the Oval Office.

I'm not calling Danny Court to give him permission to be human. I'm calling because I want to know *exactly* why Secret Servicemen were following Hank and Bennie. During my fifteen-minute drive to work, the anger, which I can never retain for long, gave way to a weird anxiety. My mind started jumping all over the place, catching on dozens of loose little threads, then zoomed back to one simple fact—the Secret Service tries to prevent people from getting killed.

The second thing I do is check my appointment book and find that I'm scheduled to meet with Melanie's biographer, David Weinhardt, this afternoon at three o'clock. Katy brings in an article from a magazine she lifted from her dentist's office last week. It's profiling Weinhardt. "He's a bachelor," she points out—that's the third time since he first contacted me that she's alluded to his marital status. He's also written a bunch of highly acclaimed books, but Katy figures I'm likely to already be informed about his writing credentials. "Not a bad-looking bachelor," she adds.

When you're unattached at my age, the well-meaning awareness of those around you is so acute that even the most professional encounter with a single man born in the same era takes on the uncomfortable edge of a fix-up date. I nod. His photo makes him look . . . well, *heavy duty.* Not exactly my type, but I am looking forward to talking to him, and to finding out how much he already knows.

After Katy leaves, I pour myself a cup of coffee and shuffle through the papers on my desk, pulling out the preliminary proposal Garth Westin, head of our London office, sent me last week, the one that's already piqued my interest. I'm reading the first paragraph when the phone rings. To my surprise it's Danny Court, already returning my call. "What can I do for you, Nora?" Just like that.

I don't know how to ask him except point-blank, so that's what I do. He hesitates a moment. "Honestly, Nora, I was a little nervous. Last week *The Washington Post* received a very nasty anonymous note directed at Senator Blackmore and myself regarding the senator's new environmental bill. The White House operator has received a couple of ugly phone calls. None of it has anything to do with Melanie's family but on the anniversary of her assassination we just didn't want to take any chances."

I'm relieved to know that it was just a precaution; on the other hand, what he's telling me is disturbing.

"I'm shifting out of my compromise mode, Nora; it wasn't working anyway. In the slim chance I don't get completely destroyed over the environment, the next move will be to work on education. I know you were a primary contributor to Melanie's ideas in that area. Can I count on you?"

A tiny fire starts to kindle in the back of my brain. I'm still holding Garth Westin's software proposal in my right hand. "I'd like to help," I hear myself say.

I hang up the phone, stare at the receiver for a second. Did I really just agree to get involved again? But this isn't politics, it's education.

It's helping translate into practical use all the things we've discovered about how the human brain works.

A long time ago, before Harvard, I studied artificial intelligence at MIT, trying to close the gap between computer brains and our own. Each computer problem I worked on also taught me something in reverse, something about the way *I* think.

This time I read Garth's proposal more carefully—and in spite of everything else that's going on, I feel myself begin to get excited.

The computer software produced by Learning Parallels is interactive, employing limited virtual-reality effects. The idea is to help students *experience* what they're learning, based on the theory that it's easier to understand how an atom reacts if you can become one for a while. Our computer programs are three-dimensional, which helps kids identify with a little stand-in persona on the screen. Because they control the persona's actions, they can discover such things as physical laws through trial and error.

Of course these programs are light-years away from full-blown virtual reality. Grown-up learning machines like military flight simulators feel just like the real thing. But my mission is to come as close as we can. Cost is still the big factor, particularly for a mass market like, say, the world's children.

The proposal I'm reading outlines a high school–level mathematics program created by this new software designer Garth has found, a guy named James Barton—and it's got some twists I've never seen. Like most of the stuff on the forward edge, this will probably turn out to be too expensive to market, but I'm definitely intrigued; I can hardly wait to talk to the owner of the mind who designed it.

At least this project shows we're working in the right direction. The research and development part of our London office is my little experiment in seeing how well creativity evolves an ocean away from the steady gaze of the corporate eye. Not that the boss, Neil Mackey, isn't every bit as committed to breakthroughs as I am. It's just that his practical side is so conservative—so tight with the buck—that he needs someone like me to slip the more speculative projects by him.

Neil is classified, in the annals of those who keep such records, as a genius. He got his doctorate from MIT only a dozen years ago and within ten months had turned it into Learning Parallels. He drives me crazy most of the time, but I adore his brain.

I ask Katy to make arrangements for my trip to London. I'm leaving tomorrow, Friday, and I'll meet with Garth Westin the first thing on Monday. I also ask her to see if Neil can fit me in today. My rank and performance afford me a pretty free rein, but Neil will expect some sort of briefing before I go.

"Mr. Mackey says he'll see you right after lunch," Katy informs me. "And, Nora, don't forget you have that three o'clock appointment with David Weinhardt."

Neil usually eats in his office, so I have just enough time to grab a quick bite. Merging with the parade of business chic that pours out into the square between the Century City towers, I find a phone booth, plunge in the rest of my quarters and dial Philadelphia. Dennis Jacobson takes my call and, with no further words between us, provides the address of a London flat. Two o'clock Sunday afternoon. I stuff the slip of paper into my billfold and head for the closest deli.

My boss doesn't believe in desks. He is sitting at his mammoth worktable, reading the newspaper midst a fortress of hardware, and doesn't look up when I enter—just launches into another of his conservative political commentaries. Neil loves to lay his opinions on me because we disagree on practically everything, even though the gap closed considerably when he became one of those swing Republicans who voted for Melanie Lombard. Normally I refuse to participate, even listen, but today Neil is clicking his tongue over the environmental bill Court mentioned to me earlier, the one that inspired the hate mail, so my ears perk up.

"Danny Court must have left reality in his other pants," Neil says. "The first thing Congress zapped from that earlier bill was the emissions control schedule. What's this new bill almost completely about? Emissions control. Court has to know the bill hasn't got a prayer; the oil lobby alone will kill it—not to mention the unbridled rage of our friends in Detroit. What a big fat waste of time." He ends his speech with the suggestion that President Court put on a blond wig if he really wants to accomplish anything.

An image, unbidden and definitely unwanted, darts swiftly through my head: Danny Court in a woman's wig with the red letter *A* stenciled in the middle of his forehead.

"I see the reporters caught up with you yesterday," Neil says, closing the newspaper and handing it across to me. "I hate retrospectives—they just stir up the pain." Neil, of course, hates anything "retro." He's the sort of man who thinks nostalgia is a brand of nasal spray.

The front-page story, commemorating the anniversary of Melanie's death, has a photo of her with Hank right after the inauguration. There's also a blurry picture of Bennie on his cycle, probably taken yesterday. I skim through the article; as far as I can tell, the reporter quoted me accurately.

"We have a proposal from Garth Westin for a high school geometry program," I say, handing the paper back to him. "I think you should take a look at it."

Neil peers at me curiously. "Has Garth actually come up with something that requires less than a million bucks of hardware per unit?"

Admitting that I haven't run a cost analysis yet, I give him a quick rundown, including my conviction that this project has some angles worth checking out. Since my previous hunches have contributed to making him rich, he listens. "Besides, I think it's time for me to meet the British whiz kid," I say. "I've scheduled a trip to London, if that's all right with you."

"James Barton the third. I've been watching him. Smart. Very smart. He's also supposed to be a slovenly little nerd, but we're not prejudiced about things like dirt, are we?" Picking up the newspaper again, he pulls a section from the middle and flips a few pages. "Go ahead and check him out, Nora. Let me see a copy of that proposal so I'll know what you're talking about when you get back."

Whenever Neil calls somebody a "nerd," I sense he's trying to exorcise the years of teasing he probably got when he was a boy obsessed with computers. He certainly goes out of his way to be anything but nerdlike now, from his expensive suits to his glamorous wife. Apparently he finds what he's looking for, because an obnoxious grin spreads over his face. "Ah, yes. I knew I saw in here that Blaine Hennessey is starring at one of London's West End theaters. What a coincidence."

I shut my eyes and sigh—wouldn't you just know it! Blaine Hennessey and I are an ongoing office joke. I met him at a Santa Monica coffeehouse when he was a twenty-six-year-old unemployed actor who had just flubbed an audition and needed a good listener. We went out together for just three months, during which time I—big mistake—dragged him along to one of Neil's famous cocktail parties. Six years later, with two major films under his belt, Blaine is big news and Neil absolutely adores teasing me about him.

I head back to my office, telling myself that Neil can think whatever he likes. He knows he pays me well enough that I wouldn't have to mooch this trip if all I wanted was to visit a boyfriend. Interesting, though, that Blaine just happens to be doing a play in London—it would be fun to see it.

"Don't forget—" Katy begins, looking pointedly at her watch, after I've asked her to get me a ticket to Blaine's play Saturday night.

"I know, I know. The writer." I check the mirror behind my door, run a brush quickly through my hair. The article with David Weinhardt's picture still sits on top of the papers on my desk. I read through it quickly. Let's see . . . he was born in Philadelphia forty-five years ago; he graduated from Georgetown University; he lives in Los Angeles; and, as Katy said, he's never been married. Once a reporter for *The Washington Post*, he's written three books, all biographies of famous people. I've read two of them, and have to admit I was impressed. I start to put the article in my desk drawer, then change my mind. Guys like this always have the upper hand because they've done their homework. It won't hurt for him to see I know a little about him, too. I decide to leave the article where it is, his picture lying in plain view on top of my desk.

SIX

"Y ou're the other woman in the photo," David Weinhardt says as we shake hands across my desk. Katy just ushered him into my office and he's looking at me as if I were a missing puzzle piece. "I'm right, aren't I? That's you in that old picture of Melanie's, sitting on the floor with Dennis Jacobson. Your hair was shorter, but—yes, I'm sure it's you." He lets go of my hand and smiles.

"Dennis Jacobson," I reflect, hoping I sound as if I haven't heard his name in years. "That was a long time ago, and I'm afraid I don't remember him very well. Have a seat."

He settles into one of my leather chairs, his face momentarily pensive as if my words didn't quite ring true. "Well, I'd assumed that the woman with Jacobson was his wife, Cynthia, but I guess you all knew each other." He looks at me for a second; then smiles again and explains the sequence of events I've already heard from Hank—how he's diligently tried to interview this friend of Melanie's, been thoroughly rebuffed and can't understand why. Behind the friendly expression, I sense a bulldog tenacity that both concerns and interests me.

"Would you like a cup of coffee?" I ask, pointing to the pot on my credenza.

He swivels his chair to the side and helps himself, pouring coffee into a bright green mug emblazoned with the Learning Parallels logo. "You'd almost think these people have some terrible secret to hide and don't want to risk being mentioned in my book," he says. "I called the University of Pennsylvania; they say the last address they have for Cynthia Powell is in Chicago. Do you think it's possible we've got a case of mistaken identity here?"

Whoa! His words tumble over one another in my ears. "I'm afraid I can't help you," I say. "Unlike Melanie, I never kept in touch." That's certainly true enough.

"What about the other guy in the picture—the one with Melanie?"

I guess I can't pretend I wasn't there, or that I'm completely brain-dead. Besides, "Jacques's flat" was written on the back of the photo. "His name was Jacques—Jacques something. Sorry, I can't remember."

I'm uncomfortably aware that the smile he continues to flash has nothing to do with the rest of his face, which has doubt written all over it. He must have had to work at doing that—maybe he practiced by rubbing his head and patting his stomach at the same time.

"All right. I'd better start by telling you why I want to write about your friend Melanie Lombard," he says.

He stares pointedly into my eyes, as if he's not talking to me but to someone inside of me, as he outlines his belief that truly creative people rarely go into public office, therefore making the reality of President Melanie Lombard a phenomenon that must be explored. For a man of no more than average size, he has a commanding presence. The skeptical undercurrent has been replaced by total enthusiasm, and his face, framed by an ample supply of curly salt-and-pepper hair, seems to move constantly. He punctuates his words with a twist of the mouth, a raised eyebrow, and his voice takes on an intensity that reminds me instantly of *Patrice*, the passionate book he created out of the long and tragic life of painter Patrice Solana—a portrait in vibrant, living colors, a translation of the artist's soul.

For a second I'm humbled by the depth of his talent; then, just as suddenly, I feel a spurt of anger. I've been thinking that the book about Melanie's life would be a kind of memorial—a recounting of something that was, with a touch of mourning for what might have been. But I know that won't be enough for him.

"Well, David, I can tell you that the astonishing phenomenon of President Melanie Lombard grew out of years of work and hope and dreams—and that all of it was blown to bits in an instant. You see, I'm afraid I still have this little problem with the ending."

The irritation in my voice doesn't faze him. "The ending can't change what she was," he says, speaking slowly as if it's critical for me to hear between the lines. "You know, Nora, I made up my mind to write about Melanie during the first days of the presidential campaign. When she was killed, I almost put the idea aside. It took me a while to remember that her life was not about the shattering of a nation's hope, her life was about creating hope. And my book is not going to be about death. Somebody has to write about her—and *nobody* can do it better than I can."

I'm used to the mental-verbal duels of the business world, but David Weinhardt is a different sort of challenge. I feel a subtle shift in my head as if a score of errant thoughts are scurrying back in line. Silently, I give myself permission. "All right, then. Shall we start out with Melanie's secret?"

His eyes light up and I give myself ten points on the invisible scoreboard. Her biographer wants to know how it all began and I'm going to tell him. I'm going to tell him a secret that no one else knows, dazzle him with confidential information, and then maybe—just maybe—I can lure him away from the real secret about her lover. He reaches into his briefcase and holds up a mini–tape recorder. I nod and he sets it on the edge of my desk.

I quote Melanie's words exactly as I've replayed them to myself dozens of times over the years. It feels odd to be saying them aloud. He listens intently as I describe her expression, the questioning look in her eyes, how I almost laughed at the little girl who believed she'd grow up to be president because her mother told her so.

"That's absolutely amazing," he says. I picture his mind spinning behind those lively brown eyes, reworking thoughts on the book he plans to write. "On some level, her whole life must have been directed toward one end."

"I'm not suggesting this is any clinical study on childhood conditioning. Melanie might have turned out pretty much the same if her mother had told her she was destined to become a ballerina."

"Maybe. But anybody who denies that history has been formed by the words fed to our children will at least have to sit up and pay attention."

Taking a deep breath, I tell him more about Melanie's mother: that she taught philosophy at the University of Wisconsin; that she was over forty when her first and only child was born; that the pregnancy had been difficult and she didn't return to work. She never saw her prediction come true, because she died while Melanie was still in law school. Surely these are details he already knows, but he listens patiently, letting me unfold the story my own way.

Melanie's mother always intrigued me because she was so different from my own. She didn't talk a lot, but when she did her words were fluid, never getting caught on spurs of judgment. Her opinions seemed to grow from the input of the moment, rather than leak out from an established mind-set. She didn't deal well with structure at all, a fact that may have contributed to her ongoing frailty. Melanie used to say it was as if she were from another, better world.

All of a sudden, from the corner of my eye, I notice a shimmering of leaves on the large ficus plant by the window—it's subtle, like most of the stuff that happens just offstage in your peripheral vision, a flicker. But then, as I watch, the whole plant begins to tremble, then really shake. Everything is shaking—lamps, desk, chairs, floor—jerking violently up and down, back and forth. For the barest instant,

David and I stare at each other, frozen; then he lunges to the doorway; I dive under the desk.

As quickly as it started, it's over. Climbing unceremoniously to my feet, I see that coffee has sloshed out of both of our mugs—streams of dark liquid race gleefully toward each other across my desk.

Neil's voice echoes down the hall: "Everybody okay?" Katy, her face blanched, peeks around David, who still stands with his arms spread against the door frame. I ask her to please bring me some paper towels.

David crosses the room and lifts his tape recorder out of a puddle, then helps me rescue my papers. "We're on the fortieth floor," he says, as if the fact has just occurred to him, as if I didn't know where my office was located. "On the fortieth floor, it probably doesn't make a hell of a lot of difference if you take cover or not. *Jesus.*" I see that his forehead is damp.

Katy arrives with a roll of paper towels and a report that Caltech gauges the earthquake at 5.1, with an epicenter about ten miles away in the San Fernando Valley. A jolt, but nothing serious.

David holds up the magazine article with his picture, now soaked in coffee. "Hey, maybe I should spend more time at the beach; I look pretty good with a deep tan," he jokes.

Now that my breathing has returned to normal, I can laugh too, albeit nervously. One thing about an earthquake—it's simple. No one, not even Hank, could imagine someone conspiring to create it.

David dries off his tape recorder, checks it and sighs with relief. "Now where were we?" To remind me, he plays back the last few seconds of the tape and we both laugh. I was recounting that Melanie said her mother was from *another, better world.* Quite a cue line for an earthquake. Leaning back in my chair, I realize I feel more comfortable with him than I did earlier. I suppose the fleeting thought that you're going to die in the company of someone instantly eliminates several layers of the getting-to-know-you process.

Melanie's father had adored them both, his soft-spoken wife and the beautiful child they had created in their middle years. Mitchell Lombard was the son of a blue-collar worker who had an idea for a more efficient tool and sent his son to college to learn how to make the idea work. The manufacturing company Mitchell and his father developed didn't make them wealthy, but it made Mitchell respect himself enough to attract a college professor wife, a fact that never ceased to amaze him. He had one of the sharpest business minds I've ever encountered, but he truly believed the brains had been given to the women of his family. His pride in Melanie was selfless, as if he had nothing whatsoever to do with her success.

"He died last year," David interjects.

"Yes." I wince, feeling a sharp pain. I can't forget Mitchell Lombard as I last saw him—an old man in a nursing home, bewildered by the cruelties of life and dying of a broken heart, having outlived both of the women he loved.

I adjust the window blinds to deflect the late afternoon sun. When I turn around, David is changing the tape and, for the first time, I can watch him without being studied in turn. I can't help wondering what his story is—what fluke is behind his bachelor status. He's nice-looking, a fairly well-known writer. Men like this have no trouble attracting women. In fact, men like this typically attract younger women—and go for it. Not that I have any right to criticize.

He looks up, his expression suddenly curious, as if he's been alerted by my thoughts and is now trying to remember something he's heard about me. He returns the recorder to the edge of my desk and asks me to tell him what she was like—in the beginning.

I seldom think about our college days, although in retrospect I know they weren't typical. Academically, we were lucky to be paired. Melanie had an excellent memory and amazing powers of concentration, so the studies came easily to her. I was a whiz in math and science and had no trouble staying on the dean's list. Someone who required more concentrated hours of study would have deconstructed if they'd lived with Melanie—she always wanted to do something else.

But what she really studied—more than economics or government or any of the subjects clustered under prelaw—was human nature. She learned about people—how they thought, what they wanted and needed—and she did that by seeking out those whose interests were as different from hers as possible. And that, more than anything else, is what made her come as close as she did to being all things to all people. David nods, as if he knows exactly what I mean.

I tell him about our early years in New York; the little apartment on East Eighty-fifth Street where Melanie joined me after she finished law school; how we wandered the museum only a few blocks away, played in the park, ate more than our share of German sausages in the Yorkville delis, took the Second Avenue bus to work. We owned the world in those days: I was writing and editing for a major computer magazine; Melanie, who'd been solicited by every prominent firm in the country, chose the law offices of Cruikshanks and Harding because they had agreed to let her take pro-bono cases. We worked round the clock, bounced problems off each other and never seemed to run out of energy.

I describe her first campaign, a long-shot race for city council against a well-heeled incumbent. Melanie must have spoken to half of the people in the district. She was tireless, walking the streets, climbing rickety flights of stairs, knocking on doors that had to be unbolted in three or four places. I tacked up signs, did cheap radio spots and made a million phone calls. She won the seat by only a few hundred votes and we celebrated along the bank of the East River with our motley crew of four campaign workers and a bottle of Gallo wine.

"I don't have any friends like that," David says wistfully. "I think sustaining that level of friendship for so many years is kind of remarkable."

I force a smile but say nothing.

"You know, there's one thing I've always wondered about," he continues. "How did a pretty blond white woman, definitely part of the American political system, manage to nail the support of someone like Nathan Marks, who hates everything political and isn't keen on most things white?"

Nathan Marks is a renowned scholar, author and head of the controversial Freedom Foundation; he's also the most powerful black man in America. I'm not sure I know the precise answer to David's question, but I can tell him that they'd met long before.

It was in a subway station at 190th Street. Melanie and I were waiting for a train home from the Cloisters, where I had taken her to see the unicorn tapestries that first week she was in New York, when we were approached by four hostile youths who drooled surly suggestions that had nothing to do with handing over our purses. When one of them grabbed my arm, Melanie whirled, hitting him hard on the chin with her fist, splitting his lower lip against his teeth; blood spurted everywhere.

The boys were surprised more than anything; I'm sure that wouldn't have been the end of it if another man, several years older and nearly doubled over with laughter, hadn't intervened. With one word from him, the four scattered. Still laughing, he bowed to us; then, in a voice suddenly ferocious, he ordered us to get the hell on home.

Years later during Melanie's presidential race, Nathan Marks mentioned our little subway incident on a national talk show. "You know all white women look alike to me," he quipped with his notorious sarcasm, "but when I started seeing that campaign poster all over town, yellow hair, red scarf—well, I realized she was the same woman."

David, who hasn't heard this tale before, laughs. "That must've happened about the time Marks was first gaining power in Harlem. You wouldn't have known him, but those four hoodlums obviously did. What a story."

"Well, you've come to the right place. I'm just full of them."

"I guess that answers my question about the campaign poster Marks was talking about—was she really that brave, facing down that gang, or was she just performing?"

"Believe me, Melanie Lombard was Superman, Mighty Mouse and Wonder Woman, all rolled into one," I assure him. If Melanie was anything, she was courageous; of course it helps when you think you're invincible. I wonder, fleetingly, if she'd managed to survive Jennie Wheeler's bullet, would she still be so brave today?

Katy buzzes to tell me she's going home and I note that it's after seven o'clock. Catching me checking my watch, David turns off the tape recorder and tucks it back in his briefcase. "To a biographer, Ms. Whitney, you are priceless, but there's never enough time. I hope we can continue as soon as you get back?" Noting my surprise, he explains. "I overheard your secretary say you're going to London."

Careful, I remind myself. This guy misses *nothing.* I tell him I'll only be gone for a few days and will be happy to meet with him when I get back.

"Fair enough," he says. "And, if you're ready to go home now, I'll walk you to your car. These huge garages get kind of eerie after hours, don't you think?"

He's right. I've been traversing these garages at all hours for a long time, but it always makes me nervous. Besides, I've just remembered something I want to ask him. I scribble a note to Katy and toss it in my out-box, stuff a copy of Garth's proposal into my briefcase and I'm ready to go.

"What do you think of President Danny Court?" I ask when we're alone on the elevator. If I'm willing to tell this man everything I know about Melanie—or most of it, anyway—he can do his share in helping me get past Hank's distrust of the man who replaced her.

"That's a broad question. Presidentially, I'm going to reserve judgment a bit longer: the man in the impossible position may surprise us by pulling a few tricks out of his own hat. About Danny Court, the person, I interviewed him, and—well, I like him. He's sincere, he's a political animal, raised and pampered by the Democratic party, but he's no figurehead. I don't think Melanie chose him as her running mate just to placate the party—even though that was a side effect."

He was her first choice, but the groundswell of support and enthusiasm Melanie elicited during those days would have allowed her to draft just about anyone, just as the huge disappointment that followed her death couldn't help but fall like a shroud over the survivor.

Although his own car is two levels below in visitor parking, David follows me off the elevator and walks with me through the nearly empty garage. "The public lost interest—or lost heart," he goes on. "We elected the first woman president; she was snatched away from us. So much for making a difference. That's why, when Court tried to get Lombard's program going, when he introduced the first environmental bill, Congress balked and got away with it. It takes a lot of energy to keep the wheels moving in the right direction, and this country was still in a state of shock. It doesn't matter whether her gender made her more important to you, or scared the hell out of you; when a president is assassinated, everyone experiences trauma—it makes us ashamed of ourselves.

"But I think Daniel Court can be a good president if he's allowed to be. Look at the gutsy move he's pulling with this new bill. The first one was full of compromises and Congress still buried it; typically, it'd be the president's turn to give up a little more, but instead he's countered with the Blackmore bill, which is hard-line Melanie Lombard, no compromises at all. No doubt, he'll get creamed, but it's a beaut of a symbolic move."

I'm listening to him, but at the same time I'm acutely aware of the echo of our footsteps through the garage, a hollow, lonely sound, made menacing by a thousand slasher movies. I'm glad he's with me. I stop walking and fish in my purse for my car keys, David stops too and the echo trails off.

"I'm sure you're going to be busy when you get back," he says, as I slide into the front seat of my car. "But since you still have to eat, maybe I can buy you lunch. Say, on Tuesday. I don't mind if you talk with your mouth full."

"That'll be fine. Just call Katy and let her know what time."

We shake hands through the open window and he turns to walk away as I start the motor—or try to. Instead of its usual vigorous roar, I get a pathetic whine. David comes back and pokes his head in the window. "Sounds like your starter."

Great. I have a plane to catch tomorrow; my car won't start; I'm exhausted. It's times like this when I'd like to scream or cry or both, if it would do any good, but of course it won't. I pick up the car phone and start to dial the Auto Club, then change my mind. I guess I should take the hint—my poor vehicle is long overdue for a checkup and I'm going to be out of town. Why not just leave it here tonight, call my mechanic in the morning and let him deal with it?

David, still peering through the window, sees me replace the phone and gather up my briefcase. "Tell me you don't live a million miles from here before I offer to drive you home," he says.

In LA, that's a fair, if not very chivalrous, question and, for some reason, it makes me trust him a little more. In fact, I live only a few miles away. Together we walk back to the elevator, ride down two levels, cross another expanse of empty garage and climb into his BMW. Again, I'm infinitely glad that I'm not alone down here. As we wind up the ramp, I contemplate the tons of cement in which we're encased—if that earthquake had tipped the Richter scale a few points higher, this whole building, garage and all, could now be a pile of rubble.

Neither David nor I say anything until we reach the exit and I realize that Katy left before us and I forgot to validate his parking ticket. Reaching into my purse, I pull out a twenty-dollar bill and lay it on the dashboard in front of him.

"You were supposed to stamp my ticket?"

"Uh-huh. If it's any more than that you can just leave me here as collateral."

David gives the bill to the man in the glass cage and receives a quarter in change, which he passes over to me. We both say "thanks" simultaneously; then say nothing; then start talking at once—he's asking directions while I'm giving them.

During the short drive home, he tells me a funny story he heard during an interview in Washington about a retort Melanie made on the Senate floor to the distinguished gentleman from Florida. When we pull into my driveway, we're both laughing. "I can make it to the door all right," I say, stopping him before he gets out of the car. "Thanks for the ride."

"I was thinking—I'm tied up tomorrow, but I've got a meeting right by the airport late Monday afternoon. It should be over just about the same time your flight's due; I could pick you up and maybe you'll feel like talking for an hour over coffee or something. The quicker I gather my information the better—and, don't forget, you're without a car."

He even knows my flight schedule. "Thanks anyway, David, but I'm always a mess after such a long flight. I'll see you for lunch on Tuesday."

Worn out, but too wired to go to bed this early, I stare at the untouched copy of this morning's newspaper on my kitchen counter, then pick it up. Except for the business section, I barely read the paper anymore. It's too hard, reading about what *isn't* happening, remembering what news was like when Melanie was making it. Still, I need to start paying attention again. Neil can be bluffed because he never expects an answer, but if I plan to keep up with someone like David Weinhardt, I'd better be informed.

In particular, I read the article about the Blackmore bill, which Court is behind. As Neil and David both indicated, it's a lot like Melanie's original initiative and includes a stringent emissions control schedule, the same schedule endorsed last year by the World Environmental Council after new satellite photos confirmed bad news in our planet's future. Last year, it was "Omigod"; this year it's ostrich time.

An auto industry spokesperson predicts such unnecessary controls would lead to economic disaster, an opinion seemingly shared by representatives from various other sectors of corporate America. World Environmental Council members express pleasure at the bill, but doubt that it can survive. The Libyan representative to OPEC's board of governors, caught by a reporter in a Venezuelan airport, comments that OPEC is not concerned with United States policies, it would simply adjust prices accordingly.

Exasperated, I toss the paper aside and head into the bedroom to pack for tomorrow's trip. The same kinds of economic alarms sounded when Melanie first talked about environmental action, but public outcry drowned them. Opponents were forced to soften their tones, speak of workable solutions. I cringe at the reminder: Hank's right about this much, at least—no matter what the Commission concluded, a lot of people clearly had a vested interest in getting her out of the picture.

SEVEN

A childish rhyme runs through my head as I fasten my seat belt: *I'm going to London to visit the queen.* Put in the context of this particular trip, the line should be: I'm going to London to *save* the queen, or rather, to save the queen's reputation—but, no, Melanie never thought of herself as a queen.

Absently watching people file past me down the narrow aisles, I can't help smiling to myself. Melanie Lombard was terrific at everything she did, but in one tiny contest, I was better. No matter how hard she tried, she could never beat me at chess. I think of the countless hours we spent sitting across that board over the years. Our last game was on election night. She said she was never going to be luckier than she was that night, and she made me sit down midst all the chaos and play chess. I would have beat her again, but we didn't have time to finish. The election was a landslide and she had to go downstairs to claim her victory earlier than we had expected. Inside my head, I can still hear people cheering and yelling, jumping up and down; I can still see her blue eyes, the way they danced at me across the chessboard.

"You're just like the chess queen, Nora. You rush straight at things. Nothing gets in your way." I thought that description was more apt for her than for me, and told her so. *"No . . . I'm the queen's knight,"* she

said. *"I go around corners, jump over things and show up when I'm least expected."* Then she left to address the nation.

The steward brings me a pillow and I settle in for the flight. I suppose her analogy the night of the election was fairly accurate in terms of how the two of us operated—me, like the queen, moving in a straight line; she, like the knight, playing the angles—but it didn't touch the essence. *Melanie Lombard became a king.* Only on a chessboard is the queen more powerful than the king, and even there, no one forgets for a second what piece the game is all about.

A man about my age in a crisp gray suit claims the seat beside me. He has short curly hair like David Weinhardt, but the face beneath it is fleshier, softer, less relentless. I wonder if there's even the slightest chance of keeping Melanie's affair from David, persistent as he is. Maybe the best I can hope for is to arm myself with information that might help me bargain with him. I talked to Hank about it on the phone last night and he agreed; I also told him I'd spoken to Danny Court, asked Court about the Secret Service escort, said I'd consult with him on education. Hank freaked. "Don't you understand that there are people, dangerous people, who might want you to keep your expertise to yourself?" he said ominously. There was no point in telling him that I *don't* understand, that my brain doesn't understand at all; his words feed directly into my body, keep me jumpy, on edge.

The cabin behind me fills with youthful laughter as groups of students work their way to the rear of the plane. Their exuberance strikes a distant chord—reminds me of a time before Hank, before everything was so complex, before the weight of responsibility.

I've probably been to London a dozen times, but my first trip across the Atlantic was a graduation present. It's hard to believe it was really twenty-five years ago that Melanie and I, squeezed into narrow economy seats, pored over travel guides, plotted adventures, circled cheap restaurants. After months of debate, we had decided to forgo the whirlwind tour in favor of a two-month sublet on the Left Bank in Paris. Now, comfortably seated in a first-class cabin, embarking on a painful mission directly related to that summer so long ago, I can't help thinking that something has gone wrong with time.

"Smile, Nora. Give me a big grin." Melanie's voice chimed through the bright glow of a dazzling afternoon, the first after days of drizzle. Wearing her khaki pants and WOMAN T-shirt, her hair a blond nimbus circling the camera, she knelt on one knee like a fashion photographer, snap-snapping.

In the wake of two full days at the Louvre, immersed in past glories, we'd burst forth with the sun, spilling our pent-up energy into Place de la Concorde. Tourists and locals weaved around us as I struck pose after pose to contribute to our collection of proof that we had, at last, made it.

We finally ran out of film, and Melanie headed off across the square to pick up another roll. I, in charge of the camera bag, strolled lazily, soaking in the delicious sun. At the fountain, I took out a coin, made a wish and tossed it in.

"Hello."

And there, standing beside the fountain, appeared the most beautiful specimen of French manhood I'd yet seen, and he was talking to me. "You're an American, aren't you? I can always tell. You look as if you're enjoying my city." Dark hair, dark eyes, warm smile and, ah yes, ze French accent.

"Doesn't everyone love Paris?"

"Actually no. Some people hate it, refer to it as an overrated old city full of rude natives. I like to dispel that image. I'm Jacques DeBrin." He extended a strong hand and I shook it.

"Nora Whitney."

"I'll bet you're part of a student tour group. Do you have time to let me give you a few tips? What I like best about Paris? There's an outdoor café just two minutes from here."

In the distance I saw Melanie crossing the square toward us. "I'm

here with a friend . . . a girlfriend. She's about a hundred yards behind you." Jacques turned and together we watched her approach;
then I introduced them.

Moments later we were munching croissants and sipping café au
lait. He told us that he, too, had been a student—of practically everything. He had studied literature at the Sorbonne, philosophy and astronomy in Munich and history in Prague, but had yet to earn a
degree in any subject. "I think my true calling is to observe and appreciate," he said, knocking us both out with his smile. To the over-
achiever twins, this man, who left even his sentences open-ended,
was deliciously refreshing.

The afternoon stretched into evening and the coffee changed to
wine. Jacques's dark eyes probed us each in turn and he listened as
well as he talked. "Why do you want to be an attorney?" he asked
Melanie, as if the choice surprised him.

She leaned back in her chair, waving her arm in that familiar
broad gesture that included all the known universe. "Law is the
structure of things," she explained. "You have to understand the
structure before you can affect it."

"Ah—then you plan to stir up the world. What about you, Nora?"

"I'm your basic behind-the-scenes sort. I play with computers."

"Nora's not just a programmer," Melanie insisted. "She's working to
teach those metal brains to *think*." The pride in her voice truly touched
me, even though I knew we had different ideas about my chosen work.

"I wouldn't have guessed you were the techie type," Jacques said,
smiling at me over his wineglass. "Too much vitality."

"See?" she chided, nodding at me. "I've been trying to convince my
friend here that her soaring IQ is not as much of a rare commodity as
her ability to get things done. Computers that think might be able to
help *people* to think, if someone as talented as Nora worked at bringing the two together."

Melanie had been determined to talk me out of what she saw as
hiding forever in the pathways of computer logic for a long time. Let

someone else sit in tiny rooms, theorize and discover, she persuaded—you should be the one to deliver such gifts to the world. By that time, I'd become adept at changing the subject.

Jacques seemed unconcerned about selecting a profession. He'd done a little of everything—taught French to rich kids in Kuwait, served as an interpreter in Saudi Arabia, worked on an oil rig in the North Sea and even considered professional soccer. "Let it come," he said of his wide-open future.

As the evening progressed, we sipped and laughed our way through philosophy, art and music, toasting our collective wit with liquid gold in sparkling glasses that changed colors beneath the glowing lanterns. Melanie's face was flushed and her eyes, in contrast, were a startling blue. The camera hung across her chest, blocking out the WO half of her WOMAN T-shirt, but no one was likely to be misled, least of all this handsome Frenchman, I thought, assessing the glazed admiration in his eyes. I can't say it didn't hurt, but I'd known it was inevitable from the moment he'd turned to see her striding confidently in our direction. What's more, I was used to it. I concentrated on counting my blessings: we were in Paris, the city of lights; the wine was smooth, the night was warm and the company was outstanding.

Jacques walked us home along the Seine. The few stars that were visible receded shyly as the Eiffel Tower appeared in a flash of instant illumination. A warm breeze carried the wet aroma of river, moss-covered stone and history, transformed by wine and love into a heady scent. We crossed to the Left Bank arm in arm, slowing our steps to stretch the night. We were inseparable already, but—"I have a friend I'd like you to meet," Jacques said. "An American. He's an engineering student, but don't hold that against him. I think you'll like him." He was looking at me.

An hour before we're due to land at Heathrow I sit up and take a copy of the new product proposal out of my briefcase. I'm doing, I think wryly, exactly what Melanie wanted me to do—trying to find a way for the genius of someone like Jim Barton to break through barriers that keep young minds from learning. I love my work and she was right: I'm more effective doing this than I would have been if I'd stayed in theoretical research at MIT. There, submerged in the study of artificial intelligence, I'd have simply been one of a dozen sharp minds, dutifully working next to an absolutely brilliant one.

It took a year for me to accept that nothing truly significant would be affected by my leaving MIT—and that there was, indeed, a big job to be done on the outside. After one year, I hopped the bus across town and joined Melanie at Harvard to begin work on my MBA. I'm not really sorry, but once in a while I remember that inner spark of excitement that exists between you and the yet-to-be-discovered—a private thing, that has nothing to do with practicality or the world.

EIGHT

My favorite hotel in Kensington isn't particularly posh, but it's unmistakable, so when I wake up in a room that's twice as high as it is wide, I know immediately that I'm in London. My heart starts to pound, flooded with the import of why I'm here. Then I look at the clock and realize it's still Saturday. I only napped for a couple of hours. I don't have to face the ordeal of Jacques until tomorrow.

And tonight I'm off to the theater. Tonight will be fun—my old lover Blaine Hennessey, parading his inimitable talent across a British stage.

I get dressed, take the Tube to the theater district and prowl around looking for a place to get something to eat. London pub fare is pretty dismal by evening, but I find a cozy spot where I make do with a large ale and a meat something-or-other; I eavesdrop on a spirited political discussion at the adjacent table. Not being up-to-date on local politics, I'm really just enjoying the rise and fall of the opposing voices, the youthful self-assurance that allows them to pursue their points with such bullheaded clarity. Then a voice, previously silent, interjects a thought in French-tainted English, and I actually turn in my chair and look. For a second my heart loses its rhythm. The speaker has dark hair and a lean, handsome, painfully familiar face. What are the odds that I'd run into—? It takes a sharp breeze as the door swings open to blow the cloud from my brain and get my heart in sync. Let's see—the last time I saw him he was twenty-eight. Add about twenty years. Uh-uhhh. No matter how much this man looks like Jacques, he simply can't be. The Frenchman at the table is—give or take a year— about twenty-eight years old. I finish the meat pie while my emotions tilt back and forth between amusement and shock. No wonder I'm nervous about seeing Jacques again. Something inside me is bound to break when I do. After a minute, I can't resist sneaking another look at the young man, savoring this last illusion.

It was four years after our summer in Paris that I ran into Jacques in a bar at Kennedy airport. I was on my way to a computer convention on the West Coast, but the snow flurries swirling about the taxi as it made its way through Queens had rapidly multiplied into a major snowstorm. I'd arrived at the airport just in time to learn my flight had been canceled.

The bar was standing-room only, packed with disgruntled would-be travelers. Elbowing my way to the rail, I ordered a scotch and water and was halfway through it when a voice I'd never forgotten said my name. "Nora."

My first thought was that I'd made him up—but, no, he was real. "Jacques! What are you doing here?"

"Trying to connect to a flight home. It's terrific to see you. Are you coming or going?"

"I was on my way to San Francisco, but it looks like I won't make it. I live here in New York now—I share an apartment with Melanie."

"Oh. Well, tell her hello for me. Look, neither of us is going anywhere right now, but we don't have to stay crammed in here." He took my arm and we squeezed out of the bar, finally managing to find a couple of empty seats in one of the waiting areas.

When I look back on it now, it seems as if this episode with Jacques took place on another planet and, in a way, it did—a way station, disconnected from our usual ties with space and time. We sat in a corner of the terminal and talked. We talked for hours. We talked about our lives, our plans, the movies we'd seen, the books we'd read, while outside the elements raged. We went back to the bar and had a few more drinks. We strolled through miles of corridors. We ate pretzels from a machine. We fell in love.

Jacques was given a voucher for a hotel room. We climbed into a van and rode there through the snow. The next day the weather was worse, adding layers upon layers of white stuff between us and the world. We stayed in the room all day making love. But then, the sun came out.

As his flight boarded, we held each other and made plans for me to visit him in Paris the following month. I had vacation time coming and I'd saved enough money. We kissed and waved good-bye. Since I'd already missed my convention, I took the bus back into the city, completely in love and happier than I'd been in years.

A week before I was scheduled to fly to Paris, Jacques called and told me not to come. "It was a mistake," he said. "I'm sorry." He might as well have yanked out my heart and ripped it in two. We never spoke again.

I check my watch to make sure I won't be late for the play, down the last drops of ale and think what a pitiful word *mistake* is—what a vague, useless, yet all-encompassing word.

At the theater I pick up the ticket Katy promised to have waiting at "will call" and find a handwritten note from Blaine inside the envelope, inviting me to a party after the show. I'm not sure how he knew I'd be here, but a party, I decide, could be just the thing. It might keep my convoluted mind from running all-night previews of coming events.

The play is a comedy and Blaine's co-star is a well-known British stage actress. From my vantage point in the third row center, I can make out every nuance on their faces as they toss witty lines back and forth, clearly having a good time and pulling the audience along with them. I've never seen Blaine perform on stage before and I'm impressed. His abundant movie charisma has been defined by cutesy macho roles, but live, and in a part that leaves room to play, he's an artist. It brings to mind the night I met him in that coffeehouse when he was a quarter short for another cup of cappuccino and he looked as if he were going to cry. My donation earned me an animated reenactment of the afternoon's audition and the seven lines he'd been allowed to read before they'd thanked and dismissed him. They were stupid lines, as I recall, belonging to a stupid minor character in a stupid thriller that later turned out to be so unthrilling it closed in a week. But with the next round of caffeine I got a touch of Lawrence of Arabia, Rhett Butler, Walter Mitty. That's the Blaine Hennessey I'm seeing on stage tonight.

Looking around during the second curtain call, I notice it's a full house, which means Katy must have had to pull some strings to get me such a great seat; that answers my question about Blaine's note. When the house lights go up, an usher promptly appears to escort me backstage. The next thing I know I'm being hugged by the star himself.

I have never been in love with Blaine Hennessey, but I like him a lot. We have the kind of rapport that may have slipped into something else for a while, but is at its strongest in the realm of understanding.

"Nora! Tell me the truth, I was smashing, wasn't I? This, of course, is Georgeanne Locke. Georgeanne—Nora Whitney, one of my favorite mentors."

The gorgeous, talented and reputedly neurotic Ms. Locke studies me with eyes that are disconnected from her beatific smile. We shake hands; I guess she is about forty, somewhere in the middle between Blaine and me. I also guess, as her slender fingers curl around Blaine's forearm, that she's quite smitten with him. It must be hard to be that beautiful, to be lured into feeling superior without ever being quite sure why; something about most of your assets being the luck of the draw.

"Nora saved my life a few years back," Blaine says, still high from the thunderous applause. "She's a big wheel in the computer biz—and a close personal friend of our late lady president."

That's me in a nutshell, all right.

At the mention of Melanie, Georgeanne's eyes grow wide, as if a slight dimension of interest has been added. I know what she's thinking—that perhaps my connection with President Lombard, my indirect link to power, is the answer to why Blaine bothers with me. After all, she must be thinking, how could such a handsome, charismatic young man, even in his pre-star days, have been drawn to a marginally attractive businesswoman so many years his senior? I smile. Let her wonder.

Blaine hustles us both into a waiting limousine. "By the way, Nora. My manager says your secretary has the sexiest voice he's ever heard. He wants to know if she looks as good as she sounds."

The party is in Blaine's hotel suite and there are at least fifty people already milling about when we arrive—the British in-crowd, mostly, with a few exceptions. I recognize a California state senator leaning against the bar talking to a thin European woman. An American recording artist whose name escapes me is holding court in the center of the room. I detach myself from Blaine and Georgeanne and start to work my way toward the bar when a short young man with thick glasses, wearing a drab brown suit, intercepts me.

"You're Nora Whitney, aren't you?" he blurts out. "Of Learning Parallels?" I nod, reaching around him to take a glass of wine from the tray of a passing waiter. "I'm Stanley Curtis, Mr. Westin's new assistant. I . . . I . . . it's a real honor to meet you."

"And I'm pleased to meet you, Stanley." I smile, not sure what an assistant to Garth Westin actually does.

"Mr. Westin said you'd be in the office Monday. I heard that you knew Mr. Hennessey and I thought you might be here tonight."

"Are you a friend of Blaine's?" Now that's hard to believe.

"No . . . oh no." He giggles, looking at the floor. "My uncle manages this hotel. He told me where the party would be."

"Ah, a gate-crasher."

He looks up, startled, and is only partially reassured by my amused grin. "I suppose so. I just wanted to meet you so badly. You've always been a real inspiration to me. I mean 'Metal Minds' changed the whole course of my life."

He's referring to a trade column I wrote for more than a decade. I'm flattered. "That's really nice, Stanley, but you didn't have to go to all this trouble. As Mr. Westin said, I'll be in the office on Monday."

His sad smile strikes an odd note in the back of my head. "But you'll be busy with Jimmy. Everything you've heard about Jimmy is true, Ms. Whitney. He's brilliant." He stares down at the floor again and actually shuffles his feet. It doesn't take a mind reader to know what he's thinking . . . and feeling.

"So I'm told, Stanley. You and I ought to be thankful we're just normal smart folk—being a genius can be a mixed blessing."

He looks grateful, even though we both know it's just as hard to be the one standing behind the genius; it takes a special kind of commitment. Gazing across the room, I notice the bevy of rapt faces hanging on Blaine's every casual word and amend my thought. On the other hand, maybe this nice young man and I are just an evolved form of groupie.

Stanley is reciting the development of his personal belief system, which sounds a lot like the birth of the Industrial Revolution. He's a nice person, but I've heard this story before. "I'm going to get a refill," I say, edging toward the bar. He nods and scoots along beside me. While the bartender pours me another glass of wine, I scan the crowd seeking the right polite words with which to move on.

Georgeanne has settled on the couch next to the recording artist; he's entertaining her with dramatic gestures and silly faces. Blaine is standing in the doorway greeting a couple of late arrivers, a portly man with a neat gray beard and a small redheaded woman. The woman turns to face the room and I nearly drop my glass.

"You'll have to excuse me, Stanley," I say. "I see someone I need to speak to." Skirting the Victorian furniture and half-drunken bodies, I cross the room in a dozen giant steps and clasp both of Deena Brennan's hands in mine. Deena was Melanie's most trusted adviser—and the only person in her political entourage I could really relate to. I haven't seen her since the funeral.

"Nora! Wow . . . what a coincidence. You won't believe this! I was planning to call you as soon as I got back to the States."

Deena reminds me of a grown-up Little Orphan Annie, which helps her get away with saying things like "wow." She introduces me to her date, a pleasant-looking man, the head of the New York modeling agency where Blaine worked when he was financing his first acting classes.

"Jake and I are trying to decide whether we want to get married. They say that traveling together is a valid test." She throws back her head and smiles up at him winningly. "Why don't you check out the beautiful faces, sweetheart. Nora and I have some catching up to do."

We sneak around the corner to a relatively private spot in the adjacent sitting room. "That was Georgeanne Locke, wasn't it?" Deena says. "Whew, she looks dangerous. So what brought you to London? Don't tell me you're seeing Blaine again?"

"No, I'm just here on business—the same old business. But what are you doing these days?"

"Well, after I picked up the pieces, I went back to New York and took a job at Melanie's old firm, Cruikshanks and Harding—they made me a partner. It felt good, you know, just to be there practicing law in the same office. I met Jake six months ago. For a while I even thought I might be able to have a sane and normal life; but I've never been cut out for that. This is a little between-jobs vacation."

Deena smiles at me hesitantly. "If I do decide to marry Jake, our marriage would probably have a better chance if we're not in each other's hair so much, don't you think? If, for instance, I commuted home on weekends."

"You're going to go back to Washington?" I'm not particularly surprised. Deena has one of the keenest political minds ever to grace our nation's capital. She was with Melanie from the early Senate days and her compact body and firecracker personality are legendary on the Hill. I smile, wondering what brave rebel lawmaker is taking on Deena Brennan.

"I'm going to work for the president. For Danny Court," she says.

I lean back in the chair, aware that my chin has dropped and my mouth is hanging open.

When the smoke cleared after the assassination, the first thing to go was Deena—a highly visible symbol of what Democratic party leaders viewed as Melanie Lombard's uncompromising independent bent. Danny Court, more polished, willing and experienced in the wheeler-dealer arts, made that concession right off the bat, hoping no doubt to narrow the breach with those politicos whom Melanie had offended. Lacking his predecessor's personal mandate, Court simply didn't have the power to play the game Melanie's way.

Of course, a year later the president is still treading water, trying to trade this for that in an effort to accomplish something of the platform on which he was elected—or at least that's the way it seemed up until a few days ago. Still, I'm stunned. Deena Brennan is the epitome of the in-your-face style of political action, and she's heading back to the White House!

"Does anybody know?" I ask.

"Not yet. Danny's planning to announce it next week, so keep it under your hat. He called me two weeks ago. He's been so frustrated. He didn't sign on to be a wimp, Nora. We're going to try to go all the way—first the environment, then education, then the senior health initiative."

"What do you plan to do about Congress?" I ask doubtfully.

"Stick to our guns, veto anything half-assed. Yeah, I know, that'll just give us more legislative gridlock. What we really have to do is get back the public support, the outrage, put the pressure back on our elected representatives. I know Danny Court is no Melanie Lombard, but it's time for people to stop feeling sorry for themselves, to let go of the woman and back up the man who's trying to do the job."

The inflection in her voice sounds as if she's asking me something. It can't have anything to do with approval or permission, because Deena never asks for either one. "You said you were going to call me when you got home."

"I did. We need to persuade some key people very fast. I thought maybe you'd like to help us."

She may as well have picked up her large black purse and slammed me in the chest with it. An educational consultant, that's one thing; being a lobbyist is something else entirely. I look at her blankly; all at once I'm drowning in decades of conversation, listening to Melanie's soft voice alive with ideas, pushing, throwing tasks at me, absorbing me into her master plan—that plan she always carried with her like a flight bag, the weight of the world, light as a feather, but only for her.

Deena's wild red hair, encouraged by London dampness, leaps like tiny flames about my senses. Her sharp eyes probe for an answer. "There are obstacles, blocks we simply can't get over without considerable public pressure," she says. "I need to get on board with Danny and talk it out. I'll call you next week."

"I'll think about it," I say, as Jake's shadow precedes him into the doorway.

It's late. I realize only a dozen or so die-hard guests remain. I accept Jake and Deena's offer to drop me off at my hotel and follow Blaine's trail into the bedroom, where he and Georgeanne are having a heated discussion about someone named Ginger. I apologize for the interruption and assure Ms. Locke that meeting her has been an honor of the highest order. Blaine excuses himself and walks me to the door.

"There are times, you know, when I yearn for the anonymity of my former life," he whispers in my ear as he hugs me good-bye.

"But it passes."

"Yes." He laughs. "It passes. So why do we have to come all the way to London to get together when we live about three miles from each other? If this thing ever ends I'll call you. Take you out for cappuccino."

"Deal." I give him a peck on the cheek and join Deena and Jake at the elevator.

In the cab we talk about the modeling business, how New York has changed, how I've learned to come to grips with LA—everything except her new job. As we pull up in front of my hotel, Deena takes my hand and squeezes it in a gesture so like Melanie's that it sends a shiver up my arm. "We're heading back to the States in the morning. I'll call you."

I nod. I'm almost out of the cab when another thought occurs to me. "Deena, do you remember Melanie spending weekends in Philadelphia?"

"Sure. She used to visit an old college friend there. Cynthia something."

"Ah, that's right. David Weinhardt asked me about it, but my memory's not so good."

She smiles. "David interviewed me in New York and I definitely think he's hot. He'll do her up right, Nora."

He's hot, all right . . . or at least he's getting warm. That doesn't make it any easier being on the other side, valiantly trying to keep another one of Melanie's secrets. I bid them goodnight and go into the lobby, stopping by the desk to leave a wake-up call. The desk clerk, an elderly man with prim gray hair, notes my request reluctantly, as if I wouldn't need such an accommodation if I kept respectable hours. He hands me a slip of paper; Garth Westin called, but he didn't leave any message.

As I ride up in the elevator, I sort through a bag of confused loyalties. I sense, from the ease of her response, that Deena doesn't know about the real purpose of Melanie's weekends in Philadelphia. For a second, because she's one person I've always trusted, I feel like telling her about Jacques, about Hank's concerns. Ask her advice. But then I remember that she's now working for Danny Court; it wouldn't be right to tell her.

I undress and climb gratefully between the cool sheets, fervently hoping not to dream. At this moment I just want it all to go away and leave me alone—Melanie's affair, Hank's suspicion, David's book, Deena's job. I can feel the jet lag closing in like a giant thundercloud. Just before I fall asleep, I see for the briefest second, flashing against the inside of my eyelids, the face of that young Frenchman from the pub—not the face I have to meet tomorrow, but the face of a fantasy embedded in my mind. I guess I still feel more comfortable with things that aren't real.

NINE

Jarred to consciousness by the wake-up call, I sit up in bed and blink my eyes to orient myself. In an instant the Task-of-the-Day looms before me like one of Dickens's Christmas ghosts. Jacques. Two o'clock.

Sinking back under the covers, I tick off one by one the little diversions I'd planned to get me through this morning: Kensington Gardens, Trafalgar Square, a bit of window-shopping on Regent Street. Instead, I roll over and bury my head in the pillow. I don't want to go anywhere—the mass of anxiety growing inside craves only one thing: oblivion.

It's nearly noon when I finally climb out of bed. I splash cold water in my face, call room service for a pot of coffee and a Danish, then pace the floor.

How will it be for me, seeing Jacques after all these years? Sipping muddy, lukewarm coffee, I soberly remind myself that I'm here because this man's lengthy love affair with the most important woman of our time is on the brink of exposure, and the repercussions of that exposure could vibrate through the American mind-set for a long, long time. I'm here to trace down Hank's slim hope that it might be some other reason that brought these two people together at regular intervals over a quarter of a century—to find out if Jacques DeBrin can tell me anything that might cast an innocent light over years of secret meetings. In short, I'm here for damage control.

I peer out the window at gray streets. The day is dismal, London damp, January cold. It feels wrong somehow to be meeting Jacques on a day like this when all my memories of him are sun-washed, even the ones that were born in a snowstorm. There's a gnawing in my stomach—what am I afraid of? That I'm still in love with him?

More likely I'm afraid of hearing the truth. Do I really want to find out why he treated me the way he did? Do I want to learn how he could make love to me while he was still in love with her? What good will it do, now that I've chased his fantasy image through a lifetime of dysfunctional relationships?

I gulp the coffee, dress quickly, then stare into the mirror at a face he'll surely recognize. I have been told that I'm aging well. My skin is still good; most of the lines on my face, I realize, have formed over the last year, as if time had stood still while Melanie was alive.

The address Dennis gave me is on the other side of Hyde Park; I have an hour to kill, so I decide to walk. Within a block of the hotel the heavy air condenses into a light drizzle. Searching for a scarf in the pocket of my jacket, I find instead the old aviator's cap I picked up decades ago at a thrift shop in New York; I still wear it once in a while, when I feel whimsical. After a half second of doubt I pull it on, tucking my hair inside and letting the strap dangle—my Amelia Earhart look.

The park isn't deserted despite the thick weather. Ahead of me on the path, two little girls in pink coats and matching hats skip along on either side of their father. One of them squeals and runs ahead; the father laughs; the other child spins around, sees me—a grown woman wearing a funny cap—and giggles. She has a round, happy face. She makes me think of all the other little girls who lined the streets as Melanie passed, eager young faces with bright, adoring eyes. Little girls wrote Melanie hundreds of letters, dedicated poems to her, named their kittens after her. A hard lump in my stomach starts to smolder. They don't deserve to have their biggest role model diminished by something they don't understand.

It seems to me that the universe ought to give President Lombard a break on this one, let it slide, but I don't have a lot of confidence that the universe I live in will do that. Thanks to the double standard, a woman president's lapse will be far more shocking than all the philandering of her predecessors.

The father and his daughters emerge from the park, chase each other down a street and disappear. I pull out a city map to recheck my bearings and head in the direction of the address Dennis gave me. I find the building easily enough, but before I let myself through the gate I remove the aviator's cap and run my fingers through my hair. No matter what my mind has created over the last twenty years, I really don't know this man at all.

For several minutes I stand in the small courtyard staring at the number above the knocker. My hand reaches, hovers, then freezes— *he* is on the other side. A burst of chill air sweeps through the wrought-iron gate, penetrating my skin as easily as it does my jacket. I back up a few feet and sit down on a heavy stone bench, wincing as the cold spreads through my jeans. It's a quaint old building, only a few stories built in a semicircle around a tiny courtyard of brick and stone, with a dirt bed that would hold flowers at any other time of year. Today it is lifeless. No sooner does that awareness enter my head when the edge of a drape in the adjacent flat creeps back to reveal a curious woman who peers out at me, returning my tentative smile with a scowl. *Trespasser, begone!* I get up and move purposefully to the door of Number Four, grasp the knocker firmly and announce my presence.

No footsteps. No sounds from within.

After a minute, I knock again. And wait.

And again.

And wait.

No, I tell myself, *this can't be!* Searching through my purse I pull out the slip of paper with the day, time and address on it. Everything checks. I knock again. Then I back up and sit down once more on the stone bench. Maybe he's just late. Why would he agree to meet me here and then not show up? The mean-looking woman peers out again; I stare back at her until she drops the curtain.

Restlessly I shift my body on the cold bench and slide my emotions up and down the scale between anger, disappointment, confusion, concern. It's nearly three o'clock. Questions dart about my head like tiny gnats. Where is he? Did he just stand me up—or did he suddenly have pressing business elsewhere? Could Hank be right? What if Jacques's role is more complicated than that of a lover? Could something have happened to him?

Finally I knock on the door of the apartment where the scowling woman lurks; she answers immediately. "There's no one home next door," she snaps smugly, as if her clipped British accent should assure me of her superiority.

"I was supposed to meet a friend there an hour ago," I say.

"You're wasting your time. He hasn't been back all month, travels a lot, just keeps this place for when he's in town."

She starts to close the door, but I place my hand firmly against it. "The person I was supposed to meet doesn't live here, he was just borrowing the apartment. Do you know where I can reach the manager? I'd like to make sure he isn't in there, that he's not hurt or ill or something?"

"Just *borrowing* the apartment?" Her mocking tone says she suspected all along that I was here for some dirty little tryst. Then her eyes narrow. "You don't mean that Frenchman, do you? He uses the place once in a while, but he's not there now."

"The manager?" I repeat. "I'd just like to make sure."

Heavily lidded eyes look me over carefully, up and down. The wrinkles on her face are pulled taut into pursed lips, producing the same effect as a drawstring bag. "I run this place," she says finally, "but I don't see why I should let you into Mr. Zayad's apartment. He never said anything."

"There could be a dead body rotting in there."

For a couple of seconds, she actually seems to consider the possibility of what I've said. Then, frowning, she takes a key off a hook by the door. "I'm certain no one is there, but we'll take a little look just to satisfy your curiosity."

Apartment Number Four smells empty, looks untouched. It also oozes opulence; I feel as if we've stepped into a museum. Fine art, tapestries, what looks like authentic period furniture. The woman stands properly in the hallway as I peek into the kitchen, the bedroom, the bath. More of the same. The building may be modest on the outside, but this apartment certainly is not. Still, it's a small place and there's clearly no one here.

"Mr. Zayad has some nice things," she comments, locking the door. I wonder briefly if she thinks I'm casing the joint in preparation for a burglary, that I might come back and steal the Persian rugs.

"He's from somewhere in the Middle East?"

She nods. "One of those Arab countries; I can never keep them straight."

I thank her for humoring me and leave, proceeding down the street toward the nearest Tube station. My head isn't functioning properly, clogged as it is with a wide variety of emotions. As I round the corner, I sideswipe a stylishly dressed young man who fumbles the package he's carrying, but catches it just in time.

"I'm sorry," I say quickly. "I wasn't paying attention to where I was going."

His look of annoyance transforms into a winning smile. "No problem. It's always nice to run into a fellow American." He's in his twenties, a cocky young prince, and he looks as if he just stepped out of the window of an expensive men's boutique. I get this wild thought that I ought to pick him up—lure him back to my hotel, let him help me forget about that empty apartment full of rich lonely things. I've never done anything quite that decadent before.

He's still smiling at me. This is not a naive young man, I can tell. All at once, a part of me zooms out to see myself standing on a London street corner, thinking what I'm thinking. *Oh, Nora,* I sigh to myself sadly. Aloud to the young man, I say, "Have a nice day."

"The same to you," he replies. "Walk carefully."

And I do—very carefully, down the street and into the Tube station. What in the world got into me, anyway?

Back in my room, I order a sandwich from room service and wait until I've eaten it, then I dial Hank in New York. When he picks up on the first ring I get this eerie feeling he's been sitting by the phone for days, even though his voice is steady and unemotional. He insists on calling me back from a restaurant down the street.

"Jacques didn't show up," I tell him. "I waited over an hour."

For several seconds, he doesn't speak; then he asks me if I think there could have been a mix-up. I'm pretty sure that's not the case, but I tell him I'll check with Dennis Jacobson, in case Jacques left a message for me. I also tell him that the apartment where we were supposed to meet belongs to a man named Zayad, obviously one of Jacques's friends or business associates. He says he'll ask *his* friend, the same one who made discreet inquiries into Jacques's travel habits, if he can check out Mr. Zayad. Then he exhales through his teeth, emitting a soft whistle.

"I've got a funny feeling about this, Nora. I don't like it. I think you should come home now."

"I can't come home *right* now; it would look strange. I have a meeting in the office tomorrow. I'll leave tomorrow afternoon, as planned." I take a mental step backward, remembering that Hank's strong bias toward intrigue is contagious. "I probably just got stood up; it wouldn't be the first time," I say.

Hank, of course, has no intention of letting me plead business as usual. "Nora, somebody could have gotten to DeBrin. Any number of people would love to see Melanie's memory dragged through the dirt, maybe the same people who wanted her dead."

"She was killed by a lunatic," I remind him.

"Yeah, right. But think for a minute: if someone doesn't want Court to get Melanie's momentum going again, what better way to crush it for good than to tarnish the woman who originated it? On the other hand, if DeBrin really is an informant, that ups the ante all around. It would mean that somebody else is even more interested than we are in keeping the relationship quiet."

"Just who *are* these people you keep talking about, these *somebodies?*"

"Well, I think you can rule out the Mob—this isn't their kind of thing. Beyond that, it's wide open; you can include every radical fringe group that opposed anything Melanie Lombard stood for." Sounding a lot like Bennie's satirical account of his father's dinner-table conversation, Hank reels off a list of pompous names and descriptions. Some I've heard before; some I haven't—there are the Children of Righteousness, exemplifying what happens to religion in the hands of mean people; there are those strange folks who call themselves Chaos and are against anything that seems to make sense; there's an ultraconservative organization with some French name that sounds like *patronize*, Le Patronage; there's a weirdo group of male chauvinists who go by the collective name of The Father; there are skinheads—the list goes on—everything but the Bavarian Illuminati. Very enlightening.

"And there's the United States government," Hank concludes. "Certain individuals and factions within it. I'm not talking about Danny Court, I'm talking about powerful, nonelected forces within the government. Other governments, too. Those third-world countries where DeBrin apparently conducts business are always suspect."

I'm overwhelmed. "What did you mean when you said somebody could have *gotten to* him, to Jacques?" I ask.

"That depends on who the bad guys really are and what the whole story is about Melanie's connection to him. I don't know—but I don't think you can assume that he didn't show up because he lost track of the time."

It never occurred to me that Jacques might have simply forgotten the date, lost track of the time, as Hank so quaintly put it; but it did occur to me that he may have changed his mind about seeing me. Maybe our brief interlude at the airport years ago had faded in his mind . . . and then he suddenly remembered, and didn't have the nerve to show up and face me.

"I shouldn't have asked you to go over there in the first place," Hank says. "I don't know what I was thinking. You shouldn't be involved."

The question of my involvement naturally reminds me of Deena. I tell him about running into her at Blaine's party, that Court is bringing her back to the White House, that she's asked me to lobby for that new environmental bill. Hank groans loudly. "Damnit, Nora, if they wouldn't let Melanie carry out her programs, they sure as hell won't let Court do it. I'm telling you it's dangerous. If they think you can make a difference, they'll stop you."

They! I'm sick of all these pregnant pronouns. "From what you just finished telling me, Hank, practically everything is dangerous. Life, for sure." I promise to call him as soon as I get back to LA, and ring off, drained. I shouldn't be involved, he says. But the question is: who should be?

Next I call Dennis Jacobson—reluctantly, because I told him we wouldn't bother him again. No, he hasn't heard from Jacques, has no idea why he didn't show up, absolutely will not give me his Paris address or phone number and would appreciate it if I didn't call again. I don't blame him. Just for the heck of it, I try long-distance information, but I'm not surprised to find that Jacques DeBrin's number in Paris is unlisted.

I give it up and concentrate instead on tomorrow; I check the closet to make sure my suit is relatively wrinkle-free and pick through my case to find the appropriate accessories. Jacques or no Jacques, I refuse to view this trip as a wild-goose chase. Tomorrow I get to meet the kid who's created a computer program that may border on mind-boggling; at the very least, it's going to brighten my day.

TEN

The London branch of Learning Parallels occupies the two top floors of a modern office building near Paddington Station. It's almost ten o'clock when I step off the elevator and walk through the glass double doors. The receptionist is new since my last visit, a studious-looking woman with an unusually pointed nose. "May I help you?" she asks, zeroing in on me.

Of course she doesn't know me by sight, so I can't pass up the chance to have a little fun. "I have an appointment with Stanley Curtis," I say, keeping my voice low. The door to Garth's office at the end of the short hallway is probably open. "My name is Susan Calvin."

She doesn't balk at the name but does seem surprised that I've asked for Stanley. He must not get many callers. I can't help smiling as she repeats, twice into the intercom, the name of science fiction's most famous female roboticist. "Calvin—that's what she said. Susan Calvin." The genre being rather narrow, I figure Ms. Pointy Nose won't recognize the heroine of the books I read as a child, but I'm willing to bet a year's salary that Stanley Curtis will pick up on it—we computer types have more in common than our work. I hear a scuffling sound in the hallway and a wide-eyed and breathless Stanley rounds the corner into the reception area. I raise my finger to my lips quickly so he won't give me away.

"Ms. . . . . Calvin." A sound escapes him that can only be described as an incredulous giggle. "It took me a second, but then I realized it had to be you."

"Can we go to your office? I thought we could chat a few moments before I meet with the others."

Stanley's office is really just an extended cubicle. "It's so funny," he whispers. "When I read your column I always imagined you looked like the woman in those robot books. I mean the way I imagined she looked, when I read them as a kid."

I ask Stanley how much he knows about the geometry program Jim Barton's working on and the sophistication of his answer surprises me. He claims it could teach the most advanced concepts of geometric space and relationships to a five-year-old child. The actual concepts. He admits that the language part, the voice module, is pretty standard textbook voice-over—nothing special. Language is necessary, though, to communicate what you know, certainly to pass tests. But he describes the program itself as spatial trial and error, the learning process at its most elemental.

My initial hunch had been right. Stanley wrote that proposal for Garth. I recognize the words—and the zeal. I have an affinity for smart kids like this; they're a scant spark short of the Neils and Jimmys, but still close enough to see the crazy fire. I realize he's like me.

We both freeze as Garth's voice bounces down the hall. "Angela? Isn't Nora Whitney here yet? I thought I heard you talking to someone out there."

"It was a woman to see Mr. Curtis. A Ms. Calvin."

"Oh, good lord. *Susan* Calvin, I suppose?"

"That's right. Did I do something wrong?"

"Oh, good lord."

Stanley and I smirk at each other as Garth's footsteps near the cubicle. "Nora," Garth says, smiling to cover his annoyance, "you're playing games with my staff. Curtis, this is Ms. Whitney from Los Angeles." He introduces me, as if Stanley really believed I was Susan Calvin, a fictional character come to life. Garth's sense of business etiquette is far more rigid than mine and schmoozing with an underling in the office before being properly announced comes across to him as rude.

"It's okay, Garth. I wanted to know what a young person thinks about this new geometry program." I thank Stanley for sharing his thoughts with me and follow Garth down the hall.

"I left a message at your hotel," he says, after we've settled in his plush office. "Pamela was hoping you could join us for dinner on Sunday."

I explain that I ran into some friends at the theater Saturday night and Sunday got booked up. "Give my regrets to Pamela, will you? How are the kids?" I'm stretching this out because I want him to bring up business first. I'll be able to tell a lot about this project by the way he plunges into it.

"They're fine. Wonderful, in fact. You must have seen the new Georgeanne Locke/Blaine Hennessey play. I hear it's quite good." He's doing the same thing, hoping that I'll give away the strength of our interest. It's a small-talk duel.

I decide to let him win. "I like what I've read so far, Garth. It looks like you're making strong progress. I'm here for a firsthand look."

He smiles, gets up and escorts me to the door. "Well then, Ms. Whitney, prepare to be astounded."

The room where Jim Barton plies his genius is an expanded version of Neil's office, lined with tables stacked with every imaginable sort of equipment. Barton is sitting in front of a large monitor; he doesn't acknowledge our entrance until Garth walks over and addresses him. I can almost see the data-filled bubble above his head burst as he turns with a start, focusing on Garth as if he's never seen him before.

"Jimmy, this is Nora Whitney."

James Barton III is pretty much what I expected, a thin, unkempt, intense-looking young man with intelligent eyes in an otherwise for-gettable face hidden behind a couple of days of stubble.

"You're the one who knew Melanie Lombard, right?" he says.

"That's right."

"Then you must know her son—Ben Cochran. I saw his film at the university festival last week. Unbelievable. If I ever get to the States maybe you could introduce me to him."

I'm hit with a split second of disorientation. People are always ask-ing me about Melanie, but this is a first. Bennie will love it when I tell him. "I'm sure he'd really like to meet you. I'm here to learn geome-try, Jimmy."

He bows elaborately, waving me toward the only table where chaos has been subdued. Garth is standing in the center of the room hesitantly. He knows I like to do this sort of thing without an audi-ence, but he doesn't want to leave. "I'll come back upstairs when I'm finished," I say, smiling at him. "Maybe Angela can order in some lunch, since I don't have to be at the airport until three o'clock."

Jimmy's watching the way I handle his boss. Typical of supertal-ent, he probably ignores Garth most of the time, but he must have fig-ured out by now that he could wind up a maniac wasting away in a tiny dark room filled with silicon and crystal if it weren't for the Garth Westins of this world.

After Garth leaves I raise my hand for Jimmy to be silent while I study the paraphernalia on the table. The dataglove is more like a plastic bag than a glove. It doesn't have all the sensitivity of the bulky types, but it's a lot cheaper. The headset is also as economical as we can get, with wire bracings and wide-screen goggles that stretch over the ears. The big money is in the box. Digital optics—stereoscopic laser scanners projected through photoreactive crystals. It's a lot less powerful than the supersimulators, which means it won't be able to do as much, but it's big bucks no matter how you weigh it.

"Set me up," I say to Jimmy, climbing into the secretarial chair as if I were taking the helm of a spaceship. I adjust the headgear and slip my hand into the dataglove. Here we go.

The voice-over introduces me to the world of shape and relationship. It's a world in which I am completely immersed, having escaped Jimmy's workroom with the flip of a switch. I am told that there are theorems which describe this world and measure its relationships, but that I must discover them for myself. When I do, it will be the voice's job to reinforce them and help me remember. Stanley had this part down perfectly—mundane.

But visually I'm really here; I'm floating in blue-tinted nothingness, being approached by a large square that grows as it nears and stops, framing my body. My hand moves in the dataglove and its virtual representation grasps one side of the square; the square stays intact, but I am provided with a rod the same length so I may build on to it, creating a skeletal house around me—a cube. As I build, the voice explains what I am doing in tried and true geometric laws. Suddenly, one side of my box fills with bright red; then each side in succession. I'm learning about area. Then color spills into the box, filling it as I swim to the top.

The experience is more real than anything I've seen in the virtual-reality entertainment centers—nearly as real, in fact, as the big flight simulators. Of course, Jimmy doesn't give it all to you; he second-guesses you and fools you into thinking that it's all there. It's like a movie set. I play with lesson one of the program for nearly an hour. When I emerge from the headset and pull the dataglove off my hand, I see that Jimmy has gone back to his spot before the large monitor and that the screen is dancing with two-dimensional representations of the same material I've just experienced.

He notices that I've disconnected, but doesn't get up. Instead, I walk over and sit down beside him, paying homage to what I've just seen. Most software designers wait impatiently for engineers to make their work first possible, then affordable. Jimmy Barton, on the other hand, has manipulated perception in order to design software that works with less, creating convincing simulation in memory that shouldn't be able to hold it. What this means is that it looks, tastes and feels like a million-dollar system, but it isn't. I know now why Garth was so excited. It isn't a ten-thousand dollar system either, but it's a giant step in the right direction.

In fact . . . I'm thinking of what Stanley said about grasping the concept regardless of the language. Kids who don't speak English could still learn the basic principles of geometry, even without a translation. Kids with learning disabilities could *experience* what their teachers have been trying to explain. My heart begins to pound and I feel that crazy rush sweep through my brain. This is just what Melanie was talking about, way back in college.

Misunderstanding my silence, Jimmy shakes his head and points to the monitor in front of him. "I can give you this with the headgear that'll make it seem three-dimensional, and limited interaction with a joystick. But then again, so can anyone else."

"No thanks. I like it the way it is."

"I can't cut back any further. The program is already plugged with tricks. Until someone comes up with a cheaper stereoscope, this is as lean as it's going to get."

"I know. We won't be able to mass-produce yet, but I think we should complete it anyway—and give it away if we have to."

He sits up straight and spins his chair around to face me. Whatever he's about to say doesn't make it out of his mouth. Instead he begins to giggle. I tell him I'm not exactly sure what I have in mind, but that it starts with putting him under contract to Learning Parallels—at a reasonably lucrative salary, of course.

"You're going to pay me handsomely for it and then give it away?" He's getting the chuckles under control, but his eyes are watering. "Is Neil Mackey planning to run for president, chief saint or what?"

Neil will consider him our ace in the hole for the future, I explain.

As for giving away the program, I ask him to keep that our secret. That's certainly not the way I plan to present it to Garth. "You just keep working; complete as much as you can, because very soon we'll have to haul you over to LA and let Neil have a look at you."

His grin, enhanced by glistening eyes and stubble, makes him look insane. I can't tell whether he's smiling at my bizarre business approach or just keen on the thought of coming to Los Angeles. I toss out some numbers, parameters and perks and he nods, still grinning.

All of a sudden I'm ambushed by a memory of myself struggling away in a computer lab at MIT. I could have sat there forever and never come up with anything as innovative as Jimmy's work, but it would have been fun trying. Stanley Curtis isn't the only one who imagined I was the twin of fictional chief roboticist Susan Calvin. I wonder for a second if I would have been happier. I guess it depends on whether you believe that results are everything. Melanie did, of course. Maybe I do, too. I glance again at Jimmy Barton's computer screen. Damnit, I spent most of my life trying to prove myself to her and she went and died before I could do it.

By the time I let myself out the door, Jimmy's already retreated into his head and his hand is tapping rhythmically against the side of the chair.

The conference table in Garth's office is laid out with sandwiches and coffee. He sits behind his desk reading a trade paper, pretending he doesn't know I'm standing in the doorway.

"He cheats," I say, walking to the table to claim a mug. "I particularly like the way he cheats."

Garth looks up and smiles tentatively. It occurs to me that he doesn't really know how Jimmy manages to pull this off. He only knows that it works. Over lunch we discuss the thin market for high-end educational equipment and the need to position the company for the future with a high-profile product. I don't confide all my thoughts to him, but I talk about learning centers and how I hope to convince

Neil to go with this system as a sort of loss leader. I also tell him Jimmy's agreed to a contract.

He looks stunned; it's clear to me that, despite his brave face, he never really expected the program to do more than impress me. He hoped I'd be willing to sign Jimmy and that I'd tell Neil what fine work was going on here.

"You're doing a terrific job, Garth." I really mean it. He picked Jimmy Barton out of a dozen hotshot hackers. He picked the right time and the right level of progress to make a serious proposal to the home office. And he was smart enough to seek the counsel of a fresh kid like Stanley Curtis. "I'll have Katy send Jimmy's contract to you as soon as I get back."

In the taxi speeding toward Heathrow, I stare out the window at the overcast English sky. I didn't accomplish what I came here to do. I didn't see Jacques; I'm not any closer to figuring out how to keep Melanie's beacon of inspiration flickering . . . how to keep a generation of little girls from losing their role model. But I did find something else.

And that something might, over the course of time, be almost as big. My mind is running on fast-forward now. I'm not exactly sure how I'm going to do it, but I've got to make sure Jimmy Barton's program is used by real kids, not a few years down the road, but soon! Which means I'm probably going to need government funding—Neil can't carry all the research and development with funds from the corporate pocketbook.

For Danny Court to have enough clout to help me get what I need, he'll have to survive his current battle. I'm pretty sure I know what Deena has in mind for me to do—and I'm thinking *I can do that*, when Hank's warning leaps forth, waves a red flag in front of my face. Determined, I will it away—well, most of it anyway.

Why didn't Jacques show?

The low ceiling of colorless clouds suddenly seems appropriate. No big ugly black rolling thunderclouds. No lightning bolts. No persistent sun casting silver linings. Just a flat, gray, no-comment sky. I lean back in the cab and close my eyes. At least I'm not sitting around watching sunlight dance on my office walls; at least I'm excited again. Besides, I tell myself, I must be pretty special—it's not everyone that gets hugged by a movie star.

ELEVEN

There's a trick Melanie taught me when we were in school. You look at something for a while and then you separate the colors, concentrate on each one. Then you close your eyes and re-create the picture in your mind, seeing only the blue. Then you add the green . . . the brown. It was a game she'd made up as a child and she said it helped her focus.

I never got very good at it. But now, gazing out the airplane window somewhere over Greenland, I'm entranced by the way the sunlight melts over the sky. If I close my eyes and concentrate on the bits of cobalt blue at the outer edges, I can make the sun's rays pull back into their source and then flow forth again, bathing the sky.

I awake as we're landing in LA, the dream still vivid in my head. I was floating in Jimmy's blue-tinted world, but instead of a square there was a yellow ball coming toward me. At first I thought it was the sun, but when it got closer I saw that it wasn't a ball at all but a woman with yellow hair, sunlight reflecting off blond curls, bright blue eyes wide with surprise and fear. "Melanie," I called, trying to swim to her through an azure field that had suddenly become thick as soup. Her expression didn't change. In all my life I've never seen her face like that—so lost, so vulnerable. "Melanie," I called again, still trying to close the distance between us, but my arms and legs refused to respond.

Finally I remembered I was in a computer program. Reaching up, I tore the headgear from my face and found myself standing in an empty room. Melanie wasn't there. The illusion was gone. Then, hearing a sound behind me, I spun and, to my horror, encountered the tight purposeful mouth and narrowed eyes of her assassin, crazy Jennie Wheeler, who lifted her hand, pointed a gun at me and fired. No sound, only light—light everywhere. And then there was sound, but it was only the pilot's voice waking me out of my nightmare with the welcome news that Los Angeles was imminent below.

It isn't until I get through Customs that I remember my car is not in its usual spot at the Valet Garage. With the residue of that dream fluttering sickly around my stomach and a head that's beginning to ache, I pick up my bag and start outside to catch a cab when I hear my name resound over the paging system's loudspeaker. At the white courtesy phone, I'm given a message from Katy—that Mr. Weinhardt will meet me outside the baggage-claim area. My first response is annoyance. After all, he offered, I clearly refused, and now he's taken it upon himself to ignore my wishes, show up anyway. I'm tired; I don't want to make small talk or, worse yet, *real* talk, and have to watch out for everything I say. At the same time, I feel a flicker of amusement. He's a pushy guy; the challenge kind of intrigues me. It would be childish at this point to refuse a ride home, but nothing says I have to talk to him.

As soon as I exit through the glass doors, I hear him call my name. David's BMW is parked a little ways down on the other side of the center divider; he's standing in front of it, waving his arms at me. Switching my bag to the opposite shoulder, I wait for the light to turn green and start across the street. Suddenly a large dark blur explodes out of the peripheral vision of my left eye; someone screams and a blow to my back sends me sprawling to land facedown less than a foot from the far curb. Pain shoots through my hands. A young male voice, very close to my ear, asks if I'm all right. I realize, as his weight lifts from me, that he was lying across my back.

"I don't know." I try to move and my body responds stiffly. "I guess so." There are voices all around me and I recognize David's.

"Your hands are bleeding," he says. "Careful, let me help you up." He and the young man lift me to my feet and I balance precariously, then lean against David for support. "You saved my life," I say to the young man. He's wearing a leather jacket with a dragon stenciled on the front; he looks about eighteen.

"Just lucky," he answers. "You sure you're all right?"

A policeman arrives and takes names; David and a couple of other witnesses describe what they saw. Everyone agrees that I was nearly struck by a dark blue Dodge van with tinted windows. No one could see the driver.

"It had no plates and I'm telling you it headed straight for her . . . came out of nowhere," David says, breathing heavily. The policeman looks dubious.

"It was parked over there," the boy in the leather jacket adds. "Left the curb and went right through the light. When I saw it wasn't going to stop, I just leaped at her." I memorize the name and address he gives to the policeman. I won't take away from his heroism by offering him something today, but I owe him.

An airport official comes out to confer with the policeman, who then tells us that the van has already been found abandoned on the other side of the airport. "Can you take this woman to a hospital or should I call an ambulance?" he asks.

"I'll take her." David scoops up my garment bag and puts an arm around my waist. I turn to offer a final thanks to the boy in the leather jacket, but he's already left. As I climb into David's car I notice that the knee of my pants is badly ripped. My leg has begun to throb.

David is silent as we drive to the hospital and looks almost angry when I tell him he doesn't have to wait for me. Luckily it's a slow day, and in less than an hour my hands and knee have been cleaned and bandaged and several stitches hold my left palm together. We sit in the car in the hospital parking lot, looking at each other.

"Nora, that van came right at you. It looked intentional."

"That's crazy." I don't want to hear this; not after telling myself over and over that Hank's theories belong in the movies, not in real life. I haven't even *done* anything yet!

"Yeah, I know it's crazy," he says, "but the guy did run the light, and you were right there in the intersection. He had dark windows, no plates, and he just walked away from an expensive van."

I feel as if I might start crying—I don't *want* to be afraid. David looks at me for a minute, then lets the subject drop and starts the car; I lean back and close my eyes. They didn't give me any drugs, but I'm feeling no real pain. I'm just sore and upset. I'm also, I realize, very hungry. Most of all, I don't want to go home.

"I had hoped to convince you to go to dinner with me," he says, as we pull out of the lot. "Now, of course, adding trauma and pain to your jet lag, it sounds like an exceedingly bad idea."

"I'll take you up on it anyway—that is, if we can stop by my house so I can change my pants."

He looks at me, surprised. "No problem. Italian okay?"

Actually, a couple of pounds of pasta just might do the trick. We drive to my house and go in; I head for the bedroom, while he wanders into the den, drawn no doubt by my walls of books.

"Are those college yearbooks I see on that top shelf?" he calls out.

"High school and college mixed together. Go ahead, but don't pull the bookcase over getting to them."

By the time I've cleaned up and changed clothes, I find him sitting at my desk staring at Melanie's senior class picture; the expression on his face is one I recognize very well. This man—join the club—is in love with her.

"She looked extraordinary even then, didn't she?" I say, breaking his reverie.

He nods, lifts the corner of the page and flips it forcefully as if he can't allow himself to look at her any longer. He turns a few more pages, then stops, trailing his finger across the row of smiling students until he apparently finds what he's searching for. "I don't mean to sound unkind," he says, looking up at me, "but it's hard to believe Dennis Jacobson married this woman—don't you think?" Peering over his shoulder at the picture, I get his point. Cynthia Powell is— was—a very homely girl. "No activities listed," he mumbles. Flipping a little further, he scans the list of names opposite the full-page orchestra photo. "Nope." He closes the yearbook and lays it on the corner of my desk. "Funny she wasn't in the orchestra, especially since Dennis's wife is a musician."

Uh-huh. In fact I'm sure the *only* thing Dennis's wife has in common with that girl in the yearbook is that they're both named Cynthia. I feel a flood of resentment at Melanie for manufacturing such a weak cover story and leaving me to deal with it. She deserves to have her affair plastered on the front page of some slimy tabloid, but I have to make sure that doesn't happen, because as usual she's attached herself—and me—to things that matter too much to be sacrificed.

"Hank must be confused about this woman," I say lamely. "He must have the names mixed up or something."

"Looks like it. Well, are you ready?"

David chooses a small restaurant in West LA, the classic neighborhood spot with only eight tables, checkered cloths and a rotund proprietor in an apron. We order fettuccine and it comes quickly.

"How was your trip?" he asks.

Steering the conversation in what feels like the safest direction, I tell him about Jimmy Barton and the geometry program; I have him close his eyes and I walk him through lesson one with as much detail as I can remember. He's amazed. Despite the fact that he'd rather hear about Melanie, I've definitely got his attention.

"Can you do that?" he asks, incredulous. "Are we really at a place where that level of technology is available to schoolchildren?"

"It's so close, David." I'm leaning forward in the chair and my eyes are probably shooting sparks. "Still too expensive, but Jimmy uses shortcuts that give you top-notch experience for a lot less cost than anything out there now. I'm hoping to get the full program written and the system working in prototype form. You can't have something like this without letting at least *some* kids learn from it."

"Maybe you should go straight to the top and talk to the president," he suggests. "Melanie put together a pretty aggressive education package, and if things work out for him he might be ready to go for it."

I tell him that Court has already asked me to consult on an education initiative, but if he's impressed, he doesn't show it. Instead, he reminds me of the time City Councilwoman Melanie Lombard made an unannounced visit to the governor of New York and walked away with a promise of two state-supported recreation centers and a free health clinic in her district.

I remember her going to Albany, and I remember the results, but I don't think I ever heard the full report as David tells it—the photos she tossed on the governor's desk, exactly what she said. Listening to him, I feel slightly disoriented. What else does he know about Melanie that I don't know?

"You might give her technique a try," he says, grinning.

I wrestle another piece from the loaf of Italian bread, dip it in olive oil. Did he recount that incident as a suggestion for how I should deal with Danny Court—or is he just hoping I'll try to outshine his story with another of my own? That's why we're here, after all; that's why the conversation always comes back to her.

"Okay, now I've got one for you," I say. "It has to do with what we were talking about before."

Apparently he doesn't have his tape recorder with him and, for some reason, that pleases me. He puts down his fork, instantly attentive, and listens to the story of a little boy who drew wonderful pictures. Peter was the son of a woman in one of Melanie's college classes and, though his skill at translating what he saw was exceptional, he couldn't learn to read or follow any kind of linear instruction. His disability obsessed Melanie. One day she turned to me, as I labored over some question of computer theory, and asked if I thought it would ever be possible for a computer to show children like Peter the sequences that made their visions come together—*show* them, so they'd understand the process. It's a perfect example of how Melanie worked: all of a sudden it became my responsibility to make that happen.

David's eyes are large and alive; I can see him sifting this latest revelation through the volumes already recorded in his head. "And now you work for Learning Parallels," he says. "Does this program you've developed in London do what she was talking about?"

"I think it can . . . it will." I hear the soft wonder in my voice; I'm in awe myself, once again, at the scope of her vision.

He shakes his head. "Pretty effective delegation, I'd say. That story sends shivers through me."

"Yeah, me too."

We stop talking for a while and shovel in the pasta; I'm not doing too bad a job of it, considering the bandages on my hands. Just as I'm beginning to relax, David puts down his fork again and leans across the table.

"Nora, what can you tell me about Jacques DeBrin?"

He's managed to catch me completely off guard. I force myself to meet his eyes, chiding myself for being so stupid. "He's a man Melanie and I met in Paris a million years ago," I say blankly.

"Yeah, I know. He's the guy with Melanie in that photo. It took some digging to find out his full name, since you couldn't remember and the Jacobsons won't have anything to do with me. Jacques DeBrin is a business broker, specializes in setting up investment deals for filthy-rich oil barons all around the Persian Gulf."

"You certainly know more about him than I do," I say. That's true—I only know *one* thing about him. "What's the point?"

"I don't want to blow this out of proportion," he persists, "but when I get a hunch and it becomes an obsession, I've learned to listen to it. I tracked down your old college classmate Cynthia Powell in Chicago—she hasn't seen Melanie since freshman year, except on television, of course. It looks like Melanie was just using her name. I knew this stuff with the Jacobsons wasn't right, but Melanie wouldn't bother to cover up something unless it really mattered. That's when I decided to trace down the other guy in the picture. I thought maybe he could tell me something about Dennis Jacobson."

About Dennis? David must think—I try to keep my voice even, only mildly interested. "And?" I say.

"Strangest thing. Jacques DeBrin left his Paris apartment a few days ago and no one's seen him since. He's disappeared. Uh, Nora, you've got alfredo sauce on your chest."

I look down, and sure enough, there's a nice fat stain above my right breast, but I resist the urge to dab at it. *Disappeared!* Suddenly I'm exhausted; I can't do this anymore. I lean back in my chair, meet David's eyes. "I'm sorry, David. This is all very interesting, but eight hours of time difference is finally beginning to catch up with me. You filled me with good heavy food, now you're bombarding me with confusing innuendos regarding things I know nothing about and I'm beginning to feel used. Let's call it a night." I stand up and he follows suit, tossing a few bills on the table.

"Are you mad at me?" he asks, after we're in the car and on the way to my house. "I really don't want you to be mad at me."

"No, I'm not mad. You're simply a man doing his job. But I can't tell you what I don't know and you won't get anything extra out of me by feeding me or chauffeuring me around."

"I see. Obviously, you think I use any and all forms of scummy wiles to get my victims to cough up fodder for my books."

"Well?"

"Maybe just a little bit—the scummy wiles part, that is. But let me tell you something else. I knew a lot about you before we even met—

a lot. I'd talked to people, read about you. But I wasn't prepared to be attracted to you. That just happened. Yes, I want to know everything I can about Melanie—that *is* my job. But at the same time I find you very interesting." He looks absurdly serious, almost ferocious. Then, although his mouth doesn't smile, his eyes do. "I warn you, I never lie about my personal interests. What usually happens, though, is that I mess up a lot—like I guess I messed up tonight. If you must know, my mess-up rate up to now is a perfect one hundred percent."

He couldn't have said anything that would have surprised me more, and suddenly, in spite of myself, I'm smiling. Of course, he notices. "Is that a silent 'me too'? Never mind, I won't pry. But sometime I'd like to know more about what makes Nora Whitney tick."

"I'm not famous enough for you to write about."

"No," he agrees as we pull into my driveway. "You're not."

David walks me to the door, waits until I unlock it and then hands me my bag. "I understand you used to date Blaine Hennessey," he says.

There it is again, somebody's idea of my claim to fame. "Yes, but I don't intend to tell you a thing about it."

"I went out with an actress once. It was a pretty gruesome experience." He looks at me intently as if I were one of those pictures in which you're supposed to find thirteen things that start with Q. "Can you fit me in for another interview on Wednesday?" he asks finally.

I nod. I feel sort of awkward; I don't know how to behave with a man like this. He leans forward and kisses me lightly on the cheek. "Be sure to lock the door behind you," he says as he leaves. It's the same casual tone you use when you say *drive carefully* to a departing guest, but I hear the concern behind it. He hasn't forgotten about the van at the airport. Neither have I.

TWELVE

My boss arrives at the crack of dawn, so he's already waiting for me when I limp into his office, favoring the knee that now sports a large Band-Aid beneath its nylon sheath. My body feels as if I've spent all week in the charge of a sadistic personal trainer. I sit in one of Neil's leather chairs, careful not to wrinkle the impeccably tailored charcoal gray suit I wore today to remind him of the equally impeccable nature of my professional judgment.

"What happened to you?" he asks. I explain how I did a belly flop in the middle of the street and about the brave young man who flew through the air to save my life. Neil insists that I have Katy check into the young man's situation. "If he needs a job, I'm sure we can find something; if he's going to school, a little scholarship is in order."

"Thanks. I appreciate that." I don't mind being treated like a corporate asset; it's flattering.

"Got your inner clock readjusted?"

"I think so. Slept through the night anyway. Katy's typing up the agreement I proposed to Jimmy Barton. It'll be ready for you to look at this afternoon."

"Obviously you think the kid's got more than the usual dazzle?"

Earlier this morning, while waiting for my car at the mechanic's shop, I prepared this speech; I crafted the phrases in my head, anticipated Neil's arguments. I don't want to push too hard at this point, but I have to get him to agree to take a look at Jimmy's project. In the end, it will all depend on his ego—how much it means to him to be the leader.

Setting my tone at what I hope is just the right level of enthusiasm, I tell him this program is better than any existing package under six figures; that, if we're this close, someone else might be too. "Sleight of mind at its finest," I say, leading into the homestretch of my close. "Shall I schedule a demo here in LA?"

Neil's head is slightly cocked as if he's trying to hear between my words. "All that in one breath, Nora? Woman's intuition? All right, you've roused my curiosity. Coordinate with Lyle. I'll want the kid here when I look at the program, so tell Garth to give him a good scrub and send him over." He closes the subject by shoving a stack of sales reports in my direction, making the point that we'd better tend to the bucks that allow me to play in the land of research and development. We're in the middle of a volume-pricing discussion when his intercom buzzes. Neil snatches the phone, listens and then puts it down again, leaning back in his chair and eyeing me with surprise.

"Well, I'm certainly impressed. It seems you have a call from the president of the United States. You can take it here. I have to run down the hall anyway." He gets up, sticks his Mont Blanc pen in his shirt pocket and hands me the phone. "First a movie star, now this. I can't keep up with you, Nora." After he closes the door I buzz the front desk and have the call put through.

"Nora, this is Danny Court. I'm here with Deena Brennan."

"Hi, Nora."

"Mr. President. Deena."

"Deena tells me she talked to you in London. She's convinced you're the best person to help us stir up some public enthusiasm for the new environmental bill."

"Someone besides the government needs to remind people that this is exactly what they voted for, Nora," Deena chimes in. "What they said they wanted when they handed Melanie one of the biggest mandates in history." I can't help smiling. The way Deena pounces on things reminds me of my conservative Republican boss—and both of them would absolutely hate the comparison.

"I'm sure you're aware that everybody in Washington thinks I've lost my mind," Danny says. "Congress is convinced that constituents gave up caring whether their great-grandchildren had a planet to inherit the day Melanie was shot. That's why public opinion, public pressure, is going to be everything when it comes down to the wire."

Court says they're going to announce Deena's appointment today, which will be akin to sounding a siren all over the Hill, and in a couple of weeks he plans to go on TV to make his own plea to the nation. "Deena's working on the message right now. She insists that the people who believed in Melanie can be reinspired. To tell you the truth, she's a lot more optimistic about that than I am."

"What do you say, Nora?" Deena persists. "You're the only one I can think of who can access the kinds of people we need this quickly. We need a very fast, very major show of hands." To emphasize the immediacy, she speeds up her already breakneck speech. "I spoke to Enrico Perez this morning; he says Nathan Marks won't even talk to him, but that he might talk to you." That's *the* Enrico Perez, once a street punk, next a famous poster boy and now an ACLU superstar, champion of the underdog.

I start to answer but the words don't come. Despite the fact that I've already decided to do whatever I can to help Danny Court—so that he'll be in a good position to help me—I feel a sudden flutter of panic, like a flapping of dark wings. Sitting in Neil's office, surrounded by polished wooden tables, computer paraphernalia and expensive art, I have a powerful urge to set the receiver quietly back on its cradle, walk to the big picture window and take a dive down forty stories into the Century City Tower's fountain. How can I even think of getting involved again—after what happened the first time? All at once I'm terrified of things I can't see, that might be able to see me.

"Nora?"

"I'm here," I say, pulling myself together. *I'm here.* I take a deep breath. "Well, I can't completely ditch my job right now, but I'll help. I'll do as much as I can."

Danny rings off and Deena waits until he's out of the room, then lowers her voice. "The truth, Nora: if we can get the right support, Danny may be better at working ideas through the system than Melanie would have been. She was terrific at getting mortal enemies to smoke peace pipes out there in the world, but here in Washington she ruffled a lot of feathers. I'm an inveterate feather-ruffler myself, so Mel was more my style—but we have to be realistic."

I blink a few times and let the logic roll around in my head. This is the first time I've ever heard the suggestion that someone else might be a more successful president than Melanie would have been. I tell Deena I'll get back to her as soon as I have a plan in place.

What a strange idea! Melanie Lombard took hold of a nation's emotions, but what if that frenzy wasn't sustainable? Maybe the layers of bureaucracy—the structures, rules and niceties that, like her mother, she didn't handle well—would have stymied her eventually. It never occurred to me that disappointments might be buried alongside the triumphs.

Neil raps politely on his own door. "Well," he says. "While you were busy chatting with the leader of the free world, I was on the phone with an old mentor from MIT. He says James Barton's a bargain at any price." Neil is obviously in a good mood, so I take the opportunity to exit on a high note and escape back to my office.

There, in my working sanctuary, I make a list. I write down the names of everyone I can remember who was part of what the press termed Melanie's "network"—the power people who formed the foundation of her grass-roots strength. Not one of them has ever held public office, but each is more influential than any senator. The tough part is that some of these people trusted only one politician in their lives, and she's dead.

At the very top of the list is Nathan Marks, because over the years his influence has grown beyond the boundaries of race, to touch anyone who has ever been mad about anything. He's a formidable man and has a reputation for being decidedly unfriendly to anyone connected with "the system." Even so, Melanie managed to gain his respect and develop a pretty amazing rapport with him.

I doubt very much whether Nathan will remember me—since I'm not the one who wore the red muffler—and I suspect it'll take a feat of wizardry to get him to even meet with me, but the seed of an idea has already begun to germinate.

I put down my pen and ask Katy to order me a pastrami sandwich. I've been trying not to think about the surge of panic I felt earlier; it was too powerful, too debilitating. I'm not even sure I can function inside a fear like that. Like a heat-seeking missile, this particular doubt cuts through all my layers of rationale, to the heart, it seems, of everything. Until now, I never had to decide whether to duck my head and merge with the crowd or stick out my neck and risk someone shooting it off. I could always stand tall—*because Melanie was standing in front of me.*

I look up to see Katy in the doorway with my sandwich, her eyes sparkling. She wants to know what I think about the writer David Weinhardt—I give her points for not saying *bachelor* writer again— and to tell me that she's found out more about him, if I'm interested. In the course of the next few minutes I learn that David was once linked romantically with the renowned photographer Germaine Bauden, as well as with Patrice Solana's oldest daughter; was more recently involved with some unknown artist whose name she can't recall; and that his favorite food is Chinese.

David Weinhardt confuses me because he doesn't behave like I'm used to men behaving. What he said last night about being attracted to me was somehow unnerving. For a second, I felt . . . well, I was surprised by the way I felt. I'll have to be careful, I remind myself. David is, as I observed earlier, *heavy duty.* Not the kind of man who can be *handled.*

I spend the rest of the day tending to the more mundane aspects of my job and, by the time I leave work, I'm feeling reasonably good. My physical aches from the airport incident have subsided; my emotional aches are safely wrapped up inside a million details—who, where, when and especially how I'm going to keep this ball rolling. I'm driving across Sepulveda when a tiny Honda makes a left turn in front of me and I hit the brakes to find that I haven't any. I end up sideways in the street, the nose of my poor car smashed against a lamppost. I'm a little shaken, but unhurt.

The policeman who takes my statement suggests irritably that I ought to have my brakes checked more often and I inform him that I just got the car out of the shop this morning; I'm certain they checked the brakes. Something in my tone must sound convincing because he confers for several minutes with the tow-truck driver, then escorts me to the auto-repair shop, treating me on the way to a nasty monologue about the scams mechanics pull and how he's sick to death of it.

Fortunately the shop is still open and we're assured that my brakes were indeed thoroughly checked and in good condition. Martin, my mechanic, looks mortally insulted when the officer suggests that he might have neglected to put things back together right. Stomping to the tow truck, he unhooks my car, orders a couple of assistants to help him push it to the rack and pump it up. After a few minutes, he calls to the officer to join him and in another minute the officer is back, suggesting that I accompany him to the station. Someone has definitely tampered with my brakes. In his hand is a newspaper clipping that he tells me was taped to the inside of my car's hood. It's a two-week-old piece from *The Washington Post*; the headline reads: OP-POSITION VOWS TO STOP BLACKMORE BILL. I don't have to scan the whole article to find the brief mention of that nasty anonymous note Danny Court told me the newspaper had received. Someone has underlined it in red.

THIRTEEN

"Hydraulic fluid leak . . . partially severed brake line," I tell David, plucking the words directly from my memory of the police report. Standing on the sparse patch of grass in front of his Laurel Canyon house, holding three white cartons by their skinny wire handles, I feel lightheaded, as if a rug has been pulled out from under me and I haven't yet regained my balance.

It's been a bizarre day. After spending a sleepless night peering out the window at the police car parked in front of my house, I arrived at work this morning in a rental car, explained the bags under my eyes to my boss and got to experience for the first time in all the years I've worked for him what it's like to see Neil truly angry. First he called the police station and yelled at them for not providing me round-the-clock protection; then, having determined the tampering with my car must have happened during work hours yesterday, he alerted the building supervisor that they'd better have someone patrol my garage level at all times; then, he leaned across his desk and asked me if I was crazy.

Crazy's too tough to define; I quickly assured him that my political moonlighting would be a short-term thing, not like the near-sabbatical I took during Melanie's campaign. Hearing the determination in my voice, having heard it before, he didn't argue; instead, he nodded grimly and suggested precautions, such as varying my schedule. Businessman that he is, I'm willing to bet that he also phoned to increase our executive insurance policy the minute I walked out of his office.

I took Neil's suggestion and left the building shortly before noon. I drove toward the ocean, winding through back streets and finally leaving the nondescript little rental car in the parking lot of a supermarket I've never been in before. I bought a diet Coke and walked the few blocks to the beach, where I spent a couple of hours sitting on a bench thinking.

Soft waves lapped over the sand. Surfers in slick black wet suits bobbed on the horizon, eagerly waiting for more turbulent waters.

Up until the moment that police officer told me about my brakes and handed me the newspaper article he'd found stuck inside my car, the idea that I might be dramatically upping my risk factor for living in an already precarious world was simply that—an indistinct idea, a speculation, Hank's heebie-jeebies.

Not anymore. Whoever was responsible for that act must have a big stake in making sure this country doesn't adopt a more radical emissions control schedule. The auto industry, oil companies, any of the scores of manufacturers that throw off polluting by-products? And just how far are they prepared to go? I wonder. Are they willing to actually harm me? Or target Danny Court? What about a year ago, when a petite blond president of the United States was almost certain to turn such a bill into law?

I couldn't let myself think about that for too long—the leap from tampered brakes to murder. Fear and a sense of helplessness had already started to smother my anger; I knew I wouldn't be able to do anything if I slipped too deeply into Hank's cloak-and-dagger consciousness—as valid as it's beginning to seem.

Then, as I closed my eyes against the winter sun, into my mind floated an image of that empty apartment in London. And Jacques, who makes his living, so David said, negotiating deals for rich oil barons. All of a sudden the world seemed very small and the disappearance of Jacques DeBrin loomed large within it.

Thinking of Jacques reminded me of David, that I had an appointment with him this afternoon. When I called him from a phone outside the supermarket and explained why I was not in the office, he was clearly distressed. The concern in his voice touched me, but when I suggested we could still keep our appointment, that we could meet someplace outside the office, he changed his tone and practically barked at me. "Keep our appointment? Can't you just say you're in trouble and you need a friend? Never mind. You can come to my place. Oh, and you might pick up something to eat; the cupboard is bare."

Now, as I finish reciting the police report, I hold out the white cartons like a peace offering.

"Is this Chinese?" he says. "I love Chinese." Relieving me of two of the cartons, he takes my hand, leading me into the house. "So what are you going to do?"

"I'm guessing the point is just to scare me off," I reason. "Whoever is behind this obviously had good information, must know my regular routes. Traffic on Olympic Boulevard tops at twenty miles per hour and that's hardly a killing speed."

"What about the van at the airport?"

I sigh. "That could be a coincidence, we don't know for sure. Anyway, I can't back down just because someone says 'boo' to me."

David looks thoughtful. "I don't think it was a coincidence, but I'm not sure what it was." Setting the cartons on the table, he smiles. "Did I tell you Chinese is my favorite food? Make yourself at home; I'll be right back."

He disappears to go shut off his computer and dig up a bottle of wine. Taking him up on his offer to make myself at home, I stray from the kitchen in search of clues; I'm curious about how this man lives, what his house can tell me about him. His decor, I see, is a hodgepodge of style, as if each item of furniture was selected separately, each accessory was a gift from a different friend. On the wall by the entryway is a large Patrice Solana print, elaborately framed and, of course, signed. On the mantel is a family photograph—two adults and four children: three boys and a girl; the oldest is obviously David. Over the couch is an empty spot where a painting has been removed, leaving a rectangle a shade lighter than the wall around it. As I work my way back to the kitchen, I notice several such vacancies.

"Did you suddenly change your taste in art?" I ask.

"Those bare walls are all that remain of one of my more disastrous attempts at a relationship. Gwen was—is—an artist. She moved out over a year ago, but I've been busy."

We pile garlic beef and sweet-and-sour chicken over the lumpy rice and eat, sipping the sweet wine. He was working before I arrived and his curly, gray-flecked hair is flatter on one side, as if he's been leaning his head on his hand. His faded Georgetown sweatshirt has an ancient ink stain on the sleeve. I keep expecting him to start talking about Jacques again, to pick up the conversation where I ended it the other night, but he doesn't.

"Aren't you dying to ask me why she left?" he says finally.

It takes a moment for me to realize he's talking about his old girlfriend. Sadly I note that the question never occurred to me. Don't people always go? "All right, why did she leave?"

"Because I made her miserable; I'm impossible to get along with."

"Oh, and here I was picturing some sordid sadomasochistic revelation," I say, reaching for the rice.

"I will tell you one—just one—revealing thing about me," he says. "It's not something I'm really proud of, but it's the truth. I'm an excitement junkie."

"Uh-huh, and what exactly is an excitement junkie?"

"I've always been attracted to people with interesting, exciting lives—sort of a vicarious thing. The famous ones I write about; the others I just hang around. Like I told you the other night, you interested me before I even met you."

I understand why he's telling me this: excitement is temporary, it wears off. "Thanks for the warning," I say.

"But you don't take warnings, you see them as challenges. Could it be that you're the one to help me work through my little fixation?" He tips his wineglass to me.

I'm thinking that I have problems enough of my own. Why does his candor make me feel so uncomfortable? I change the subject and briefly outline my lobbying plan, whom I'm going to contact. David is a savvy guy; his advice could be helpful.

"What about Dorian Wayne?" he asks.

"I'm passing on him. The Reverend Wayne and I don't even speak the same language; it'd be a waste of time."

David grins. "What do you know—another challenge. Don't forget he beams his message to a pretty huge flock every Sunday. Tell you what, I'll drive you down and we can pitch him together."

I like the idea of having a teammate, even it's just for a tiny part of this endeavor. I agree, although I have no idea what possible good it can do. The Reverend Dorian Wayne had far less interest in Melanie's plans for the country than he did in the phenomenon of Melanie herself.

We go into David's den and he turns on his recorder while I settle on the couch and, at his request, begin to describe the day Melanie first met Hank at the rally in Central Park. He seemed so perfect for her—intelligent, undemanding, comfortable with strong women—a college professor with a schedule flexible enough to coexist with her hectic itinerary. He was the ideal partner for life in the public eye: handsome, steady, supportive and squeaky clean. It also didn't hurt that he was so rich.

And she loved him. I can say that to David with a straight face because, Jacques DeBrin notwithstanding, I know it's true. Melanie loved Hank the way she loved her life, her work, her country; she loved him as her husband, the father of her child; it was all one thing to her. Jacques was outside of that, something else. I don't know how I know that, but I do.

That Hank loved her is a monumental understatement. When Mitchell Lombard walked Melanie down the aisle in that small church in Wisconsin, I thought Hank would faint with joy. And when Mitchell relinquished his darling daughter to her adoring fiancé, Melanie—an angel in white—turned to me, her only bridesmaid, and winked. That was another of her successful techniques: with a blink of her eye she included me, made me special, chose me out of all the rest; the secrets of the world were just between her and me.

Bennie was born a year later. Lying there in the hospital bed with a beautiful baby boy in her arms, she winked again; from that instant on, her child belonged to both of us. I know—I knew then— that she included me because she needed me to make her life work. But I didn't care.

I tell David about the years when Bennie was little—how the Central Park West apartment where Hank and Melanie lived became a hotbed of political activism; how when things got too hectic I'd sneak Bennie down to my little place in the Village. I taught him to play chess before he was five.

"That was the period when she was holding those 'invitation meetings' at the apartment," David comments. "And when she started up the People's Hotline."

He's right. Twice a month, invitations to join Melanie for coffee and conversation were sent to twenty constituents in her city district, randomly chosen from the voter list. The meetings were only moderately successful in helping her gain new insight, but turned out to be immensely popular with the media. People's Hotline, which I manned on occasion, was an even bigger public relations hit. It became a symbol, blown out of all proportion.

David laughs. "Didn't Mustafa D. ask to see the Hotline when he met with her five years ago?"

"He sure did. He thought it was an historic landmark." After spending half an hour strolling the White House gardens with the president of the United States, visiting Syrian cabinet member Mustafa D. told the press he had also agreed to discuss his country's problems with Senator Melanie Lombard, but only if they could meet at her home in New York because he wanted to see the fabled People's Hotline.

I can't help smiling at the memory. To Washington's amazement, Mustafa D. spent three hours at the apartment, talking with Melanie, Deena Brennan and a couple of other aides, under the steady gaze of a dozen Secret Servicemen. Two hours into the discussion, the secretary of state just happened to drop by.

It was an incredible political coup—and all because a city councilwoman believed in customer service.

I stop talking as the proverbial lightbulb begins to flash. It was a great story. The press bought it; we all bought it. But now I'm betting the real truth is that Mustafa D. agreed to meet with Melanie Lombard at the urging of a mutual friend.

Where is Jacques now?

I ask David, "If you had to guess, who do you think is most likely to be responsible for my severed brake line?"

"Someone who doesn't want the Blackmore bill to have the slightest chance." He shuts off the tape recorder without missing a beat. "I'll pick the United Automobile Workers' Union. You aren't going to repeat this, are you? I'm only playing along here—no slander intended."

"What about oil interests?" I ask.

"Who? Refineries? Gas stations? Arab sheiks? Do you think OPEC is after you?" He makes it sound so incredibly bizarre, as if I'd said I was afraid of being hit by a Scud missile. "Look, Nora, that bill slaps at a lot of industries. I don't think you can narrow it down that way."

"I don't know. I just—all of a sudden everything seems to, like, touch, somehow. Tell me, do you think there's a chance that Melanie's assassination was a conspiracy?" I ask him.

"A *chance?* There's always a possibility. But, no, I don't think her death was the result of a conspiracy. You want to know why?"

I nod mutely. David gets up and walks to his file cabinet, takes a folder off the top of it and comes over to sit beside me on the couch. "The Commission was very thorough," he says. "I read every word of their report and didn't find a single thing that would link Jennie Wheeler to any kind of subversive group. Beyond that, I have two reasons for believing as I do. One—Melanie was only in office for three days. Any sane entity would have waited to see how effective she was going to be before resorting to murder." He opens the folder, removes a photograph and hands it to me. "This is the second reason," he says.

I know the woman in the picture is Jennie Wheeler, though she only remotely resembles the photographs that plastered the newspapers last year. The wild mane of hair has been cut and neatly combed. The clothes are prison-hospital issue. The features of her face are not violently contorted as they were when the Secret Service marched her away just minutes after the shooting, when she'd twisted her neck around to scream "Satan woman!" at Melanie's body. This Jennie sits at a wooden table, looking in the direction of the camera, but her eyes seem to focus just short of it. It's her eyes that captivate me. They're not dull and lifeless; they just seem to swim in the moment; they harbor no cause, no point, no reason at all.

I hand the picture back to David. He's right, it's hard to imagine this woman being part of anything outside her own head; this is what crazy really looks like. Then, without warning, tears spring forth, all the pressure of the past two days condenses into salty drops that run down my face. David quickly moves over and puts his arms around me; I cry softly into his shoulder.

He holds me for a few moments; then he gently turns my face to his and kisses my wet eyelids. First one, then the other, then my cheeks, my lips. He kisses me lightly at first, then harder; I feel my body start to tremble. Half dazed, I draw back slightly and peer into his clever brown eyes. And I see it—that familiar look, the one I first saw on his face when he was studying Melanie's yearbook picture. David has spent months learning everything he can about Melanie Lombard and now, like everybody else, he's in love with her. The pounding in my chest stops cold. I don't want her men anymore.

"Something the matter?" he says, as I pull away.

I mumble an excuse: I have to go home; my boss badgered the police into one more night of protection; a police car is sitting outside my house right now; it'd be rude to show up late.

FOURTEEN

When I tell Deena Brennan about my severed brake line and about the clipping, she swears into the phone, then puts me on hold. In a few minutes, she's back. "Danny wants you to forget about helping us. Whoever it is probably just wants to scare you, but it's not worth the risk."

"I thought government policy was not to give in to terrorists."

"You're not the government. We want you to drop it." I can tell this is the official version. Personally, she's livid at the thought of losing my help.

I remind her that, on the bright side, somebody must think we've got a chance—besides, I'm too stubborn to quit now.

"Yeah, I thought so," she says. "Look, Nora, we'll have the FBI do some checking, but we can't authorize any twenty-four-hour federal protection; you're a civilian and the brake thing is a police matter. What if we treat you to a private bodyguard, somebody whose salary doesn't come from taxpayers?"

The idea doesn't appeal to me; the bigger we make this, the scarier it gets, and I'm trying to keep myself calm. "I don't think so, Deena. All I'm doing right now is making a few phone calls."

"Well then, I'll give your local cops a buzz, emphasize Danny's concern."

I'm thinking how much the Santa Monica police department will love me. First Neil hollers at them, next Deena dangles the president's wrath over their heads. I promise to be careful and we hang up.

I am being careful. In fact, so far today I haven't even left the house; I've been on the phone all morning. Rubbing at the tension in the back of my neck, I take a sip of coffee and punch some more buttons. This time, the young man at the Freedom Foundation is even ruder than he was the first time I called. Mumbling an epithet under his breath, he insists that Mr. Marks already said he had no interest in talking to me, so I should quit wasting their time.

I guess my first approach, identifying myself as a friend of Melanie Lombard, didn't include the secret password, so I take a deep breath and ask him to tell Mr. Marks I'd like to repay an old debt . . . from a subway station incident twenty-two years ago. "I'm the woman *without* the red muffler. Do you have all of that?"

"Who cares. I told you, he doesn't want to talk to you."

"And I'm telling you I have something to give him, something *he wants*—and I'm not going away."

"What was that about a subway?"

I repeat the message twice until I'm sure he's got the gist of it, then doodle an elaborate concentric circle during my ten minutes in the limbo of "hold." I'm nervous, and I have a right to be.

"Yes, Ms. Whitney?"—the unmistakable booming voice of Nathan Marks, directly descended from the god of thunder. He listens without comment while I assure him that I'll only need a few moments of his time and what I have to talk to him about is truly astonishing. "I'm not interested in your talk," he growls. "You said you have something to *give* me."

Ah, *give*—that's the secret password. I draw another deep breath and hold it. I made up my mind last night that this is my best bet for killing two birds with one stone. At the same time, I'm overstepping my boundaries by about a million miles. Nathan Marks is not a man to toy with, and if I commit to him now, I sure as hell better be able to follow through. "I have an important gift for you," I hear myself say.

"In that case, you've won a trip to Harlem."

Yes!

Marks is a big coup, but not all my efforts this morning have been successful. Freda Lowe of the California Women's Coalition, for example, said she wasn't about to divert any energy from their primary purpose of promoting women; Danny Court was the wrong gender. Had I ever considered running for public office? she asked.

Other not-so-helpful responses included an offensive suggestion from Youth Power leader Lucifer Brown, whom Melanie had managed to tame but from whom I expected pretty much what I got. Lucifer is an ex–gang member who's formed a nationwide support group, but politics-as-usual isn't his thing. I only contacted him because I believe in being thorough.

Far more interesting was the reaction of Mort Hanley, an outspoken political commentator, who agreed with absolutely everything I had to say, but refused to actively help stir up support. His reasoning had to do with careful rationing of a good thing. "The momentum we accomplished with Lombard was rare and wondrous," he explained. "If that level of outcry becomes a regular din, Washington will just put on earmuffs."

Uh-huh.

I brush my hair and apply some lipstick. I'm meeting Bennie in a few minutes, and after that I have an appointment with Elena Bendle, who writes a nationally syndicated column that does a better job of waking people up than their morning coffee.

Outside it's a sunny day, birds twitter, all of nature conspires to convince me that things are right with the world. Still, I take a different route to La Pâtisserie, walk a block out of my way. I only have to wait in the parking lot a few minutes before Bennie's bike sputters up behind me. He buys us each a cup of coffee and a huge pastry to share, while I find a table that isn't obscured by plants. I want Elena to be able to find me.

"Guess what?" Bennie says, barely able to contain himself. "There's a guy who wants to invest in my film. A friend of Dad's— which put me off at first. Then I talked to him on the phone."

His long hair flops over one eye as he bends to take a bite of the pastry. "He's a young guy, not much older than me, and he's rich—with a lot less strings on his fortune than I have. Dad told him about me, so he went to see my student film at a festival in New York. He swears that Dad won't be involved at all, no looking over our shoulders."

"That's great, Bennie." Inside, I applaud Hank wildly.

I've already filled Bennie in on my trip to London, both Jacques's default and Jimmy's discovery, but I haven't told him about my brakes; I don't want to alarm him. Instead, I chat about my morning and speculate about tomorrow, when David and I are scheduled to drive down to Orange County and meet with Dorian Wayne. I learned of and agreed to the Wayne meeting via answering machine. David and I haven't actually spoken since I squirmed out of his arms the other night.

Bennie pushes the plate aside and folds his hands on the table. "That man is hot for you, Nora. When he interviewed me he asked as many questions about you as he did about my mother. I know he's not your usual type, but you ought to take advantage of his lust; you might con him into being kinder with his mighty pen." I get up to refill my coffee, punching him in the shoulder as I pass. I know he's joking, but his words jab at the heart of a game David and I may both be playing.

When I return to the table, Bennie is toying with the saltshaker and his face is serious. "You know, for six months after she died, Dad never phoned me once. Now he's started calling every week, for no particular reason. It pisses me off." He twirls the saltshaker one more time; then he shrugs his shoulders as if he can make his concerns slide off onto the sawdust floor. "So when is the great Ms. Bendle due to show up?"

"Any time now."

"I knew her daughter at UCLA—brilliant, studious; she spent six days in the library and went psycho on Saturday nights. Speaking of Saturday, you haven't forgotten our party, have you? Your mother called me; she's positive you've forgotten."

Damn, I did forget. And Mom, though I've talked to her twice this week, would rather revel in my forgetfulness than remind me. Mother, Bennie and I were all born in February and the joint birthday party has been an annual event since he first came west to school. It's a week from tomorrow, I now remember, plenty of time to order a cake and figure out the menu after I get back from New York. "Are you bringing somebody?" I ask Bennie. It's our policy to encourage additional guests to keep the ritual from growing stale.

"Yeah—Karen—the girl I met in Ferris's waiting room a few weeks ago." Dr. Ferris is my ex-shrink; Bennie began seeing him the week after his mother died. "How about you?" he says.

I think for a minute. "You know that programmer I told you about, Jimmy Barton? He'll be in town, he wanted to meet you and he's strange enough to get a kick out of this."

"Ah, a twenty-something techie weirdo," Bennie chides, making a face at me. "That should really please your mother."

Mother is a former high school math teacher and she believes everything should follow crisp, logical rules laid down at the beginning of time. She's still mad at Dad over the divorce, even though he's been dead for years. As for me, I'm a spinster executive, definitely an aberration; besides, computers being an outgrowth of the cursed calculator, my chosen profession borders on corruptive. I shudder to think what she would say about Jimmy's geometry program.

"I believe your outspoken friend has arrived," Bennie alerts me.

I turn to see Elena standing in the doorway. Well over six feet, with flowing silver hair and a body as straight as a sapling, Elena Bendle can't make an entrance without commanding attention. Sensing a change in the air, people all around us stop their conversations, look toward the door. Bennie stands as she approaches our table.

"Nora," she says, taking my hand. "This must be Ben Cochran. You know my daughter, Britt, I believe, from school."

"I never would have made it through astronomy without Britt's help. It's nice to meet you, Ms. Bendle." They shake hands and he offers her his chair.

"Looks like his father," Elena comments as Bennie heads toward the counter to get her some coffee. "I've always considered Henry Cochran to be a terrific-looking man—sort of a subdued style of handsome, if you know what I mean." She settles into the chair and tosses her hair behind her shoulders. "Well, are you back among the living?"

I've watched Elena in action enough times to know that she chooses her words carefully; that she's always direct and often rude. She could have asked if I'd decided to come out of hibernation or something less tactless than the reference she used, but she did it on purpose. She likes to prod and provoke as if she has no emotional stake in anything herself, but it won't work with me because I remember the hollow, pained look on her face at Melanie's funeral.

I mention Deena Brennan's appointment to the president's staff, and she grins. "Washington's talking about nothing else," she says. "Have they drafted you, too? Are you going to tell me what's gotten into Danny Court?" She leans across the table, resting her chin on the tips of her fingers; her gray eyes probe my own more boldly than I'm used to in the ritualistic world of business.

I explain how serious Court is about getting tough with Melanie's original agenda, starting with the environment, the Blackmore bill, and that I'm trying to drum up public support; I thought she'd want to help.

She looks thoughtfully into the distance. "I don't know, Nora. I love Deena and, even though I'm sometimes hard on him, I have a lot of respect for Danny Court. But—and I know it sounds odd coming from me—I'm inclined to think he should compromise on this one, make a few friends and throw his weight behind education or the senior problem. You know . . . politics. This is too tough a sell."

Bennie returns with a cup of coffee and a plate of tiny muffins. He bids Elena farewell, asks to be remembered to her daughter and favors me with a kiss on the cheek. "Call me when you get back from New York," he says over his shoulder.

"Too bad he and Britt never got together," Elena muses, watching him walk away. Her face is not nearly as harsh as the words she loves to throw around.

"You're saying we need to choose which kid we're going to pull into our tiny little lifeboat, is that it? And then learn to live with ourselves? Damnit, Elena, if we renege on Melanie's promise to the World Environmental Council, if we let this slide—then everything else will end up just as diluted." I've caught her off guard, nibbling on a muffin, so I hit her again, a strategic from-the-heart dissertation that boils down to this: that the package of ideas, energy and courage we all fell in love with has a life of its own. If it died with Melanie, that's only because we let it die. Deena understands that, and I think Danny Court finally understands it, too. Melanie Lombard taught us something extremely important and we weren't listening.

Elena says nothing. She simply stands up—the whole vast length of her—and reaches out to take my hand, an odd expression on her face; then, halfway to the door, she turns, whipping her silver hair to one side, and calls back to me, "I'll think about it."

I wait until she makes her exit, then scoop the remaining muffins into my bag and head out the other door. Coming from Elena, "I'll think about it" is an excellent sign. And I can't help being privately impressed by what I said to her. I hadn't exactly planned it that way, but it seemed to come out right. All at once, I feel this odd sense of bravado. Look at me—I'm doing this. I didn't run and hide, I've brazenly defied an impolite order to cease and desist; I've called somebody's bluff. Oh, I'm a million miles from feeling invincible, I'll never feel that, in fact, I'm still very scared. But I'm doing this. I'm really doing it.

I begin to wonder what in the world I'll say to the Reverend Wayne, not to mention how I'm going to ride forty miles side-by-side in a car with David after my strange behavior the other night.

FIFTEEN

I don't own a gun but I always keep a baseball bat beneath my bed. Twice during the night, stirred from the edge of sleep by unfamiliar sounds, I reached for the bat, climbed out of bed and prowled the house, peering out the window at the empty, darkened driveway, opening the back door a scant inch to peek into the backyard. Santa Ana winds whipped the palms into a frenzy, but the orange trees, heavy with ripe fruit, responded sluggishly, shifting their branches in slow sweeping arcs that cast grotesque shadows across the lawn. When the first light blinked through my kitchen window, I was wide awake, sitting at the table and drinking my second cup of coffee.

Today is the day I agreed to drive to Orange County with David. I dress with little enthusiasm, aware that my reddish eyes and weary demeanor won't go a long way toward impressing the Reverend Dorian Wayne. Pausing at the hall mirror, I catch myself pushing aside the woman Wayne will behold and wondering instead how I'll look to David. Tired? For sure. Determined? Maybe. Attractive? For a split second I see in the mirror the most appalling hunger, just a flash, but that's all it takes for me realize how much I want him to look at me as lovingly as he did at Melanie's yearbook picture. The magnitude of my need is a little overwhelming, and the apprehension that accompanies it is almost as strong as the one that kept me up half the night.

I hear his car in the driveway and grab my jacket. For some reason I don't want David to come inside: it's as if my mirror image is still etched on the glass and I'm afraid he might see it. I may have become expert at juggling young men's short-term needs and short-term promises, but I have no idea what to do with a not-so-young David Weinhardt, who can likely match me hangup for hangup and has his own complete set of romantic baggage, mountains to overcome as big as my own.

David stands on the sidewalk looking both perplexed and annoyed. "Good morning," we say in unison. He stares at me for a moment, then walks to the car and opens the door. Once we're buckled in, he backs a few feet down the driveway, then stops, kills the engine and turns in the seat to face me.

"Nora, whenever I'm working at this stage of a book, my head is a swirl of facts, ideas, theories. I've got a lot of things on my mind and what I don't need right now is to sit around wondering why you backfired out of my arms the other night—what I might have said, done; if I misread the moment; if I have bad breath; whatever. So why don't you just tell me, so I can quit thinking about it."

I'm nonplussed. He's asking me about a very personal reaction to a tender moment, yet he's asking it as if it were a housekeeping detail he'd simply like to get out of the way. What's more, he doesn't leave any room for me to hedge, or joke, or make up something that sounds more dignified than the truth.

Vaguely irritated, I describe the expression on his face as he looked at Melanie's picture in my yearbook, that it was a look I've come to know well over the years, having seen it on male faces from college boys to wistful junior congressmen. Everyone was in love with her. "When you kissed me," I explain, "that look flashed through my mind; it sort of hit me with a bucket of ice cubes. I guess I've played second fiddle to Melanie too many times."

He eyes me steadily, his face nearly expressionless. "You're aware that I never had the good fortune to meet the lady in person?"

Doesn't he get it? He can be as much in love with the *idea* of her as with Melanie herself, and there's no way I want to compete with that. I gaze at my hands for a second; then, feeling childish, I force myself to meet his eyes.

"I think I'm beginning to understand your problem," he says pensively, then sighs. "You've got some glitch that says every time a man looks at you romantically, he's comparing you to Melanie Lombard. God, Nora, you caught me admiring a photo of a dead woman, feeling respect, a little fondness for what she was, all that—but not love. I don't fall in love with dead women, or even with memories of dead women; relationships are tough enough with the living."

"It was an automatic reaction," I admit. "I suppose it had nothing to do with you."

"So, are you ready to give it up? Maybe Melanie beat you out of a boyfriend in the past—or maybe your overwhelming conviction that she was so superior to you pushed them in her direction. But you can't hide behind her forever."

That does it! I feel a rush of anger. What gives him the right to pick me apart like this? "It's not as if I work at feeling that way," I snap at him.

His eyes and the tone of his voice have that same stubborn tenacity I glimpsed the day we first met. "I hear that most of the men you've been involved with are a lot younger than you are," he persists. "Does the fact that they're not from the same era—yours and Melanie's—make a difference?"

I'm thinking I should get out of the car right now and go back into the house. This is impossible. "You'd have to ask my former shrink about that. He has a number of theories."

Reaching over, he takes my hand; I feel an instant stab of annoyance at the way the gesture melts my anger. I try to hold on to it, but I can't. "Here's what I see when I look at you," he says. "I see Nora

Whitney, a complex, intelligent, enigmatic and challenging woman to whom I find myself very attracted."

"You left out sexy."

"I was trying for a more lofty appeal."

He starts the engine and backs out of my driveway. In a few minutes, we're easing onto the San Diego Freeway and I settle in for the ride, wondering what it would mean to do what he said—to give it up—and exactly how I would go about doing that.

"Oh, by the way," he says, "I got a lead on your French friend, De-Brin. He was in Cairo on Thursday, signing the papers for some business deal. The transaction made the Cairo newspaper, naming him as the broker. An old associate of mine picked it up off the wire, checked it out for me and, sure enough, DeBrin was there in person." David is watching me out of the corner of his eye, hoping, no doubt, for a reaction. "At least he hasn't dropped off the face of the earth," he says.

Jacques is all right! Nothing horrible has happened to him! I let the relief play around inside, carefully keeping it off my face. "I'm glad about that," I say. "If memory serves, he was a pretty gorgeous specimen of the human race; it would be a shame to think he didn't exist somewhere. Of course, I haven't seen him for a couple of centuries— he may have changed." *There, that sounds detached enough, sufficiently glib.*

"Well, I can guarantee you he's not in his twenties anymore," David says. "He must be way too old for you by now."

The "F-you" idiom comes to mind, but I don't say it.

David continues. "Anyway, *you* may not have seen Mr. DeBrin since your playful summer in Paris, but my guess is that Melanie did—and that he doesn't want me to find out about it. Why else would he be making himself so scarce right now?"

Turning to face him, I see a mass of silver metal looming down on us; I scream. "David, watch out!" A horn blares, David swerves, a pickup truck streaks past, its driver glaring at us with loathing. Engrossed in our conversation, he'd let the car drift dangerously into the next lane. I was looking for a way to change the subject, but this isn't exactly what I had in mind.

David glances sheepishly in my direction, then fixes his eyes on the road. Taking advantage of his embarrassment at having nearly killed me, I scoop up the topic of conversation and try to force it to a close. "Melanie never once said a word to me about seeing Jacques again, David." *True enough.* "That's why I think you're on a wild-goose chase. It's nice you have a hobby, though."

His eyes remain firmly on the freeway, so I can't tell if he believes me or not. "We'll see, my smart one," he says. "You may be very surprised."

After that ominous remark, we drive for a while in silence. I lean my forehead against cold glass and gaze out at the bleak stretch of long, flat industrial buildings and huge, mostly vacant parking lots that line the freeway. I can tell we're not far from the office of this evangelical preacher Melanie so miraculously brought into her fold. What a mystery that was! Contrary to the way I usually remember it, not everyone was swept away by her magnetic personality or enthralled by the human emphasis of her agenda. And foremost among her detractors were religious conservatives, whose ideas of freedom were considerably narrower than hers and for whom her program of cooperation required compromises they were unable to make.

Dorian Wayne was the exception. I never watched his televised ministry, but his endorsement of Melanie was front-page news. It took a lot of courage to do what he did—especially in light of insinuations put forth by his colleagues that he'd been bewitched.

"Well," David asks, "are you ready to play the politics of theology?"

The only other car in the lot behind the modest building that houses Wayne's televangelical production company is an old station wagon. David pulls in beside it and we climb out, shaking off the long drive and readying ourselves to meet the man who wins the Sunday morning ratings game hands down. The door to the building has a broken pencil wedged in the jamb. We push it open carefully and enter a stark lobby. Taped on the wall next to the elevator is a hand-written note on yellow lined paper directing Miss Whitney and Mr. Weinhardt to the third floor.

He's waiting for us when the elevator door opens. Dorian Wayne doesn't exactly fit the TV-preacher mold. He's young, for one thing—thirty-five, I believe, although his baby face makes him look even younger. He's a couple of inches taller than David and stockier, with short sandy hair, hazel eyes and rosy cherubic cheeks. Although I've seen his picture many times, it's always been in more ministerial at-tire. Today's light blue turtleneck sweater and tan cords throw me off until he speaks. His voice, though soft, carries a powerful sincerity that echoes down the hall with no less force than it will tomorrow morning, when his message will be heard all across the nation.

His office is as humble as his car—a small desk, comfortable worn chairs. He pours us each a cup of coffee from a pot on top of a gray metal file cabinet and pulls his desk chair around to join us. "I'm not exactly clear on why you wanted to see me," he says, the hint of a smile activating the dimple in his right cheek. "As I told you on the phone, I don't wish to be interviewed for the book about the late pres-ident. You'll simply have to rely on statements that I made at the time."

David smiles back, exhibiting no dimples, only a couple of well-worn laugh lines. He assures Wayne that our visit isn't about the book, that he's only along for the ride, but that he can't help won-dering how things are going—off the record, of course. "You came under a lot of fire from your peers. Has that healed or is there still some tension?"

"Off the record?" The minister waits for David to nod before he be-gins to depict, in a voice tinged with sadness, the terrible rift his en-dorsement of Melanie Lombard created in the Christian community. He explains his own difficulty—trying to reconcile the fact that so many of her views seemed to be contrary to the Word of God—and how his own confusion was magnified a hundred times in the believers who listened to him. His colleagues presumed he had been deceived, had experienced a temporary lapse. "I'm still struggling with it, searching my heart."

"Why did you do it?" I ask, incredulous.

His eyes flash quickly from me to David and back again. "It seemed so right at the time; I'd prayed about it for weeks. There was a selfless quality about her; in spite of the paradoxes, I saw truth in the way she spoke. I believed that whether she knew it or not the Christian spirit was working strong in her." He pauses but keeps his eyes fixed on mine. "I've always been troubled by the fact that belief—ours, anybody's—is exclusive; she brought people together, and that was good."

"It was very good," David agrees. "It was amazing considering the different points of view—"

"I know now that it was not my place to get involved," Dorian interrupts. He gazes toward the window as if he's consulting something far away on the other side. "If God had meant for Melanie Lombard to be president, she would not be dead. What happened was God's will."

David's hand reaches across to close over mine and his touch is like a spray of cool water quelling the fury that explodes like a cherry bomb inside my head. God's will, my ass. But as David's fingers exert a gentle pressure, my vision clears enough to see that the minister's confident voice is out of sync with his troubled eyes. For a second I feel sorry for him. He's not the only one who has desperately wanted Melanie's death to make sense.

"I grew up with the Old Testament God," David is saying. "As you know, He was big on lessons and they were usually pretty harsh. Maybe the murder of one very caring and courageous person will eventually awake the compassion and courage of many others who might have been more timid."

That's my cue. As I begin my spiel, I'm surprised that Dorian actually seems interested in the success of the Blackmore bill.

"I believe we have a responsibility to take care of the Earth," he offers, "and I don't think the alternative plans take that responsibility seriously. But please understand that I have no intention of endorsing this bill or becoming involved in anything political, ever again. If you've come here for that, I'm sorry."

His sincerity sets something in motion inside me. It was Melanie's gift to see through disparity, to find quality and make it shine. I've dismissed Dorian Wayne because his brand of logic is foreign to me, but this is a good man and even if we come from different planets, we're both struggling and searching our hearts; we both care.

"It's enough that you've helped me remember how ultimately we're both on the same side," I tell him. It occurs to me also—and I'm not even sure exactly what it means—that I need to remember not to take Melanie too personally.

We talk a bit more, an interesting, friendly exchange about the country, the world and our separate missions in it. He remains absolutely true to his perspective and, of course, David and I each stick to ours, but as I stand in the parking lot waiting for David to unlock the car, I realize that I have probably learned more today than I possibly could have learned from an encounter where my powers of persuasion had a chance.

"Kind of a nice guy, don't you think?" David says. "Despite the heavenly bias."

"Yeah, thanks for talking me into coming."

"You're welcome."

David snaps on the radio, punches through a few stations and turns it off. Hoping to sidestep another dangerous dialogue, I quickly ask him to tell me what he was like as a kid. "Okay," he says, and like a true biographer, he begins at the beginning. "I was born, the eldest of four, to nice Jewish parents in a middle-class suburb of Philadelphia."

Over the next several miles, David describes in detail the fine-furniture store owned by his family through three generations, now being run by his youngest brother Andrew. He tells me how it looked when he was a boy—the rich scent of polished wood, the dainty table legs; his father, handsome and proud in his three-piece suit, wearing his best-customer smile. He tells me about his mother, an obscurely published poet with a keen intellect, who still sits down at her rolltop desk and writes a new poem each week. "They swear they love each other," he tells me, "but they never talk."

He's closest to his sister Sara, a stockbroker in New York. His other brother, Ted, lives in Miami and sells insurance. Although not particularly religious, his parents were always socially active. At various times in his childhood, David marched on behalf of the poor, the homeless and downtrodden, usually pushing a sibling in a stroller. He talks as vividly as he writes and by the time we're halfway home, I know these people.

"Now it's your turn," he says.

Not a chance—I'm on a roll. "First you have to tell me the real reason why your artist girlfriend moved out on you," I say.

He looks at me warily. "You really want to know about that? All right. Her name is Gwen." In a voice devoid of its previous narrative energy, he recounts the last six months of their relationship, how he couldn't seem to help acting moody, irritable, unfriendly. He'd convinced himself that he still cared about her, and only later did he realize how much he'd wanted her to leave. "She got the message long before I did," he admits.

"Sounds as if you just grew tired of her," I comment. That fits what he's already told me about himself.

"It's more than that. When I first met Gwen, I saw her as this ethereal creative spirit. There was a certain look she got on her face when she painted—this intense excitement; I just *had* to have her in my life. The first year was okay, even though, like my mom and dad, we rarely talked. After that, I started pushing; I wanted to understand who she was, you know, connect with her, but I couldn't find anything to connect with—there wasn't anything there." Catching my eye, he quickly amends his statement. "That's not true, of course. Gwen's a fine person; we just had nothing in common."

The story of David and Gwen requires no comment and I have none to give. David and I should run away from each other as fast as our seasoned legs will take us. I find myself touching his arm lightly. "Thanks for telling me that."

It's four o'clock when we pull into my driveway. At least a dozen preteen boys are playing touch football on the lawn across the street. "Next time it's your turn," David says.

I think for a minute. "I'm better at show than tell. How would you like to attend a traditional family birthday party and actually meet my mother? It's a week from today, and we don't do gifts, not even disgusting funny ones."

"I'd like that. Shall I come in now and help you rustle up some dinner or do you want to call it a day?"

With hardly any sleep last night and an early flight to New York in the morning, I convince myself it's not a good idea. Besides, I haven't yet figured out how I'm going to accomplish what he suggested earlier—let go of my old habits. "Thanks, but I fly out at seven A.M. and I'm not fully prepared for the inimitable Mr. Marks."

"Gotcha. I'll just come in and check the house."

I'm warmed by his concern, but the rebel inside reminds me that I can't have somebody looking in closets and checking under beds every time I come home. Besides, it's broad daylight. "You don't have to do that. As you can see, the house is in full view of a football game and two gardening neighbors. Thanks, it's not necessary."

"If you say so. Call me when you get back from New York—and watch your step in Harlem." We look at each other for a very long moment before he leans over and kisses me on the cheek. I have the distinct feeling that the ball is in my court.

Just inside the door I stand for a moment, breathing deeply and listening to the sound of his car receding into the distance. Tired as I am, I already miss his company. The house feels so empty—and cold.

Suddenly my mind snaps to full alert and I move slowly through the living room into the den. A sharp breeze greets me. Glass is everywhere. In the center of the room a rust-colored brick has made a shallow gouge in the polished wood floor. Could someone be in here? Carefully I pick up the phone and dial 911. I should run, I think, listening to my voice speak meekly into the receiver. "Window . . . shattered . . . please come."

SIXTEEN

"Things like this—usually just kids messin' around." Officer Galloway picks up the brick and turns it over as if he might find a message scratched on it. "I doubt if they even came inside. Anything missing?"

"I don't think so. But I had an earlier incident." These policemen were in the neighborhood when I called; the dispatcher sent them over, but they're unaware of the problem with my brakes; I quickly fill them in. "I've been talking to a Lieutenant Hacker."

"Hacket." I'm corrected by the other officer, an older, gruffer man with thick black eyebrows. Peering through the jagged remains of my picture window, he scowls. "Looks like someone wants to scare you. Ex-husband? Boyfriend, maybe?"

I shake my head, trying to ignore the old movie scenes flashing by in rapid succession—tough plainclothes cops with hard eyes and cigarettes drooping from the corners of their mouths. *Got any enemies, lady?* Lieutenant Hacket has been alerted to my political involvement; I think I'd better let him decide who else needs to know.

"We'll check to see if your neighbors noticed anything, but there's not much chance of catching 'em." Galloway scribbles some notes on a small dog-eared pad. "Got something to board this up?"

"I phoned my insurance company; they're sending a man over right away."

Galloway picks up the telephone, calls the station and asks to speak to Lieutenant Hacket, who isn't there. "I'll make sure he gets a copy of the report. And we'll keep an eye on the place, drive by periodically." I tell him that I'm going to be out of town for a couple of days and I'd feel a lot better knowing someone was watching. "We'll do what we can," he promises.

The two policemen bid me good-bye and head across my lawn in separate directions to question the neighbors. I set about collecting the tiny shards of glass scattered over every inch of my den. There's less than half an hour of light left. The sun, low enough to have a clear shot beneath the eucalyptus branches, bounces its rays off the edges of what used to be my picture window and splashes into the room in crisscross beams. Ordinarily this is the time of day when dust particles dance visibly in the air, but today all I see is the sparkle of thousands of bits of glass, as if some unseen hand has waved a magic wand, seeding the room with diamonds—more like razors in disguise, deadly glitter.

The effect is mesmerizing, making my arms and legs feel heavy, clumsy. I poke the broom at a few bits of sparkle on the black leather seat of my desk chair, sweeping them off onto the floor, then place my body carefully into the chair. It's a weak February sun, more show than warmth. I'm aware of the chill in the room, but it seems appropriate. Each second stretches endlessly as I watch the light play over my violated sanctuary. When the trance lifts, no more than a minute or two later, I am intensely alert. Outside a blackbird shrieks. Across the street, boys shout to each other. I hear, or imagine I hear, the slap of a ball against the pavement.

For some reason beyond my understanding, I'm not afraid. Sitting here by myself in the last traces of daylight, with my house exposed to the coming darkness, I'm surprised that not one of the emotions welling up inside me is fear. What I do feel is alone—ultimately and most completely alone—and at the very core of that aloneness is the stark knowledge of how and why I came to be this way; I see myself as architect of a life that may have missed the point.

Next week I will be forty-eight. I always say that I never married because I never found anyone I wanted to marry who also wanted to marry me, but the deeper truth is that I made sure it happened that way. For years I've pushed good men out of my life with the same stiff arm I used on David this afternoon when he offered to come inside and check the house. The rebel didn't need them, couldn't let herself need them—so here I am.

For the most part it's been okay. My life has been full of big exciting things, time sped by so fast and I was always busy, striving to be better, worthier, smarter. When you're active and involved, there are always companions, temporary lovers, come-and-go friends. There are always the Blaine Hennesseys.

Of course, no children. Bennie, I force myself to admit, is not really my child. Somewhere down the road, Bennie's kids will call me "aunt" and his wife will likely wonder why she has to put up with me at all. After all, I'm not his mother.

I have friendships that center on work, change from job to job or project to project, and I have friendships that grew out of common causes, reviving themselves from time to time. I have special friends like Hank, where Melanie was the bond. But since she died, I have no true-blue, "just-because" friends anymore—and maybe I never did.

Sitting alone in my den, I am absolutely aware that there is no one in the world who belongs here with me, whose place is by my side. That doesn't hurt nearly as much as I think it ought to—it just feels empty and slightly pathetic.

The room goes gray on cue, as if my little window of illumination has run its course. I think of David, his relentless probe into my psyche, his admission that he thrives on excitement and presumably gets bored with its lack, his assertion that he's impossible to get along with. I see a million pitfalls—but maybe I've also glimpsed something special, something that could make it all worthwhile? How do I recognize that when I see it? I vow to think about this very carefully, not to forget that the saddest thing about loneliness is that there are worse things than being alone.

Punctuating my thought, the doorbell and telephone jingle simultaneously. I direct a nice-looking youth with tousled brown hair and a huge piece of plywood around to the back, and catch the phone on the fifth ring. It's Hank.

"You sound funny," he says. "Are you all right?"

"Yeah—I'm fine." I don't tell him about the window because I don't want to listen to the inevitable lecture. Or maybe I'm afraid he'll talk me out of finishing what I've set out to do, convince me I shouldn't risk this meeting with Nathan Marks. "I was going to call you tonight," I say. "I'll be in New York tomorrow, do you want to have dinner?"

"I won't even ask why you're coming to town," he says. "I called to tell you I've got some information on your Mr. Zayad."

At this moment, I'm far too tired, too drained, to deal with anything else. "Save it for tomorrow, okay? I'd rather we talked about it in person."

After a prolonged silence, he agrees; we arrange to meet for dinner and hang up. The young man, having quickly installed his plywood patch, waits at the front door for me to sign his clipboard. I scrawl my name and lock the door behind him, but not before I note the patrol car passing slowly by the house.

Back in the den, I review the gruesome glass with a more practical eye, chuck the broom and dustpan and attack the mess with the heavy-duty shop-vac I bought last year in anticipation of someday cleaning the garage. When the glass is gone, I collapse on the couch. The room basks in the brilliance of Mr. Edison and I have an excellent, very comforting view of a large piece of impenetrable wood. Sure, I know security is an illusion, but for the moment I let myself pretend.

SEVENTEEN

The ride in from Queens is dismal at any time of the year, but in February it's particularly depressing. The cab shoulders its way down Lexington, pulls around and jerks to a stop before the familiar awning of the Waldorf. A bellhop leaps to attention and relieves me of my garment bag, and I stop for a moment, breathing in a different variety of pollutants. Down the street I can see the building where I toiled for a few years writing what-if computer scenarios in a tiny office on the thirty-second floor. Later, after moving across town to a competitor, I became fairly well known in our narrow trade world with my "Metal Minds" columns, but it was right there down the street that I earned the very first buck from the fruits of my extensive education.

A polite desk clerk hands me two small envelopes along with my room key. One is a message to call the White House; the other is from Enrico Perez, offering himself as an escort on tomorrow's trip to Harlem.

The flowers in my room are from Hank, although the card will credit them to an admirer—it's a long-standing tradition that always makes me smile. Years ago, when Hank and Melanie were first dating, she and I confessed to him and my now-forgotten date that once in a while we sent each other flowers. "For show, you know, to each other's office—once or twice a year and always on Valentine's Day if nothing else is going on—from an admirer." Together we explained how pitiful it was to sit at the only unadorned desk on Valentine's Day. From then on, Melanie and I never spent a flowerless V-Day or put in a florist's order on the other's behalf. Often when I come to New York, the admirer's touch greets me.

I fluff up a couple of pillows, lean back against the headboard and dial Pennsylvania Avenue; I ask for Deena Brennan, only to be informed that Ms. Brennan is not in her office today, that she'll be in tomorrow at eight. Sunday, I remind myself, but the message has today's date on it. "This is Nora Whitney. I received a message to call."

"Yes, Ms. Whitney. The president wanted to speak with you. Hold on, please."

I only have to wait a minute. Danny Court's voice sounds tired—not exhausted, just that strained edge, the chronic state of someone always walking into the wind. "Deena tells me I won't be able to convince you to table your activity," he says soberly, "but I'm asking you anyway, as a personal favor. I'd order you to stop, but I'm sure you'd remind me that you're a free agent. Nora, I hate bullies as much as you do, but that doesn't mean they aren't real. I'd be extremely relieved to have you out of it."

He wants to frighten me and he's succeeding, but now I'm finding out, no matter what I thought before, I *can* function inside of fear. "I'll stop, right after I meet with Nathan Marks tomorrow," I say.

"But that's my point—I don't think you should meet with Marks. Whoever is responsible for harassing you, Marks is likely to be the reason."

He's right. A nod from Nathan Marks would be worth its weight in gold. Nathan almost never gives one, and the fact that I even managed to get an appointment with him is impressive—or a cause for concern—to someone. "I'll stop after tomorrow," I repeat, sounding a lot braver than I feel.

"I don't suppose you'd consider any form of armed escort?" he asks.

We both know I wouldn't even get in the door with an armed escort. "Enrico Perez is going with me," I say.

Court sighs. "I give up. I said before that I didn't know Melanie very well, but I certainly saw both her stubbornness and her courage. In those ways, you're a lot like her."

I have no response to that. But I do appreciate the call and I tell him so.

By the time I leave for the restaurant, night has already laid its starless blanket over the tops of the buildings; street lamps, neon signs and brake lights join to keep the dark at bay. As the cab honks its way uptown, I watch the people of New York stream along the slushy sidewalks, going somewhere; I think how, at any second, any number of things could change their lives. We're all vulnerable—not just to purposeful acts of those with evil intent, but to accidents, illnesses, all the ominous possibilities that zap madly about the world bumping into folks at random.

The traffic has us gridlocked two blocks from the restaurant and I'm already a half hour late for dinner, so I pay the cabbie and get out, wiggling my way between bumpers to the sidewalk. The wind rushing down Third Avenue is far more wicked than the one that chased me across Hyde Park on my way to visit Jacques last week. With no aviator's cap to protect it, my hair whips about wildly and I tuck my chin into the neck of my coat, hugging the buildings and stepping around slush piles as I plunge ahead into the biting current. I was a New Yorker long enough to have the technique down pat, but nine years of Southern California winters have thinned my blood and definitely weakened my weather-fighting spirit.

With the restaurant's sign midway down the next block as my goal, I squint my eyes and push forward into the wind, easily outpacing my abandoned taxi and humming to myself against a background of blaring horns. I didn't leave this city because of the cold. I left because Neil Mackey made me an offer I couldn't refuse and because, with Melanie and Bennie down in Washington and my romance with that second-chair violinist nearing its inevitable end, I had no real reason to stay. I went to California filled with purpose. I would help Neil create and market products that could make a difference in a progressive world led by visionaries like Melanie Lombard.

Hank is waiting in the bar. "I was beginning to get worried," he says, offering his arm and guiding me into the dining room. "Then the bartender told me traffic hasn't moved on Third Avenue for more than an hour." The restaurant is warm and elegant with fine linen, flickering candles and good art, enough to fool one into thinking the world is a civilized place.

"Scotch—neat," I tell the waiter as soon as we're seated.

Hank's eyebrows lift. "It's been a long time since I've heard you order that. Didn't you used to drink scotch when you were a young editor blazing trails in those computer magazines?"

"Yeah. I don't think I've tasted the stuff in fifteen years."

The waiter brings our drinks and I take a sip of the Chivas Regal. It tastes like steel. Hank swirls the stick around his vodka martini, staring into the liquid whirlpool. "You managed to convince Nathan Marks to meet with you, didn't you?" he says. "That's why you're in New York."

"Uh-huh—and don't bother trying to talk me out of it, Hank. Danny Court already tried."

"At least Court understands the risk you're taking. You know the general consensus of my CID friends is that you're treading a pretty fine line with this sort of lobbying." Seeing my perplexed look, he explains. "CID—that's short for CIDTS, which stands for 'Coincidence?—I don't *think* so.' It's supposed to be a joke." He pauses for a second, but neither of us laugh.

"CID is just a little group I belong to, mostly professors, academic

types, men I've known for a long time; we meet on Thursday after-
noons." He takes a sip of his martini. "It started out as social, a little
scholarly discussion over a glass of brandy, but then a few years back
we got intrigued by what we saw as a preponderance of coincidences,
and began to talk about the idea of forces moving behind public actions—in short, conspiracy theory. For everyone but me, who has a
personal interest, it's a hobby. We adopted the CID acronym to keep
ourselves from getting too serious.

"Naturally, none of us agrees with the Commission's report on
Melanie's death, and when I mentioned you were going to try to help
Court by reviving some of her grass-roots support, well, everyone
thought it could be dangerous."

How charming to know I'm the subject of some Thursday afternoon highbrow discussion. "I didn't know you were interested in that
kind of stuff—I mean, before Melanie died."

A bitter smile crosses his face. "I think I've been looking for insidious connections since I was a kid—when my dad, the most selfish
man I've ever met, supposedly killed himself." He shakes his head
grimly. "Funny thing, though. I never really thought anything
would happen to *her*; she seemed above it somehow."

Yeah, I know—invincible. "You said you found out something
about this Zayad person?" I remind him.

Hank's face lights up. "Ah, yes. It seems that Jacques's friend is related to royalty. He's the nephew of a sultan in the United Arab emi-
rates. So much oil money, it'd make your head spin."

Hank must have analyzed this information from every possible
angle by now. I ask him what he thinks it means.

"It means that Jacques has powerful friends, which makes it even
more likely that Melanie was using him as part of her political information bank. I suspect that's why he disappeared. If it were to get out
that he was a direct line to the US through Melanie, it could be dangerous to him, embarrassing to his friends."

All that could be true, but my mind is running down another path.

"Hank, do you think it's likely that oil-producing nations would get involved in trying to stop the Blackmore bill?" I tell him about my brakes, the newspaper clipping, my shattered window. Does he, an expert on connections, see one here? His forehead creases with worry as I describe my harassment, but to my surprise he looks just as doubtful as David did when I suggested my nemesis may have to do with oil.

"I don't think so; they wouldn't get involved like that, Nora," he says. "Those sheiks and sultans just wouldn't understand the import of your activity. Grass-roots pressure is pretty uniquely democratic; the subtlety would escape them. I'd be more inclined to believe some White House aide spilled word of your activities to an industry lobbyist, somebody representing the interests of a major manufacturer, a big polluter. I think your danger lies a lot closer to home."

I swallow the last of my scotch. "Well, I may be scared, Hank, but I'm not going to let myself be intimidated."

The waiter comes and we order; then Hank reaches across the table and takes my hand. "Remember when Melanie was first running for Congress," he says, "and we all sat around the apartment spinning grand plans, wonderful ways we could contribute to changing the world?" He doesn't wait for me to respond. "Forgive me, but if every single one of those things had been accomplished, it still wouldn't be worth it to me. All of those dreams put together weren't worth one hair of her head to me. And as far as I'm concerned, what you're doing for Court is a painfully foolish risk." His pale blue eyes are moist. "I know it sounds like a cowardly attitude—Melanie would remind me that such thinking would have kept us a British colony—but there are just too many forces at work out there. None of this is worth your life."

"You don't still think Danny Court has anything to do with it, do you?"

He shakes his head slowly. "My problem with Court is personal; he gained from her death and I guess I can't get past that. But no, I don't think he's involved."

I have a sudden urge to reach across and touch his cheek, smooth his forehead, as if by stroking I could melt the forlorn mask that's been frozen there since the day she died. Before I can do it, the food arrives.

Over dinner, I try to cheer him up by recounting amusing lines from my discussions with America's popular leaders: I tell him about Lucifer Brown's off-color, physically impossible suggestion; Freda Lowe's insistence on ovaries as a qualification for personhood. Hank's smile lacks enthusiasm.

Neither of us is in the mood for dessert. On the way back to the hotel, he asks me what magic I used to score tomorrow's meeting with Nathan Marks; I tell him. For a second his face is pained, reminding me how hard it is for him to think that any part of Melanie's vision could go on without her, but he recovers quickly. Life shouldn't go on, but it does.

"You don't have to say good-bye, Nora," he says, as the cab pulls to a stop. "I'll see you on Saturday; Bennie invited me to the birthday party." I try to cover my surprise with an enthusiastic remark about how great I think that is; I give him a hug.

It *is* great for Bennie to include his father, I think, as I ride up in the elevator. When I open the door to my room, the perfume from the vase of gardenias is almost overwhelming.

EIGHTEEN

Enrico Perez gets up from the plush chair in the lobby and walks toward me with his hand outstretched and a broad grin on his bronze face. I decide it's the hotel that looks out of place, not him. Bundled in a heavy plaid hunting jacket, a thick lock of black hair hanging over his forehead, Enrico is at home anyplace on the planet. I haven't seen him for a few years, but it doesn't matter. Despite the fact that he's put on a pound or two, he never looks much older than he did in that poster photo. The big difference isn't age, it's attitude. The once-surly Puerto Rican youth maintains an almost overbearing level of enthusiasm.

I wait inside the lobby door while Enrico talks to the cab driver. When you pick someone up at the Waldorf you don't expect to be asked to drive to Harlem. Obviously persuasive, he waves for me to join him; I see, as I crawl into the backseat, that the cabbie has suddenly recognized his fare and is staring at him with rapt admiration via the rearview mirror.

"You don't really know Marks, do you?" Enrico asks, turning to lean against the door and leveling those large brown eyes at me. When I shake my head, he makes a face. "Nathan's brilliant, powerful and effective, but he's not a very nice man. I can tell you right now he doesn't give beans about the Blackmore bill or anything else

Washington might come up with. He's the government in Harlem. Has been for fifteen years."

"Melanie got to him, though."

"Yeah, well she had a way—" All that intense light drains from his face; he shifts around in the seat and looks out the window. Enrico has always refused to tell the press what Melanie whispered to him that day on the sidewalk, what magic words made him change his mind and walk away. Several times I've been tempted to ask him, but I've always resisted the urge. Clearly, he feels those words were just for him.

We ride in silence for several minutes, crossing to the west side, passing through neighborhoods I rarely see since I moved to California. This is part of the district Melanie represented in her first public job, and although a lot of it has been renovated in the years since she stumped door-to-door, a lot of it hasn't. These are still poor neighborhoods, ringing with different languages. Children in ragged, outgrown clothes play handball on the sidewalk and chase each other between the dirty buildings.

As we pause for a light, I notice a thin woman crouched on the stoop of a corner building, wearing a man's jacket several sizes too big and holding what must be a baby wrapped in a rough blanket. She's obviously braving the weather to watch her children, four of them, play in the slush. My mind does a quick rewind and I can almost see Melanie leaning against that rusted wrought-iron railing, talking to her. Melanie is wearing her navy quilted jacket and the red muffler, her short blond hair flying. She stoops, reaching out to move aside the blanket and gently touch the baby's face. I see her smile.

The light changes and the cab moves on. The woman still sits on the stoop, but Melanie isn't there. Enrico looks at me sadly, as if he knows my mind was playing tricks. "I've been thinking about running for the council," he says. "Maybe even a state office, but I'm not sure I'm ready to give up the day-to-day practice of law. Maybe I'm more productive where I am—being a burr in their backsides."

Picking up the gist of the conversation, the cab driver adds his two bits in Spanish and he and Enrico carry on a rapid dialogue over the next couple of blocks. "He says I should run for mayor," Enrico explains. "He's seen my picture and read about me in the Spanish newspapers; he's sure I would be a great mayor. Too bad it isn't as simple as that."

"Why won't Marks talk to you?" I ask him as we near our destination. There hasn't been a white face in sight for blocks.

"I told you he's not a nice man. Besides, we don't work the same way and we don't value the same things. Nathan and I have done nothing but jab at each other for years. I can't think of anything I have to say that he'd care about."

"And you can't imagine anything I have to say that he'd care about."

"Right. He had a soft spot for Melanie, so maybe he'll be polite to you. More likely he'll chew you up and spit you out." The cab stops in front of an old brick building. Enrico gets out and comes around to open my door, nodding at the driver. "Bernardo and I are going to go get some coffee; then we'll come back, sit out here to wait for you. It's probably the only place in this neck of Harlem that's safe for a couple of PRs." He leans back against the cab door and folds his arms. "We'll wait until you get inside."

He doesn't have to wait long. The door opens before I have a chance to climb the steps, and a young black man wearing a purple shirt, his face framed by dreadlocks, meets me halfway. "You can go now, man," he calls down to Enrico. "We take care of the lady."

Nathan Marks has the only door I've ever seen in New York without a lock. The young man follows me in and simply closes it. I turn in the narrow entryway and extend my hand. "I'm Nora Whitney."

He looks at my hand, then up at my face, then back at my hand again. Finally he takes it, but only for a second. "Yeah, I know who you are. I'm Jonah. Mr. Marks is waiting for you."

Jonah takes me up in the elevator to the third floor, then down a long hallway past several offices where people are busy working at computers or on the telephone. The door at the end of the hallway is closed and Jonah knocks, a series of short raps like a code. A voice bids us enter. Jonah pushes the door open but doesn't follow me inside.

The room is spacious, with windows on two sides and a third wall lined with shelves of books and African artifacts. In the center is a huge desk piled with papers, and sitting in the leather chair behind it is a large black man with graying hair, wearing a faded blue sweatshirt. Nathan Marks is about sixty years old and, unlike Enrico, shows his age. I haven't seen him in person since the day he saved our hides in the subway, but, courtesy of television, I've watched his hair gray and the lines around his mouth deepen.

"Sit down, Ms. Whitney. I understand you were accompanied by that little spic." He savors the word, but does not seem surprised that I don't react. "He must have told you all sorts of flattering things about me."

I sit in the only other chair in the room, an uncomfortable straight-backed piece that looks like a garage-sale reject. Nathan obviously doesn't pamper his guests. "He said you weren't a very nice man."

He laughs loudly, a full sound like an opera singer warming up. "Nice. Oh, he's right about that. What's to be nice about?" Leaning back, he folds his hands behind his head. "Enrico Perez is just another do-gooder under some pathetic misconception that he can make the system work in favor of his Puerto Rican people. He and the ACLU." He draws out the letters as if they taste bad on his tongue. I say nothing, deciding to sit this part out. "Perhaps he's so naive because the Puerto Ricans have only been hanging out on the streets of New York for decades. Whereas we, Ms. Whitney—I mean my people—we've been around for quite a while. Isn't that so?"

Do not argue with this man, I remind myself. He wants you to argue with him. "You've been around for as long as I can remember, Mr. Marks. Please call me Nora."

He laughs again. So far, so good. "Ah. You don't look like her. You don't talk like her. But there is some resemblance in the amount of nerve. Tell me, Nora, did you think because you are a friend of Melanie Lombard, you could walk in here and talk me into something?"

It occurs to me suddenly that behind all the mystique Nathan Marks operates just like any shrewd businessman. The awareness that I'm simply making a sales call helps me to relax. "No, Nathan, I did not. My visit *does* have to do with Melanie because it concerns something she and I used to dream about—something that wasn't quite possible while she was alive, but now it is and I think she would want you to have it."

"All right, I'll bite. Just what is this gift you mentioned on the telephone?"

I sift through my inner thesaurus, seeking user-friendly words to describe the gift of cognition. Not for him, of course—for the kids. For kids who don't respond to words, whose attention spans have been kept short by minute-to-minute lifestyles; nonlinear kids; kids for whom learning has been thin and flat and pointless, without the thrill of discovery. What Nathan Marks really wants are more black engineers, more black scientists, black doctors. "You want a black president—am I right?"

He leans forward, nodding slowly, resting his heavy chin on his hand. I reach into my purse, take out a single sheet of paper and push it across the desk at him. "I've got a learning program that'll knock your socks off."

Nathan retrieves a pair of glasses from the top drawer of his desk and quietly reads the paragraphs I wrote on the plane. Using Garth's outline as a basis, I took out the technical stuff, left in what I'm sure were Stanley Curtis's enthusiastic adjectives and added my own experience with lesson one of Jimmy's program.

"You have this program?" The expression on his face is guarded, but I can sense that the person behind those eyes is at full attention. I nod. "This could change our whole method of education," he says.

"I think it will eventually. At the moment it's a little pricey to mass-produce."

"So exactly what are you suggesting?"

I explain that we'll set up three demo systems in one school and he can pick the school. Learning Parallels will donate the systems and our educational consultants will work with the local school district to evaluate their effectiveness.

"Three systems, one school—if this program is too expensive for general use, what happens after that?" He leans across the desk as if his whole body is waiting for my answer.

I don't actually have one. I tell him I'm absolutely committed, personally, to making sure kids benefit from this technology sooner rather than later, and I remind him that Melanie's education plan included federal funds for computer research and development, specifically geared toward inner-city educational problems.

"Danny Court has asked me to consult on education and if Uncle Sam can kick in, we ought to be able to set up learning centers in a number of inner-city schools."

Nathan looks up at the ceiling; still clutching the paper, he emits a rude sound from his pursed lips. "You'll never get that far. Court will have to cave in on this pollution thing if he wants to survive; he'll be forced into more political games—and *pol*itical games just trade around the pieces. You're handing me a pipe dream."

"No, I'm giving you three demo systems, scot-free, that can make a difference to somebody's kids." Admitting that the rest is speculation, I say I think it could happen, if Court could count on the same support that got him into office.

Nathan removes his glasses, opens the desk drawer and lays them inside along with my one-page outline. "Why me, Nora? Why don't you let your friend Perez find a school for your systems? Maybe those little Latino kids could get all the way through high school without learning English."

"That's not exactly the purpose of the program," I say. "Besides, Melanie had a lot of respect for you and this is her dream as well as mine."

"Of course you wouldn't mind a bit if I happen to put in a good word on behalf of Mr. Court, whom I believe to be an asshole. Admittedly, in my opinion everyone in Washington is an asshole."

Our eyes lock across the desk and I know instantly why he and Melanie understood each other. "No," I say, continuing to meet his gaze. "I wouldn't mind."

His face relaxes into a smile. "Thank you. I do remember you, you know—that look of utter amazement on your pretty face when she hauled off and slugged that punk in the mouth." He chuckles softly. "Of course, you weren't as surprised as those four hoodlums. Defied by a little blond handful of a girl."

I smile with him at the memory.

Abruptly, it occurs to me that Nathan, having himself been on a number of subversive lists over the years, might be able to give me an educated opinion about my recent harassment. He listens thoughtfully, his chin again resting on his fist. When I've finished, he sits up, folding his hands in front of him. "I think Henry Cochran is right. There is more in heaven and earth than is dreamt of in your philosophy. You should be careful, Nora; I wouldn't take it lightly."

Nathan Marks quotes Hamlet; I kind of like that. "Do you think Melanie's assassination was a conspiracy?" I have to ask.

"Of course I do. But I think everything is a conspiracy."

He pushes a buzzer on his desk and Jonah appears at the door. I thank Nathan for his time and tell him we'll have the systems set up and the teachers trained before summer.

Enrico and Bernardo are playing cards in the front seat of the cab when Jonah raps on the window. Enrico climbs out and he and Jonah edge around each other on the sidewalk in some sort of primitive inner-city ritual while I open the back door for myself.

"Well, was he a real sweetheart?" Enrico asks as we pull away from the building.

I don't answer because I'm busy doing math in my head and praying that I'll be able to get Neil to go along with me on this. Otherwise, I've just given away a year's salary.

NINETEEN

I leave New York, feeling that weird sense of relief that goes along with having done something irreversible. I had no right, really, to give away computer hardware and software that doesn't belong to me, but whatever happens, I'm glad I did it. Neil may fire me, but he'll never renege on a company commitment.

The sky is already dark when I pull into my driveway. I unlock the front door and walk through the house slowly, turning on lights. Things appear to be undisturbed. The camellias in the vase on the kitchen table have turned brown around the edges. Sunday's paper lies on the chair just as I left it. In the den, still guarded by a plywood patch, the shop-vac sits in the center of the floor. Nothing has been disturbed. I leaf through the mail, allowing myself to feel hopeful. Since my invisible adversaries knew exactly when I started helping Court, they should also know that I've finished.

On my machine, I find a message from David that starts out with a loud comic-book sound—no vowels, lots of r's and g's—and then shifts to a panicky plea about how he's drowning in words. Finally, in a normal voice, he describes himself as a bleary-eyed zombie super-glued to the chair in front of his computer, mountains of notes piled on either side; he no longer has any sense of day or night and believes his only hope lies in breaking free for a little while. He'll be at Madoros in Santa Monica from eight o'clock on this evening; he knows I'll be tired from my trip, but if I'm up to joining him, he would appreciate the company. Pretty much all in one breath. I take the fact that he chose a spot in my part of the city, rather than in his own, as an indication that he really means it. I glance at my watch; it's eight-thirty. Of course, my body is really on East Coast time, but I decide to go anyway.

David's car is parked at the far end of the lot and I pull in beside it, smiling to myself. Two cars. Neutral turf. From the doorway I see him sitting at the bar, talking to a young man with a dark ponytail; I watch his face break into that captivating grin, the wiry curls bounce against the neck of his olive green sweater. The ponytailed fellow, completely denim-clad, looks about thirty and very attractive in an artsy sort of way. I realize, as I walk toward them, that I know him; that I met him in the very same coffeehouse where I met Blaine Hennessey, and even went out with him once, to a party celebrating the first publication of some writer friend of his. Of course, I can't remember his name. I'm mentally running through the alphabet when David notices me and spins around on the stool.

"Ah—you came."

"I hope you're not too far ahead of me." I edge into the narrow space between them, my brain on fast-forward and my eyes firmly locked on David. *M . . . N . . . O . . . P.*

"Hi, Nora. It's been a while."

T . . . Tom . . . Tim . . . Tim . . . yes! "It sure has. How have you been, Tim?" Tim's eyes have a dreamy quality I'd forgotten. Now I remember that I went out with him more than once. David looks from him to me and back again.

"I'm working—have a couple of pieces at Wynn's. I'm still in the same studio—maybe you'll come by sometime."

"Tim's a sculptor," I say to David. And a work of art, I note to myself as they shake hands. They've been sharing animated conversation but haven't bothered with introductions.

"Tim Lynch."

"David Weinhardt."

"The biographer?" Tim asks, looking at me. I nod and he turns back to David with a wide smile and open admiration in his eyes. "I read *Patrice*. It was magnificent."

"Thanks. I'm glad you liked it." David stands up. "We're going to move to a table. Why don't you join us?" A nice try, but his invitation doesn't sound too sincere.

Tim glances at me quickly and shakes his head. "I need to get back—thanks anyway. It was good to meet you. And, Nora, I meant what I said about coming by the studio. I think you'll find my work has grown a lot since we—since you were last there."

David and I squeeze away from the crowded bar into the other room, where a table is being vacated by the window. "More than an old friend, I'd guess, from the way he looked at you," he says, pulling out my chair.

"Not much more. We had a few dates. I had a hard time remembering his name."

He waves down a waitress and we order a couple of beers and some nachos. "Come to think of it, he couldn't really be an *old* friend." He raises his eyebrows as if he's about to make a surprising observation. "He's not old enough."

"Okay, okay—next time we can run into one of your ex-girlfriends, one of those intense, exciting persons from your past."

"I'm just wondering if I'm wasting my time, that's all," he says. "I obviously don't fit your usual pattern."

Do I pick up the quiver of threatened masculine pride? Interesting. Didn't he see how the youthful, handsome Tim nearly drowned in his awe of the famous writer? The waitress brings our beers and I stare at him over the mug. "I suppose whether or not you're wasting your time depends on what you're after," I say.

He folds his arms across his chest. "And what are *you* after, Nora? Tell me the truth now—does it have to do with my book?"

Next, it'll be my turn to accuse him of playing up to me because I'm a treasure chest of Melanie Lombard trivia. We're both of us scared to death of each other, and if I weren't in the middle of it, hands shaking as I drain my beer, if I were watching this repartee between some mixed-up couple on television, I'd be laughing myself silly. We're not kids; what the hell is the matter with us?

The waitress delivers a large platter of nachos—fuel for the truth. "I think the subject of what each of us is ultimately after may be too advanced for right now," I submit, looking him in the eye. "But I'm willing to state for the record that I'm here because I like you, not because of anything having to do with your book." *Like* him—preteen phraseology, but he gets my point.

He looks startled, then smiles slowly. "This is what I get for finding a woman who knows how to talk." Putting down his beer, he reaches across the table and takes my hand. "*For the record,* if you had never even met our former president, I would still be making every excuse under the sun to see you."

After that we sit in silence for a few moments, picking at the nachos. I can tell that something is still bothering him. "I almost wish that were true," he says finally, "that you didn't know her. I mean— you were her closest friend and you're probably expecting the book to be one long standing ovation; I'm afraid you'll be pretty upset with me when you read it."

I'm not sure what to say. If I were to create a pie chart illustrating how David and I have apportioned the precious little time we've spent together, better than 75 percent of it would be labeled "talking about Melanie." But, of course, I've never told him how I feel about her now. I can't tell him how angry I've been with her for lying to me, hurting me, stepping all over me—for making me see myself as the kind of person she could lie to, hurt, step on. I can't let him know how close I've come to hating her, that the only thing stopping me is that I can't hate Melanie without feeling sorry for myself, and I never get very far with that.

"As a biographer, I'm a student of power," he says. "What it does to people, how they use it; and Melanie Lombard wielded power as relentlessly as anyone I've ever seen. Yeah, I know her motives were honorable and she did what she did in order to achieve splendid things, but I think she truly believed that the end—her vision of the end—justified the way she used people, molded them to be part of her plan and, in doing so, took away their freedom of choice. You told me she didn't believe in destiny, but don't you see how she assigned destinies to everyone she needed: you, Court, Deena Brennan, Reverend Wayne, that Puerto Rican kid on the poster; the list is endless."

Everything he's saying is true. What surprises me is that deep inside I still feel a tiny stir of pride to be among the very special people he just named, to be chosen—because Melanie selected only the best. Have *chosen* and *used* always been the same thing? I play with that in my mind as David, fully engrossed in his own argument, nibbles on a nacho. I decide that the distinction is too subtle, too volatile. Besides, didn't we all—didn't the United States of America—choose and use her as well? Looking at it that way, it's hard to say she took more than she gave.

David must have heard my thoughts. "Melanie had to sacrifice a lot to be who she was," he says. "And because of that, she didn't accept being governed by the same rules as the rest of us." He smiles at me tentatively. "What I'm trying to tell you is that she was a master manipulator and that will come through in my book because it's part of the phenomenon of Melanie Lombard."

"I know she wasn't perfect," I say, suddenly annoyed. So she was a master manipulator and a master politician—how unusual for a president to be those things. Like many people in power, Melanie made her own rules; it was only shocking because we didn't expect that from a woman! Just as quickly my irritation subsides; I have my own personal gripes with our late lady president, but the big gender fury is too old and too familiar to hang on to.

For one absurd second, as I sip my beer and watch David watching me, I imagine Melanie sitting here with us, listening to all this. I can practically see her blond head tipped to one side, her blue eyes studying David's face, intent on catching every word; she'd be absolutely fascinated.

"When was the last time you got drunk?" David says, his face serious. "I mean really drunk?"

"Uh—not for a very long time."

"Me neither, but maybe we should both get that way." He signals the waitress again and orders a bottle of tequila and two shot glasses. "One last thing before we change the subject; I have to get it off my chest: the more I dig, the more it seems clear to me that Melanie must have had an ongoing relationship with that Jacques DeBrin over a considerable period of time. I can't prove it yet, I still haven't been able to talk to him, but I think he was her lover—and I think you already know that." He puts his hand up as if I might leap at him across the table. "No, don't say anything; I'm not asking you to confirm it. I really don't want you to say anything, but I had to let you know where it stands."

I know where it stands—right smack between us—but for tonight at least, I'm willing to join him in putting it aside.

The tequila arrives. He pours two shots, hands me one and downs the other. Then he asks me to describe my meeting with the infamous Nathan Marks and I do so as colorfully as possible, including the part about giving away the math program: virtual reality comes to Harlem.

"Give it away? Political trade, don't you mean?"

"Nope—gift. I had to find a way to get the program out there; also, it was the only possible way to capture Nathan's attention. Of course,

I haven't told my boss yet." I toss down the shot and chase it with a swallow of beer. Whew.

David pours another round. "I have to hand it to you, Nora. Here, let me hand it to you." He gives me one shot glass and raises the other in a solemn toast. "Here's to an amazing woman—you."

"Okay. I'll drink to that." I can't believe I'm doing this. Like a gulp of fire, the clear liquid burns its way down my throat and bounces back up to ignite my brain. We grin at each other, twin fire-eaters in a state of combustion.

"I mean it," David says. "You go out there, confront a malcontent like Marks. You risk your job giving away something that isn't yours. On the other hand, maybe you're just nuts. You haven't had any more trouble, have you?"

I tell him about my picture window and he leans across the table, his hand clutching the bottle as if he might hit me with it. "You couldn't let me come in and check the house that day, could you? You have to handle everything by yourself." His voice is getting ragged at the edges.

He's right, I should have let him come in. Anyway, I'm hoping it's over now; I've done all the lobbying I plan to do. My words are beginning to slur. What are we talking about?

"Has anybody ever told you that you have three of the most beautiful eyes?" he says, losing the thread along with me. We stare at each other, our right hands moving in unison, downing the shots. Our left hands creep across the table until the fingers touch and I can feel us floating somewhere beyond the confines of the room.

"Do you do this often?" I say without moving my lips.

"Let's see—the last time I did shooters? Georgetown, sophomore year." At that, the dam breaks and he begins to shake with soundless laughter. "Mary Ellen Whatchamacallit. Come to think of it she had three eyes too—amazing coooincidence." He bursts into giggles and empties the bottle into our glasses. We drink and laugh some more. His grasp on my left hand is the only thing I can actually feel.

David pays the bill and together we manage to stand up and walk a relatively straight path to the bar, where he asks the bartender to call us a cab. We wait outside, leaning against the building.

When we pull up in front of my house, David asks the driver to wait. Surprised, I say nothing until we're standing on my front step with the key in the lock. "It's all right if you stay. Lots closer to pick up your car tomorrow."

"No thanks, but this time you're going to let me check out the house." He disappears into my dark living room, turning on lights as he proceeds. In two minutes he's back at the door. "Now for a stroll around the perimeter. Care to join me?" He doesn't wait for an answer, but grabs me around the waist and we walk-stagger along the side of the house, through the back gate and across the orchard. "Anyone here?" he calls. "Guess not." Turning unsteadily, he puts both arms around me and we stumble backward to lean against a large eucalyptus. His mouth tastes like the fire we've both been drinking and I feel the night spin as if I might pass out right here on the lawn. He pulls back suddenly and rests his forehead against mine. His voice is a whisper. "When we make love, Nora, I want to remember it."

David leads me back to the front door, kisses me lightly and pushes me gently across the threshold. The taxi still sits at the curb, ticking away. "Don't forget my birthday party on Saturday," I manage to say as he retreats down the sidewalk.

He turns, gives me a sweeping bow and saves himself from a face-first dive into the cement with a quick two-step.

"G'night, Nora."

TWENTY

"I still can't believe I did it," Bennie insists. "I think it was some alternate Self from a parallel universe that interfaced just long enough to spit out those fatal words—'Hey, Dad, we're having a party. Why don't you fly out and join us.' See, it doesn't even sound like me." He groans. "I have a miserable feeling that I'm going to regret this."

Talk about miserable feelings. My stomach is reacting as if something covered with fur is doing deep knee bends inside it; my head, closeted in a shiny blue helmet, feels full of cement and I have a definite inner-ear problem. "Ummm" is the best I can manage to say with my face buried in the back of his jacket. When the light changes the cycle lurches, my stomach bringing up the rear, and I clutch him tightly around the waist, marveling at my brilliance in allowing myself to climb on a motorcycle with a Grade A hangover.

Finally we arrive at the parking lot and Bennie sputters to a halt beside my car. I pull off the helmet and hand it to him, but my head doesn't feel any lighter. David's BMW is still there, so I fish in the bottom of my bag for a single dog-eared packet of Alka-Seltzer and leave it under his windshield wiper.

"This looks serious," Bennie says.

"I'm not talking yet. He's coming to the party too."

"Great. Maybe he'll keep Henry busy. You know I never would

have invited him, but he called me again—just to talk—and I couldn't help it."

Despite his six-foot-two frame, Bennie sometimes gets this look in his eye that reminds me of when he was eight years old. It's a lonely, uncertain look that's gone before you have a chance to deal with how it makes you feel. "I think it's a giant step in the right direction, kid. You two have to quit depriving each other of family."

"Just so long as he doesn't turn the party into a wake for my mother. You're following me to my place, right? I have the perfect cure for that decadent state you're in."

Grateful for the solid feel of my car's smooth upholstery and the protection of a metal shell, I wait for Bennie to rev up his cycle and zoom out of the lot; then I shift into crawl and pull out after him. I manage to make the few blocks to Venice without mishap.

Bennie's apartment is the top floor of a duplex one block from the beach; to enter I have to step around columns of ponderously stacked books, magazines and videotapes. Bennie's clutter always looks as if it were expressly laid out according to some strange design. A pair of discarded jeans clings by one long denim leg to the arm of a black canvas director's chair. In the center of the white tile floor, a volley-ball and basketball rest against each other, barely touching, like a shy interracial couple. A crate overflowing with multicolored dials, gears and gauges sits on top of the bookcase. And everywhere are these sculpted towers of tapes and books. The order of the room, like an inventor's mind, makes sense only to itself, but amazingly there are no layers of dust to dull its statement. I picture Bennie gingerly vacuuming each stack, holding his breath when one begins to rock and keeping score every time one tumbles.

He emerges from the kitchen with a huge glass of carrot juice and two tiny pink pills. "Sublingual B-12. You have to let them dissolve under your tongue."

"I know what sublingual means. You don't really expect me to drink that orange stuff?"

"Just do what I tell you for a change, it'll make you feel better. You must be in love with this guy—I can't imagine you getting bombed." He doesn't say "at your age" but of course he's thinking it.

I collapse into one of the vinyl-and-chrome chairs by the table and pop the pills under my tongue, where they immediately begin to melt, leaving a Pepto-Bismol kind of taste. Bennie straddles a chair across from me, ready to get down to business. "Katy called yesterday," he says. "She's ordered a banana-chocolate sheet cake from Alfie's."

I take a sip of the carrot juice—it doesn't taste half bad. "What if we get some lasagna from Harold's?" I suggest. "They make great lasagna, vegetarian and regular."

"Anything but Mexican. Your mom said the enchiladas we had last year gave her heartburn. By the way, she's bringing the champagne—and Herbert."

Herbert is a man who lives in the same senior apartments as my mother, two doors down the hall; he doesn't hear very well so he laughs a lot, assuming someone said something funny. Mentally, I begin to add: Bennie and me, his friend Karen, Mother and Herbert, Hank, David, Jimmy Barton—eight.

"Karen's going to make the hors d'oeuvres. She says she likes doing that kind of thing. I guess if you study physics, anything mindless is R&R. She's a grad student at Caltech."

"Impressive. You also said she's a patient of Dr. Ferris's?"

"Yeah, her father was Emanuel Márquez, that concert pianist who died of a heart attack onstage last year. We share the 'child-of-the-famous-and-dramatically-deceased' syndrome."

Well, there's certainly common ground. I shut my eyes for a second, remembering. "At Lincoln Center. Your dad was there, I think." I tuck the information about Karen into that pocket in the back of my head. I may want to borrow her when Jimmy demos his software, get the opinion of a student with her kind of background.

Without noticing it, I've managed to finish more than half the carrot juice. My stomach still isn't particularly happy, but I'm beginning to recognize other signs of life. "I'm feeling better. Thanks."

Bennie runs down his list; he's pretty organized for a kid, but then he had two very organized mothers. "They'll deliver the lasagna, won't they? I'll buy some good bread. Don't forget to stop and get ice cream when you pick up the cake. We should probably have something else to drink besides champagne."

Then he gets up and pulls me to my feet. "B-12, carrot juice and fresh air. C'mon, we'll take a little jaunt along the sand."

All the remnants of coastal haze have lifted, and the midday sun on this February California day is dazzling. As we walk toward the water, I'm struck by how clear everything appears, sharp-edged, as if a film has been washed from my eyes or someone has turned my perception dial up a couple of notches. It's maybe 65, with a slight breeze, just enough to stir the palms. We cross the street and shuffle through the sand to the hard-packed strip above where the waves are gently lapping. Gulls swoop across a sky that is blue forever.

"Once upon a time," Bennie says, taking my hand, "there was a young boy who lived in a huge palace with one thousand rooms." I close my eyes, letting his firm hand and the soft cadence of his voice guide my steps along the beach. "The boy, of course, was a prince who would one day be king of all the land, but now he was a boy who, like other boys, wanted to play and have fun—and, like other princes, he had a problem because of the special rules assigned to him. Worst of all, he couldn't go anywhere beyond the palace walls without an armed guard.

"Now this was a very well-read boy and he had studied how other princes had handled the problem, but he knew these ways wouldn't work for him. If he were to change places with someone else—a pauper, for example—he might miss out on important parts of his education. The truth was that he really wanted to be king and he wanted to do everything necessary to make himself a good king—if only it weren't so limiting.

"As I said, the palace had one thousand rooms—nine hundred and one of them were used to house the court and its many servants, but the other ninety-nine rooms were in the wing at the very top of the palace, inconvenient and unused. It was in these rooms that the boy played, pretending to be an explorer. Each day he would enter a different room as if it were a strange land and he would have many imaginary adventures. 'It's good simple fun,' said his father the king. 'As long as he tends to his studies,' said the queen.

"And so, each afternoon when his tutoring was finished, the boy climbed to the top floor of the palace, hoping that this time the room he entered would be the magical one. You see, he had once had a powerful dream in which he was told that one of the ninety-nine rooms was a portal through which he would truly be able to come and go to different worlds.

"At last the day came when only one of the ninety-nine rooms remained unexplored. As soon as his studies were over he raced to the top level of the palace and stood for a minute outside the very last door. Then he opened it and went in. The room was much like the other ninety-eight, filled with odd pieces of furniture draped in ghostly protective coverings. When he pulled back the heavy curtains on the window, all he saw was the familiar countryside. The boy was devastated. Standing in the center of the room, he shouted at the four walls: 'What about my dream?' Then, suddenly, it came back to him, the magic words, the one part of the dream that he'd forgotten. 'It doesn't have to be like this,' he whispered to himself—and then, gaining confidence, he said it aloud into the room. 'It doesn't have to be the way I think I see it.' And, in an instant, it wasn't.

"The boy grew up to be a very good king, but even as a grown-up he crept away now and then to the enchanted ninety-ninth room at the top of the palace and escaped through the secret portal into other worlds. He knew he was a far better king from all he'd learned on his secret voyages and, of course, because he'd always come back in time to do his lessons. The end."

Bennie lets go of my hand and steps around a large clump of sea-weed. "I was six years old when she first told me that story. We were curled up on that old green sofa in her study and she had on a blue wool sweater that scratched my cheek but I didn't move the whole time. I remember thinking that if I held real still the story might never end."

He laughs softly and digs at the sand with the toe of his shoe. "All of her stories began in that room. It was through the ninety-ninth room that I met the mysterious Jacques who led the little prince on countless adventures. You know, I've been thinking about it a lot since you brought up the Jacques affair and the stories started coming back to me. *'It doesn't have to be the way I think I see it.'* I realize that my films, every one of them, were born in that room."

I haven't said a word since we stepped onto the sand. The breeze has picked up, gently lifting my hair as we walk. The brilliance of the sun on the water is blinding. The sensations washing over me are in sync with the waves—rhythmic, overpowering surges of mixed emotion. The stories Melanie used to tell me from the top bunk of our dorm room were not like that—they were more topical, designed to heal the problem of the day. But I have been in Melanie's ninety-ninth room anyway. No one told me it was supposed to be a portal to pass through, or that I was supposed to be home in time for supper. I tried to live there.

We turn and retrace our steps up the beach, each in our own private reverie. I stayed right there, suspended. Portal, doorway, dead end. How could I go anywhere when I didn't know how to make it work? And how could I stop trying and run the risk of being . . . ordinary?

The enormity of what I'm feeling brings tears to my eyes. Jacques DeBrin was the epitome of everything she had that I wanted, so I tried to re-create him over and over, but no one could ever be Jacques—*because I am not Melanie.* It was never about him at all.

And, of course, it wasn't about Melanie either. Just me—who I'm not. That's why the ninety-ninth room never worked for me; I forgot to see it the other way around—who I am!

Walking along, leaving distinct footprints in the sand, I think about the amazing dance that was my relationship with Melanie Lombard. We stood in that college dorm room on Day One with eighteen years of separate baggage, but from that moment until the day she died, we played off each other. I've spent countless hours examining how she brought out my strengths and my weaknesses. But, of course, I did the same for her. And just as I contributed to the creation of the president of the United States, I also must have helped create the other woman, the one I didn't know.

I blink my eyes to catch Bennie looking at me intently as if my face has sprouted a surprising new feature. "Half my trust fund for your thoughts," he says. "You look as if you've just experienced an epiphany of some sort."

"Your mother's story launched a few rockets."

"Yeah, I know."

And, it occurs to me, he *does* know. There's comfort in that. We walk the rest of the way in silence, cutting diagonally across the sand and through the parking lot. "Oh, I almost forgot to tell you," Bennie says when we're back in front of his apartment, "I met that guy who's investing in my film. He was in LA on some sort of business; he doesn't have a job or anything, just invests. Anyway, we had lunch on campus; he's pretty cool—and he already gave me a check for fifty grand." I squeeze his hand; I'm glad. Bennie deserves to have nice things happen to him, and it's about time one of them is connected to Hank.

The story of the enchanted room replays in my head as I drive home. And so does the idea of Jacques the Adventurer. All of us got so involved in her imagination, but it's up to me to figure out my own version of "the end." I can't talk to Melanie, but I *could* talk to Jacques—if I could find him.

As soon as I get in the door, I pick up the phone and, setting aside my promise, I dial Dennis Jacobson. His secretary tells me he has nothing to say to me, and when I insist that it's important, that I'll only take a second of his time, she returns with the same message, an emphatic no.

I try long-distance information again—the operator could have made a mistake the first time—but once more I'm told that the number in Paris is unlisted. I wonder how David found out where Jacques lives. There has to be an office address; I could put Katy on it in the morning, tracing down some business directory, but it's probably futile. David said he hasn't reached him and, as good as David is, that means Jacques is still unfindable, even though he showed up briefly to close that deal in Cairo. He's hiding. From David? From me? Or from somebody else?

Maybe he's escaped through Melanie's ninety-ninth room, I think ironically, through the same portal that transformed him into an adventurer, a lover, a spy—or practically anything one could imagine. My head begins to ache again and I catch myself talking out loud. *You may have managed to pull it off while you were alive, Melanie . . . make it seem like magic . . . but when David Weinhardt paints your exploits with large sweeping adjectives, I don't think they're going to play in Peoria.*

TWENTY-ONE

I get up early on Thursday, hoping to beat Neil to the office, but the leprechaun in charge of little things has a different idea. One missing button, stuck zipper and previously unnoticed grease stain later, I've already blown the advantage, so I sit back down at the table and scan the paper in preparation for Neil's typical current-event zingers. Searching for buzzwords, I would have skipped right over Elena's column if it hadn't been for the headline: HONK IF YOU STILL CARE.

"This writer hears from a reliable source that President Court is not going to take no for an answer when it comes to emissions controls; in fact, in an effort to rally behind the voters' mandate, this administration may not be taking no for an answer when it comes to any part of the Lombard agenda." The column goes on to laud the rehiring of Deena Brennan, denounce national backsliding and bewail the pitfalls of win-lose psychology. Elena calls for an end to our period of mourning. "I don't know about you," she finishes, "but I'm going to drop a little note to my representatives in Washington—remind them that Daniel Court is trying to carry out what the people of the United States, in overwhelming numbers, said we wanted. We're still here, aren't we? And we're still registered to vote."

I experience a distinct stab of pleasure. As Deena must have shouted when she read these words this morning on East Coast time—wow! This may be just one editorial column, but Elena has a considerable bipartisan following.

Still smiling, I leave the house, bend to pick a rose for my desk and happen to notice a man's footprint in the damp ground of the flower bed. Undoubtedly it's the gardener's, but that awareness doesn't keep the prickly sensation from sweeping rapidly up the back of my neck. Damn, I guess it's a good thing that I'm learning to function in spite of fear, because it doesn't look like that particular emotion is going away any time soon.

"Neil was looking for you," Katy whispers as soon as I've gotten my coffee and settled behind the stack of mail on my desk. She dutifully gives me a rundown on everything that's been going on: the demo is scheduled for Monday morning at nine; Jimmy Barton is flying in this afternoon; Lyle, our hardware specialist, will pick him up at the airport so he can get a start on all his questions.

"Ah—you're here." Neil sticks his head around the door, then follows with the rest of his Brooks Brothers body, easing into one my gray leather chairs. "I couldn't wait to ask you: are you now or have you ever been a reliable source?"

"Excuse me?"

"Bendle's column in today's paper. She refers to a reliable source—that's you, isn't it? Not bad work. I'm one of Elena's most ardent Republican fans." He leans back in the chair as if he plans to put his feet up on my desk; then he changes his mind, crossing his legs instead. "So what else have you been up to?"

While I'd dearly love to put this conversation off for a year or so, I'm terrified Nathan Marks will catch Neil off guard by making some public allusion to our generosity. If that happens, I won't be around long enough to pack up my personal items. I stumble around inside my head trying to figure out how to begin—how exactly should I say this? I decide to try the back door. "Do you remember why I came to work for you, Neil?"

"Certainly. I offered you an outrageous salary and you jumped on the next plane. Of course you were also drawn by the fact that I'm a brilliant software designer as well as a dazzling entrepreneur."

"—and we shared some visions of a new approach to education."

"We shared some visions about making a living providing new kinds of educational software." He stares at me for a moment, then adds perceptively: "Spit it out."

I'm trying to ignore the sensation that my chair, with me in it, is sinking through the floor. "I promised Nathan Marks that we'd provide Jimmy's software on three systems, complete with training, to the school of his choice—free."

On the surface Neil's face doesn't change, but I can make out something moving behind his eyes. "You and Nathan Marks, that cantankerous jerk who thinks he invented integrity, have cooked up this little political contribution I'm supposed to make?"

"It's not a political contribution. I told Nathan that Learning Parallels is donating the systems to demonstrate our commitment to urban education. It's a terrific opportunity for clinical study."

He isn't buying it. "Clinical study? We know it works, Nora. It's been working at the Pentagon for quite some time now."

"But *we've* brought it that much closer to the classroom. *We're* the ones who believe that educating kids is as important as the ability to wage war. *Learning Parallels* is the company willing to stick its neck out to make a difference—donating this system where it can do some real good—at no profit and with the risk of compromising exclusive technology. It's a public relations dream. We're not only leaders in the industry, we're *the* leader in the realm of corporate responsibility."

"Very eloquent. I don't suppose you've secured some sort of a matching government research grant?"

"Not exactly, but that's something I'll pursue."

"Uh-huh, the pieces are beginning to fit. I imagine you made that scenario very clear to Mr. Marks?" Neil is obviously angry, but I can't tell just *how* angry. Then he shakes his head and his poker face cracks—I can't tell whether it's a look of disbelief or just an attempt to hide the clenched teeth that are holding him back from killing me. "I can't believe you did this without consulting me," he says.

I have absolutely no response to this. He gets up and walks to the door. "I'll look forward to this demo with a very different eye—and you'd better come clean with Lyle. It'll make a difference if he knows he's going to have to produce something that isn't just a temporary jerry rig." I can hear him muttering to himself as he walks down the hall.

For the rest of the day, I bounce back and forth between writing dynamic press releases portraying Learning Parallels as the white knight of the universe and scrambling through my budgets to come up with any loose dollars that might help offset the loss if this whole thing turns out to be a folly. I'm just about to go home when Jimmy Barton calls. We've put him up at the Century Plaza and he thinks he's in heaven. Katy says she's agreed to take him to Disneyland tomorrow, if it's all right with me; that Lyle thinks we shouldn't let him wander around alone. I guess I can do without a secretary for one Friday, and I like the idea of keeping Jimmy out of the office until the demonstration—the impact will be much stronger if Neil is hit with the full force of this kid and his genius all at once.

"Be sure to save Saturday," I tell the awestruck programmer. "You wanted to meet Ben Cochran, so I'm inviting you to a party at my house. Someone will collect you around two."

When I arrive home, the light is flashing on my answering machine. I assume it's David; he left a message yesterday, thanking me for the Alka-Seltzer, and when I tried to call him back, I too got a recording. I push the button.

"Nora?" It's not David's voice, but I recognize it immediately because for most of my life I secretly prayed to hear this voice every time I picked up the telephone. "This is Jacques. I don't think I'd better leave a message. I'll call again." I stare at the machine, overcome by the same sensation I have in a nightmare, when I escape through door after door and find myself still in the same room.

TWENTY-TWO

I change my answering machine message to refer to my office number and stay at my desk all day Friday, but Jacques doesn't call.

David does. "I don't like to bother people at work," he says, "but your message was adamant. I guess you got tired of playing phone tag." He's calling to confirm for the birthday party.

I go home Friday night and sit by the phone some more. Oh, I don't actually *sit* by the phone; I perform menial household tasks, nervously, with an expectant ear tuned to pick up a sound that doesn't happen. It's not like *that,* I assure myself; I'm not just waiting for this man to *call* me—I'm waiting for him to call for big important reasons—but by nine o'clock all my arguments have drowned in déjà vu. My inner observer keeps popping out thoughts like *piteous.*

On Saturday, I'm busy enough preparing for the party that I almost forget the phantom ringing in my head. When I do hear a ring, it's the doorbell; I open the door to find a young woman cradling an armload of hors d'oeuvres.

"Hi—I'm Karen. Ben had to get the bread before he picks up your mother, so he dropped me off. Some of this needs to be refrigerated."

Relieving her of one of the trays, I usher her into my kitchen, which is overwhelmingly suffused with the spicy aroma of lasagna. I can't help remarking on the artistry with which she's carved and curled and spritzed the myriad vegetables and goodies. "Vivian, my mother, will be stunned that we're actually serving something not commercially prepared," I say. "I presume Bennie's filled you in on all the characters."

She laughs. She has a strong face—full lips and smallish gray-green eyes with the same lost flicker behind them that I sometimes catch when looking at Bennie. She's taller than I am—maybe five-eight—and fairly well proportioned, with long legs that look great in denim. Her curly brown hair is pulled away from her face and held in place with two tortoiseshell combs.

"Yes . . . well, sort of. He's told me about your mother and her friend Herbert who can't hear . . . and about the writer who he says has a crush on you. And his father, of course. I've heard quite a bit about Henry."

Karen helps me find room in the fridge for the perishables, then follows me into the den, where we arrange the rest of the goodies on the bar. Reaching in her purse, she pulls out two packages of napkins. One is a child's birthday design featuring Spaceman Bob; the other is imprinted with the quizzical countenance of Albert Einstein, who looks as if he's trying to remember something important. "Ben picked them out," she explains.

Together we stretch the traditional pink and blue "Happy Birthday" banner across the beams above the bar, a thin crepe banner similar to the one Mother used to hang in the doorway when I was a little girl. Then I take a last glance around the room where we're likely to spend most of the day. My new picture window is startlingly clear, with none of those permanent water spots from years of sprinkler abuse.

"I think we're all set. How about a drink? I've got pretty much everything, hard and soft."

"Ben made me drink a gallon of carrot juice about an hour ago. I think I'm ready for a beer."

Bennie's girlfriends have been very few and far between, and knowing him as well as I do, I can understand why he likes this one. Pouring beer into a frosty glass, I steal a quick peek inside my heart. I guess it makes me feel a little jealous, but the feeling isn't painful or even very strong.

For the next half hour we sit and talk. She tells me about meeting Bennie in Dr. Ferris's waiting room and how good it's been to know someone who can really empathize. Her mother died when she was too small to remember, and she was very close to her famous father. Emanuel Márquez never remarried, so the only adult women Karen knew were teachers and housekeepers. "Ben and I both found our strongest role models in people of the opposite sex," she says, tipping her head to one side in a gesture that must make Bennie's heart pound. "We agree that it's been great for our personal development, but it's made our expectations in the romance area a trifle unrealistic."

I note the sound of cars in the driveway with some reluctance; I'm enjoying talking with Karen. By the time we get to the door, Bennie has already helped my mother out of the car, given her the bread to hold, and is busy pulling out Herbert. David, who parked right behind them, has made it halfway up the sidewalk only to find his path blocked by the long end of a loaf of Italian bread; I go to his rescue.

"Mother, this is David Weinhardt. David—my mother, Vivian Whitney." I make my introduction with one hand on the bread so that, if she turns suddenly, she won't whap either of us in the head.

"Mrs. Whitney." David nods, favoring her with an endearing grin. He's wearing a red sweater with an interesting geometric pattern, and I wonder fleetingly if it was a gift from his previous live-in artist. For some reason I don't think it's something he would pick out himself, but it looks smashing on him. I realize that I *am* jealous of her— Gwen, who shared his canyon home long enough for her paintings to leave permanent shapes on his walls.

Mother is looking at him with that blank smile; I can almost hear the dialogue going on inside her head. *Thank God this one's nearly her age, even if he is a little short; and, of course, he's Jewish, but that won't matter.* "Call me Vivian," she says. "I haven't read any of your books, but Nora thinks you'll do a good job with Melanie."

"Nora's confidence is important to me," he replies, not taking his eyes from her face.

"Well, you and I shall have to have a little talk. I knew Melanie too; perhaps I can help. Oh, this is my friend Herbert Bunche . . . and you know Bennie. Herbert, here's that writer I told you about, David Weinhardt."

Mother's friend is carrying two bottles of champagne, which Bennie grabs as Herbert tries to shift the load and shake hands with David at the same time. I lead the procession into the house, thinking that, if nothing else, this day has all the elements for being very funny. When Bennie introduces Karen, Vivian's focus visibly switches from the possible man in her daughter's life to the woman who's currently preoccupying her adopted grandson. I feel momentarily relieved.

"Your dad offered to stop by the Century Plaza to get Jimmy," I tell Bennie as we put the champagne on ice. He looks so happy today; it's good to see him looking so happy.

"Yeah. I didn't want you to have to chauffeur him around, so I told him I'd pick him up on my cycle." Bennie grins wickedly. "That did it; he decided to rent a car. Hopefully, he won't notice that we came in Karen's Honda."

"You'd better be nice to him or I'll drag out all your old baby pictures and show Karen what a twerp you were. I like her."

Bennie puts his arm around me and pulls me to him in a big-brother hug. When we join the others in the den, I see that Mother is on the couch next to Karen, sipping wine and probably asking about things that are none of her business. Behind the bar, David opens a beer for Herbert, who nods and laughs at the room in general. "You don't mind if I play bartender, do you?" David asks me, his eyes sparkling as if the question is a secret code for something of far greater import.

"I don't know. My head still hasn't recovered from the last time I mixed you with alcohol."

"No shooters today." He refills my mug and slides it across to me, touching my hand with the tips of his fingers. "You look great, by the way."

Before I can respond, the doorbell rings, and I'm not even halfway across the room before Hank and Jimmy have already let themselves in. They stand at the entryway to the den: a tall, well-built man who would look distinguished even in pajamas and a skinny youth with wild eyes, wearing a brand-new Mickey Mouse T-shirt. I note with amusement that Jimmy Barton, exactly the opposite of Enrico Perez, looks as if he belongs nowhere on this planet.

"Happy birthday, you three," Hank proclaims, crossing the room in a few strides and lifting my mother off the couch. "Vivian, you grow more beautiful each time we meet."

I introduce Jimmy around the room and he shakes hands absently, as if he has little connection to the physical. As soon as the formalities are over, he drops in the chair next to Bennie and launches into a multilevel discussion of Bennie's film. I watch a slow smile cross our young filmmaker's face as he grasps the extent of the young Englishman's appreciation.

Hank joins David and me at the bar. "It looks as if Ben has found himself a very nice girl. I was there the night her father died, you know, but I don't think this is the time to mention it. Do you have Perrier or anything else nonalcoholic that tastes good with a twist? How are we coming with our book?"

David's glance meets mine for the barest second as he twists the top off the mineral water. "I started writing last week," he says matter-of-factly. "I shuffled notes for about as long as I could. There comes a time when you have to go for it."

"You have all the information put together, do you?" Hank asks. His voice is low and even. "Must be a massive task. You'll let me know if there's anything else I can do to help?" David says he's sure he'll be checking with both Hank and me pretty regularly as it goes along; that he'll probably get to be a real pest near the end. "And when do you think that will be?" Hank asks. "I mean I have no idea how long it takes to write such a book."

"I told the publisher I'd have it in three months. That would be working pretty much nonstop, but that's the way I like to do it." David looks at me quickly without meeting my eyes, as if it's suddenly occurred to him that such a tight schedule might preclude other things. "I think your mother needs some more wine," he says. "Excuse me for a minute."

Hank's eyes hurt my heart. "So," he says, "how much do you think he knows? Is he going to put everything down in fancy little words for the world to misunderstand and judge?"

"Well, he's figured out the relationship, but he told me he hasn't been able to confirm it, he can't find Jacques, so I don't know what he'll write." I stop, take a deep breath. "Hank, Jacques phoned me on Thursday; I wasn't here and his message just said he'd call back. So far, he hasn't." I reach over and touch his hand; it's trembling. "I'm really glad you're here," I tell him.

"If Jacques does call back, just talk to him over the phone. I don't think you should try to see him again; he wouldn't be hiding if it weren't dangerous." Suddenly a curious look crosses Hank's face, as if he's thought of something he considers truly bizarre. "You and Weinhardt are getting to be quite good friends, aren't you?"

"That's another story," I say, taking his arm and pulling him away from the bar. "C'mon, let's mingle."

Bennie, Karen and Jimmy have moved out into the backyard while Mother has managed to wedge David on the couch between her and Herbert. Hank heads toward the sliding-glass door. "I think I'll annoy my son for a while," he says.

"Your mother wants to know what my intentions are," David explains as I join them.

Vivian protests: "I didn't exactly say that, Nora. Stop laughing, Herbert; no one said anything funny."

"And what did you tell her?" I ask.

David grins, looking back and forth between us. "Extremely lascivious."

"And I said"— Mother smirks, rising to the occasion—"that it's about time." Now when Herbert laughs she doesn't correct him.

I steal David and take him into the kitchen to help me with the lasagna, which he carves into realistic squares while I uncork the champagne. "What did she *really* say?" I ask, aiming the cork toward the laundry room. *Pop.* I spill a little into a glass and hold it to his mouth.

"That's good. We were discussing how successful you are, and Vivian pointed out that Melanie was also successful in what was obviously very demanding work and yet she still had time—"

"—to have a husband and a child," I finish. "I've never quite figured out why Mother is so adamantly opposed to my singlehood, considering that her own marriage was a flaming disaster."

"Maybe she's still a believer," he says, sneaking a taste of lasagna from the edge of the platter.

Together, we load the food and drink onto a serving cart and wheel it into the den, setting up a minibuffet in the center of the room. For the first time we all sit in a communal circle while Hank fills the glasses and toasts the health of three generations of birthday honorees. For about five minutes the only sounds are food-related. The lasagna is warm and filling and comforting. The bread is fresh from the bakery. The champagne floats along on top like a happy afterthought.

David pops the second bottle and pours another round. "Nora told me a little about your work," he says to Jimmy. "It blew me away. I had no idea such a thing was possible on that scale."

"Jimmy's designed a high school–level mathematics program that uses virtual reality," I explain. "You know, like the flight simulators that train pilots. We're going to unveil it to our boss on Monday." Jimmy wipes his mouth with a Spaceman Bob napkin, looks across at Bennie, then back at me, but doesn't say anything.

Mother grumbles: "No offense, young man, but when I taught high school math, students relied on hard work and their own brains, not some gimmicky computer to entertain them."

"But think about it, Vivian," Karen interjects. "You must have had a few students who had difficulty grasping math concepts. If I understand correctly, the programs Jim designs are experiential."

Vivian rolls her eyes toward the heavens beyond my high-beamed ceiling. "Now we have to *experience* a math problem. Pretend you're a number, I suppose. What does that mean, anyway—virtual reality? Games. It means games."

Jimmy puts his plate back on the serving cart and leans forward, still clutching the Spaceman Bob napkin. It's amazing the way his body suddenly appears graceful when he immerses himself in thought. His eyes have that glassy excited look, but his voice is calm, almost reverent. I try to catch his attention, to let him know through hand signals that he shouldn't let Vivian get to him, that there's no point in arguing, but he isn't looking my way.

"A mathematical equation isn't real," he says. "It just represents reality, explains things—right?" He turns to Karen, the physics student; she nods. "A person using my program experiences what is *being* explained—the reality. More real anyway than the number in the book. Things can be created from numbers and numbers are used to explain what's been created. We live, I think, somewhere in the middle—and my programs are meant to help people understand that relationship."

I have no idea how much of what Jimmy just said is comprehensible to my mother, but she looks thoughtful, with no trace of her previous disdain. I wonder briefly how someone as wildly different as Jimmy can get through to her when I rarely can.

"It seems real?" Karen asks.

Jimmy flicks the napkin onto the cart. "Tricks of perception. But then, who's to say? Experience is what it is. Isn't that what your film is about, Ben?"

"Yeah, I guess so." Bennie catches my eye across a tray of leftover lasagna. He's thinking, I know, about his mother's ninety-ninth room—maybe even about his mother's life, or should I say lives. She was, of course, a natural.

Draining my champagne, I catch Hank staring at me. "Was Nathan Marks pleased with your presentation?" he asks.

"He ought to be; I promised him three free systems." Quickly I glance at Jimmy, whose mouth is agape with surprise; he understandably didn't take me seriously when I said I planned to give the program away. Since I don't feel like fielding any questions about Neil's amazing generosity, I change the subject. "There's a banana-chocolate cake in the kitchen," I say.

David and I wheel out the leftovers and reenter with cake and ice cream. The number of candles on the cake equates to however many were left in the box from last year, but the real number, spelled out in bananas slices across the surface, is 145—that's cumulative years for the three of us, and we have a solemn pact not to divulge the breakdown. Mother blows out the candles with Bennie for backup; then Hank and David lead a loud round of "Happy Birthday," purposefully off-key.

Jimmy asks Bennie about his new film and Bennie provides an excited summary, noting his new financial backing. His sideways glance at his father tells me he's still not comfortable with the fact that his good fortune is courtesy of Hank, that he still sees gratitude and obligation as synonymous.

At our request, Jimmy describes his trip to Disneyland, how Katy made him ride everything, even the children's rides, and then took him on a tour of the city last night. "You got to go to Disneyland with Katy!" Hank and David chime together. Karen relates an amusing story about a fellow in her graduate program. Vivian describes the senior sit-in, protesting overcooked meals at her retirement apartment. Herbert just continues to laugh. Somewhere along the line, evening turns to night.

Hank puts his arms around me, reminds me he's still on East Coast time, and pretty wiped out. "Your programmer wants to stay a while, but I'll drop your mom and Herbert off at their place."

"Will I see you again before you fly back?"

"Ben and I are having dinner tomorrow night; I may stay over for a day or two. I'll call you."

I give Herbert a peck on the cheek and, for some reason I won't analyze, hug my mother harder and longer than usual. "I love you, Mom," I whisper in her ear.

"I know that, Nora," she replies.

After they leave, the rest of us tip Kahlúa in our coffee, top it with whipped cream and chuckle over the day. "I think old Herb has the right idea," Bennie says. "Laugh at everything." This is followed by a speculative discussion on the depth of Mother's relationship with good old Herb, which I'm just about to protest when we're stopped cold by a loud crash, and the sound of scuffling on the other side of the wall. Bennie and Jimmy race to the front door. David steps over and locks the sliding-glass door, then heads through the kitchen to the back. Karen and I gape at each other, then split, as she follows the boys into the front yard and I grab a flashlight and run through the house after David. I find him in the orchard and together we slip around the side of the house to the front.

Jimmy and Karen are standing by the front step as Bennie explores the bushes. "Over here," he calls.

David and I join him at the end of the driveway to find, hidden behind the overgrown hedge, a hulking silver-and-black motorcycle. "The owner has to be around here somewhere," Bennie says, looking at me. Then Karen screams.

I catch a burst of movement that blurs in the weak glow of the porch light—a man breaks cover from the opposite side of the house and streaks across the yard. Jimmy runs after him, David tries to cut him off from the side and Bennie takes to the air with one of those flying tackles you see in the movies. The three of them manage to pin him to the ground, where he heaves, pulling them with him as he struggles to get up. A leg shoots out and catches Bennie in the stomach. "Get the hell off of me," the intruder sputters. He's a large black man and his face is furious. "I didn't do anything."

"Why are you hanging around here? What were you doing back there?" Bennie gasps.

"Call Nathan Marks. I ain't saying nothing. You call Nathan."

TWENTY-THREE

As I stare at the arrangement of bodies on the grass, confusion and anger pound so blindingly in my temples that I have a momentary fear of aneurysm. "What time is it in New York?"

"After midnight," Bennie grunts, his full weight still sprawled across the legs of the intruder. "Just call the police."

"Let me try to rouse Nathan first. You three sit on him until I have some answers."

The man's broad features twist in a scowl, but he stops struggling. "You can let up a bit," he says, his voice raspy. "I ain't going anywhere." David releases his grip but doesn't move away. He hasn't said anything at all. Jimmy looks excited.

Inside the house I dial the number of Nathan Marks's office. I'm sure they live there—he and his groupies. Standing in my silent den, hands shaking, I count the rings. Scattered all around me are cups floating with coffee dregs and whipped-cream scum, remnants of a day that built slowly, peaked in camaraderie and changed in an instant. Everything seems so disconnected, like a string of single images roughly sewn together.

The machine kicks on and I leave a scathing message, then hang up and dial again. On the third time through this same routine, a live voice interrupts. "Mr. Marks will be with you in a minute."

Nathan's deep, full voice carries no trace of sleepiness. "Tell your gentlemen friends not to hurt him, Nora; he works for me. After our talk last week, I decided to have Eddie keep an eye on you for a few days; I didn't like the idea that someone was so interested in stopping you from trying to influence me. Would you please put Eddie on the phone now; I need to talk to him."

I want to shout into the phone that he could have warned me, but suddenly I have no more energy for anger. I turn to find David standing in the doorway and send him out to fetch our prisoner. Eddie enters, still scowling, flanked by Bennie and Jimmy, who aren't touching him, but look ready to spring if necessary. I hand him the phone.

"Yeah," he tells his boss, "I caught this guy creeping around the side of the house. I tried to grab him from behind, knocked him into the garbage cans—made a big crash and everybody came running out; the bastard got away. He had a gun, Nathan—I think he dropped it out there."

A gun! David takes my hand, his face white. I stand transfixed, listening to Eddie. "Yeah . . . yeah . . . no. Right." He hands the phone back to me and heads to the front door; Bennie motions to Jimmy and they follow him out.

"Listen, Nora, when the police get there, introduce Eddie as your bodyguard. I'm sure you'll have plenty of official city protection tonight; I'll have a couple more of my people there by morning."

Eddie returns with the revolver, using the edge of his shirt to keep it free of fingerprints and muttering that he's pretty sure the guy was wearing gloves. Bennie is right behind him, in the doorway. "Look what I found," Bennie says. It appears to be the back pocket of a pair of jeans.

"I knew I heard something rip when I grabbed him," Eddie says.

The pocket makes a crackling sound; Bennie turns it over and we see a small piece of paper stuck to what used to be the inside. Bennie is jubilant. "It's part of an ATM receipt. This is great—the police can track him down from this."

"That's from a bank machine?" Jimmy asks. "Get me to a computer and I'll have his name in ten minutes."

That's true—I'm standing beside one of the world's best hackers—but what he suggests is against the law. Besides, all the police have to do is walk into the bank, flash their badges and ask. I mention the ATM receipt to Nathan and he asks me if I've told the police about it yet.

"That's my next phone call."

"I know this is going to sound strange," he says, "but I'm suggesting you hold back that bit of information for the time being. I'm not personally acquainted with your local police, but I won't be surprised if the FBI is in this by morning. I'll feel better if you let me run that receipt through an NYPD friend I'm sure I can trust."

The implications set my head spinning. Putting my hand over the receiver, I turn to Jimmy. "Are you sure you can trace it?"

He grins at me with mock incredulity. "Ms. Whitney—please." Unlike the rest of us, Jimmy looks as if he's having an excellent time.

Nathan agrees that keeping it to ourselves is even better. "Whatever you find out, let me take a look first; then I'll feed it to the police through my contact."

I'm agreeing to break the law here, withholding evidence, not to mention a pretty hefty electronic crime. If I manage to get Jimmy Barton in trouble two days after he's signed a contract with Learning Parallels, I'd better start swimming toward Brazil. Then I remember that somebody could be dead right now, probably me, and all of a sudden I wish Nathan would send a whole army to camp on my front lawn.

"Nathan—"

"I hope you understand that I don't make a practice of bothering about every pale damsel in distress; I just want to make sure we get our computer systems. Besides, I'm curious who's behind this cowardly behavior."

"I think maybe you like me a little bit," I quip, a feeble attempt at humor.

He chuckles. "How is that possible? I don't like anybody."

Next I call the police and speak to Lieutenant Hacket, who says he's on his way. I'm trembling all over; David reaches out and puts his hand on my shoulder, an awkward, comforting gesture. Bennie sinks down on the couch next to Eddie, who's still rubbing his leg. "You tackle pretty good for a skinny white kid," Eddie comments; then an odd expression crosses his face, as if he's searching for something inside his head. "I—I liked your mother a lot," he continues finally. "She was a great woman." Bennie smiles and nods.

Jimmy sits awkwardly on the floor by the coffee table; an overabundance of adrenaline has left him bewildered. Karen has collapsed into a chair in the corner. "I don't suppose you could take me home now?" she asks Bennie, her voice not much stronger than a squeak.

"I think we'd better wait for the police," he answers.

Before Lieutenant Hacket gets here, I fill everybody in on Nathan's request not to mention the ATM receipt. Only Eddie and Jimmy seem completely okay with that, but no one refuses to go along. A black-and-white unit with two uniformed policemen arrives first, but Hacket is only a few minutes behind. He paces my den, taking names, addresses, circumstances, looking immensely displeased. They have no leads on the brake thing, he tells me—and now this.

The lieutenant is especially pushy in his queries to Eddie, but apparently Eddie does work for a company that supplies bodyguards, undoubtedly part of a complex structure, zigzagging down the secret organizational chart of Nathan's Freedom Foundation. Hacket wraps the gun up carefully, scowling at Eddie's mention of gloves. He asks each of us individually if we're sure we heard a scuffle, if we're certain there was someone else out there. I watch him as he grills

Eddie. It would never occur to me not to trust him, or the Santa Monica police, but I understand that Nathan is being extra cautious. I'm not sure why I'm so willing to trust Nathan Marks, but it's probably because Melanie trusted him so implicitly. It's true she was a phenomenal judge of character—in fact, judging character was her greatest talent.

"We don't even know it was you he was after," Hacket says irritably. "Lombard's son is here, her husband was here earlier. That makes it a federal matter." He spins on his heel and faces David. "And you've probably made enemies too, with those books you write."

I suppose he's right, the gunman could have been after any of us, but my intuition says no—and, considering the alternatives, I'm not sorry. I'd rather be the target than worry about losing someone else—like Bennie. Finally, Hacket departs, leaving the expected unit parked outside, and we all take very deep breaths.

"Tomorrow's Sunday. Can we get into the office?" Jimmy asks me. "If I have to do a lot of crunching, I'd rather have a faster system." He bobs his head at the modest computer sitting on the corner of my desk.

"No problem getting in—" I stop. Neil has the strictest principles about illegal hacking, and using his office equipment to break into bank computers, honorable motive or not, is an unforgivable breach of trust. I have to draw the line somewhere. "I can't do that; you'll have to try from here," I tell Jimmy, at the same time thinking what an interesting study it would make, figuring out why people draw lines where they do. My gesture is pretty inane—I'm the one responsible, not Neil, wherever we are—but still I feel better about it.

Jimmy shrugs and sits down in front of my computer, but I stop him before he can turn it on. "Not tonight. I don't want to know tonight." We agree that he'll stay over in my guest room. Eddie insists the couch is perfect for him, not too comfortable to make him forget why he's here, and better than crouching in the bushes.

"I'm going to take Karen home now," Bennie says. "I'll call you tomorrow." Looking at the deep concern in his eyes, I experience a sensation that's about as close as I'll ever get to motherhood. My life isn't really mine to take chances with; I can't let him be hurt like that again.

I apologize to Karen for a night of trauma she didn't need, and we make arrangements for her to come by the office next week to give us a physics student's opinion of the math software. There's a struggle behind her eyes, too. She's lived through her own tragedy and I wonder if she's reconsidering the wisdom of dating a high-profile person like the late president's son. I hope not.

After they leave, David and I stand in the doorway looking at each other, trying to figure out what needs to be said. I had thought— maybe we'd both thought—that this evening would end differently and he, not Jimmy Barton III, would remain to spend the night. The events of the past few hours have drained us and we lean toward each other in silence, only our foreheads touching.

"Enough excitement for you?" I ask.

He thinks for a long moment before answering. "A powerful lesson. I think I like my drama a little *less* real."

"That's good, because I'm not even going to try to sustain this level."

He steps back, his hands on my shoulders. His face looks tired, older. "You know, Nora, that day in your office when we first met, I kept thinking that it was really time for me to shape up. 'This one's for real,' I told myself. I don't know what made me assume that suddenly, miraculously, I'd know how to do it right, after managing to wreck every relationship I've ever had."

"You didn't hire that gunman, did you?" I kid him. In truth, I don't know what he's trying to say.

Dropping his hands from my shoulders, he shakes his head slowly. "I don't know what to do to avoid the pitfalls, keep from fucking this up."

"I thought we were doing okay, all things considered."

"But you might have gotten shot tonight and I should probably stay here with you; instead, I'm going home to work on my book. It seems like everything I do revolves around the book; I don't know how else to be." Finally, he stops to take a breath.

I hear him. There's a part of me that would be forever warm and happy if he refused to leave my side in time of peril. But that's not who he is. "Sir Galahad rides a big black motorcycle and he's spending the night on my couch. You have a book to write."

He gives me a long searching look; then he kisses his fingers, lays them against my lips and whispers a hoarse goodnight. I watch him walk down the sidewalk and climb into his car. I'm thinking that there's more than what he said—that there was something else—but he didn't want to tell me.

TWENTY-FOUR

The angle of the sun shining in my bedroom window says it's midmorning. I sit up, amazed that I could have slept so late with this much apprehension hovering over me. The door to the guest room is still closed, but the den couch is empty, a pillow and blanket neatly stacked on the coffee table. Peering through the sliding-glass door, I see Eddie in the backyard talking to two other burly African-Americans.

Overnight, yesterday's stress has converted into a variety of aches and stiffnesses. Dully, I put on a pot of coffee, then check the street in front of the house, but the police car has gone. When the phone rings, I find myself talking to an FBI agent, willing my brain to process what he's saying. I write *2:00* on a scrap of paper and promise to be here, fervently hoping that Jimmy will be finished with his little electronic investigation before the FBI arrives.

When the coffee is ready, I fill a round of cups and carry them on a tray into the backyard, where Eddie introduces me to Albie and Dexter, the rest of my protective squad. Both of them are large, and Dexter is particularly handsome. Despite the gravity of the situation that's brought them here, I feel oddly flattered to merit this level of protection. My momentary fantasy involves dragging them around to visit and intimidate everyone who's ever slighted me. Eddie assures me that they'll stay out of my way as much as possible, but they do plan to be visible wherever we go—that's the point, after all.

Jimmy is sitting at the kitchen table when I get back inside; he's helped himself to a bowl of some sugary cereal that's probably been in my cupboard as long as I've been in Los Angeles. I tell him about my appointment with the FBI and he shrugs. "By that time, I'll know where this guy's mother went to grammar school." He pours himself a half cup of coffee, filling the other half with milk and two heaping tablespoons of sugar; then he settles in the den and turns on my computer.

I don't want to distract him, so I take the Sunday newspaper and move into the living room. Between Jimmy and the men outside, I feel uncomfortably crowded; I'm used to having the place all to myself. Today's headline is a glaring message from the president: COURT COUNTS FIVE TRAVESTIES, ONE FANTASY AMONG RIVAL ENVIRONMENTAL PLANS. So far, four Republicans and one Democrat have drawn up dramatically different plans with one thing in common: they all significantly water down the emissions control schedule. *Absolutely not,* says Court. On the other end of the scale, a senator from my home state of California, a Democrat, has packaged a bright green program that includes rigid protection for insect species not yet discovered. *Way too much,* Court says.

Putting down the paper, I lean back and close my eyes. It's a little hard to concentrate on politics while I'm waiting to find out the name of the would-be shooter who lurked outside my home last night. What if he really does fit in with one of Hank's grand conspiracy theories? Nathan clearly doesn't trust the FBI. Do I tell Danny Court? Do I tell the press? At what cost?

Jimmy sticks his head around the corner and gives me a thumbs-up sign. "I got it. The guy's name is Joseph Miller; here's his address and Social Security number." He crosses the room to hand me a slip of paper. "I'm going to see what other databases I can roam through—don't worry, I'm scrambling your modem phone number."

Joseph Miller—Joe Miller. I feel a chill. It seems like too common a name for a killer. I pour myself another cup of coffee and wander through the house, peering out of windows. Dexter is sitting on a lawn chair in the backyard with the neighbor's fat orange cat on his lap. In the front, Albie pretends to trim the hedge along my driveway. Joe Miller. *"Were you ever afraid, Melanie?"* I whisper to myself. *"Did it ever seem too overwhelming?"* And I realize, I don't know. If she was, if it did, she never told me. I sit down at the kitchen table and try to concentrate on today's crossword puzzle.

"Nora, can you come in here a minute?" Jimmy's voice snaps me to attention. Joining him in front of the computer, I stare at the screen. "I couldn't find much on him," he says. "Thirty-eight years old, calls himself self-employed, doesn't have a lot of money, rotten credit. I went back to the bank and ran through deposits; that's what you're looking at now." Jimmy punches a button and scrolls through several months of scant deposit listings, stopping at the last week in January—a check for twelve hundred dollars written on a New York bank. The screen moves again to the first week in February—last week: a check for five thousand dollars from the same account. Jimmy flips the screen and we're in the New York bank—the account of someone named Bret Hauser.

I pull up a chair and sit beside him while he follows Hauser's Social Security number through what science fiction refers to as cyberspace, a realm of interconnected data. Bret Hauser is only twenty-six years old, but he has a heap more money than Joe Miller and he lives in a pricey section of Manhattan's Upper East Side. He's the son of wealthy parents, a graduate student in International Affairs at Columbia University and dabbles, quite successfully it seems, in the stock market. "Uh-oh," Jimmy says. "See that?"

His mother's maiden name is Miller, which means he could be family and have nothing to do with Joe Miller's activities. Still, why did he start sending money only two weeks ago? "Let's go back and look at Hauser's bank account," I suggest.

He's certainly not thrifty, he spends money in the manner of one who's never had to stop and think about it, but one item stands out in particular—a check for fifty thousand dollars that cleared just a few days ago. I guess that's not really unusual for someone who invests heavily. "You say he's a grad student. Do you know where he did his undergraduate work?"

"I saw that somewhere—also Columbia, I think."

Where Hank teaches.

I don't like the queasy feeling that's rising up from the pit of my stomach. "I'm going to make a couple of phone calls, Jimmy. See if you can extricate yourself from there without triggering any alarm systems—and thanks."

"Piece of cake." He grins. "When is your federal bureau due to show up?"

Mr. FBI, whose name I neglected to write down, is due in an hour, and since Jimmy's not the type to go over well with authority figures, we agree to have one of my bodyguards drive him back to his hotel. Dexter seems more than happy for the diversion.

After they leave, I sit down and phone Hank. His voice is cheery, so I assume Bennie hasn't filled him in on the prowler with the gun. "Hank, do you know a young man named Bret Hauser—he was a student at Columbia?"

"Yes—why?"

Briefly I describe the events that occurred after he left last night. The news seems to knock the wind out of him; it's hard to hear his voice. "What does Bret Hauser have to do with that?"

"Can I come by the hotel to see you in a couple of hours? We'll talk about it when I get there. The FBI is paying me a visit this afternoon."

"I'll be here."

I try to phone Bennie, but he's not home; I'm not sure what I was going to say to him anyway. Nathan Marks isn't around either, so I pass the pertinent data about Miller and Hauser to Jonah, who writes it down with nary a question and promises to give it to his boss as soon as he's available. Then I put on some makeup to impress the FBI. I feel numb, and that's probably a good thing.

At precisely two o'clock, a fortyish, stern-looking agent named Williams arrives to ask voluminous questions about what I might have done to deserve becoming a target. I remind myself that, although Williams represents a government ostensibly headed by Danny Court, he and I are likely light-years apart in our politics. I keep watching his eyes as I describe my lobbying efforts, looking for a glimmer that might indicate he thinks that all this serves me right.

He asks about Albie, whom he met out front, and I tell him my bodyguards have been provided by Nathan Marks; I might as well save him the time of tracing them down. His jaw clenches, just as it did the first time I mentioned Nathan, who is obviously not an FBI role model.

Williams's questions are thorough and detailed, as they have to be if he hopes to narrow down a long list of possible suspects. When he's finished, he gathers his papers and I walk him to the door. I can't resist asking. "Tell me, are you a fan of President Court?"

"He's the president of the United States, Ms. Whitney." The solemn official response.

"I mean personally, off the record." I have no idea whether an FBI agent ever goes off the record with personal opinions, but it doesn't hurt to ask.

He squints at me for a moment. "No, I'm not. I *did* vote for Lombard. I didn't plan to, but when I got in the voting booth, I just punched her name. If you ever tell that to anyone, I will make sure every detail of your entire life is thoroughly investigated and publicly exposed." He scowls at me fearsomely. "And if we can't find anything, we'll make something up." Then his scowl breaks and he laughs loudly. "Just kidding, of course. We'll be in touch, Ms. Whitney."

He strides rapidly down my sidewalk, climbs into his late-model, American-made vehicle and drives away. An FBI agent with a sense of humor—what will they think of next?

Albie stays back to guard the house, while Dexter rides with me to Hank's hotel. The numbness has settled into a cold dread; I would never have made the connection if it hadn't been for that fifty-thousand-dollar check.

When Hank opens the door, his face reflects the same misery I'm feeling. I introduce him to Dexter, who then makes me wait outside while he checks the room. Satisfied, he motions me inside, drags out a chair and takes up his post outside the door.

"This bodyguard stuff feels bizarre," I say.

"I know, I had to get used to it myself for a while. Can I get you a soda or something?"

I nod and he takes a can of diet Coke from the minibar, pouring it mechanically. Yesterday at the party he looked at least a decade younger than he does today. I wait until he's seated in the chair opposite me; then I give him a condensed version of Jimmy's electronic investigation—how Bret Hauser's name came up in the first place. "He's the friend you got to finance Bennie's film, isn't he?"

Hank nods dully. He stares at me, his eyes sunken; then he drops his head in his hands. "Oh my God, Nora, this could all be my fault."

"What do you mean?" I ask. But I desperately don't want to hear what he has to say.

"Bret Hauser is in my CID group, the bunch of men I told you about. He was an undergraduate student of mine, extremely bright. When he entered the graduate program, he looked me up. We started talking, and I found out he was a conspiracy buff, had read all the same books and articles, was fascinated by the so-called coincidences in our history. I invited him to one of our meetings and he fit right in; he became a regular."

Yes, the CID group, *Coincidence . . . whatever.* "That's the group you told that I was going to lobby for Court." I'm trying to keep my voice calm, but not succeeding very well.

"Yes. Mostly they're men I've known for a long time; I trusted them." I notice his hand is shaking badly. His voice falters, but he catches his breath and goes on. "Hauser is also the one I asked to check out Jacques DeBrin and his Arab friend; he said he had a cousin with a wire service. God, Nora, he got all his leads from me! If anything happens to you, I'll never forgive myself. And what about Ben? What do you suppose he wants from Ben?"

I'm hoping that Hauser's interest in Bennie was just another way to worm himself into the inner circle, but I don't know that; I don't have any answers. Hauser knew about Jacques and the sultan's nephew; how does that fit in? "Do you mind if I use your phone to call New York?" I ask.

This time I get Nathan in person. He doesn't sound terribly surprised. "Turns out Hauser's quite a mysterious fellow," he says. "A mere babe, but he manages to hobnob with some pretty powerful people."

"Did you find out anything about Joe Miller?" I ask.

"They're second cousins; Miller's just a punk for hire and it looks like Cousin Bret found a job for him to do. To be on the safe side, I'm going to feed some information into the system and get both of these guys picked up as soon as possible, but you know Hauser's not acting alone." Nathan clears his throat loudly. I picture him sitting behind that massive desk up there in Harlem, where he's as close to a king as one can get in this country. "I want the boys to continue keeping you company for a while. As for Ben Cochran, he'll have Secret Service protection within a few hours."

Hank stands at the window, peering blankly out in the direction of the ocean. Even from here I can see the sun change colors as it sinks through layers of smog, a pretty spectacular sight from this high up. "You didn't know, Hank; it wasn't your fault." But I know my words don't help.

Abruptly, a horrified expression crosses his face; his eyes fill with tears. I know what he's thinking, a monstrous thought too horrible to contemplate; it's also occurred to me. *The assassination.* "My God, Nora, what if something I said—what if—oh, my God, could—?" As I watch, his face seems to crumble and I know I'm seeing the collapse of structure, not just the slackening of muscles.

"Hank . . ." But there's absolutely nothing I can say. I force myself to think of the photograph David showed me of Jennie Wheeler; it only helps a little. I hear talking outside the door, followed by a knock. It's Bennie.

"I couldn't get you at home, so I traced you down through Jimmy. What's going on?" He looks past me to where his father sits on the arm of a chair, body stiff, face like broken glass. I explain quickly; Bennie looks dazed for a moment, then swears.

Striding into the center of the room, he stands glowering before his father. "Stop it, goddamnit; just stop it. You're not the cause of *everything.* Whatever this guy's about, we'll deal with it. But it's not all *you.*"

Hank looks up, his eyes empty and unfocused. Bennie reaches out and grabs him by the shoulders, bending until their faces are only inches apart. "Look at me," Bennie shouts, "goddamnit, why won't you look at me?" Hank's expression doesn't change, but suddenly Bennie's does. The fury melts into a pool of anguish, unbearable to see; his voice cracks. "Dad, please—please, look at me." He lets go of his father and steps back, tears running down his face. Instinctively I start toward him, then stop. Like the snap of a hypnotist's fingers, the sight and sound of his son's grief jolt Hank from his stupor. He's on his feet, pulling Bennie to him. A voice inside my head says it's time for me to leave.

A year ago, we stood in the cold at Arlington Cemetery. The planes had flown over and the guns had sounded their salute. Only then did the storm behind Bennie's eyes break, and we clung to each other, but Hank could only stand awkwardly at our side, looking at the ground; he was unable to comfort, even touch, his son.

I think about that while Dexter and I wait for the valet to bring my car. Scanning the darkening sky, I look for some sign, a shooting star, anything, to mark this momentous event, but no one seems to be home in the heavens. Dexter checks the car expertly, then holds the door for me. As we turn out onto the Avenue of the Stars, some city computer flips the switch and the night lights of West Los Angeles blink into place. I know it's not the same thing, but I smile anyway.

TWENTY-FIVE

On Monday we gather at the office for Jimmy Barton to demonstrate his math program. I can tell Neil is excited because his eyes are all funny and he's gritting his teeth like a kid riding a roller coaster. Apparently whatever he and Jimmy talked about in the hour they just spent behind closed doors was enough to set the process in motion. Now, as we stand around the long table in the center conference room, waiting for Lyle to put the finishing touches on the setup, Neil can barely contain himself.

This is a highly classified operation, so the only people present are Neil, Lyle, our local prodigy Sara Bean, Jimmy, myself and Eddie, who accompanied me to work this morning and got drafted when he admitted he's never studied geometry. Lyle has rigged up a system that's connected to an overhead screen—while Eddie experiences the program, the rest of us can put on cheap 3-D glasses and follow along with him. We won't be able to interact, and we won't have the same sense of reality, but we'll be able to observe from his point of view.

Jimmy helps Eddie put on the headgear and dataglove, then runs a five-minute play program so Eddie can get used to the equipment. By the time the geometry lesson starts, Neil's teeth are clenched so tightly it looks as if he has lockjaw. We watch Eddie build shapes by testing various lengths of rods until he finds the one that works. Each success or failure is accompanied by an explanation of how it worked or why it didn't. We watch him move inside a circle that becomes a ball and then splits into arcs and angles. When he finally emerges from the program, he's momentarily disoriented and we're all gaping at him as if he just returned from Mars.

"It makes sense," he utters, obviously amazed. "I didn't get all the words, but the basic stuff in there isn't so hard."

The rest of us already know what Eddie learned because we watched his performance increase dramatically from one situation to the next. He may or may not remember the terms contained in a theorem, but he's on his way to understanding geometry.

Neil says he just wants to try it a few minutes himself; then he'd like Sara to go through the whole thing. Jimmy and I smile at each other as Neil purposely does everything wrong, breaks rods in half—"I knew somebody would try that," Jimmy says, "I just thought it would be a kid"—and attempts to climb over barriers. When he removes the headgear and dataglove, he reaches out to shake Jimmy's hand. "Truly amazing," he says. Then he leaves the room without even looking in my direction. After about an hour, I buzz him on the intercom, but he says he isn't ready to talk to me.

I guess I can't blame him. No matter how exciting this program is, I've put Learning Parallels—*his* company, after all—at risk. We can't afford to produce expensive systems right now. Even if we could, we might create a whole lot of enthusiasm only to have someone else beat us to market with one that is affordable. I don't want to think how much additional capital it would take to speed up research and development to make sure that doesn't happen. For very selfish reasons, all tied up with personal pride and promises to a dead woman, I've forced the company to jump the gun. Neil ought to fire me, and if he does, I decide to go quietly.

I realize it's impossible for me to work. My shoulders feel as if they're held together by taut wires and my head is swimming with thoughts I don't want to acknowledge. Miller and Hauser are still at large; Jacques still hasn't called back and if I didn't have his voice preserved on my answering machine, I'd think I made it all up. Cause and effect, like the chicken and the egg, seem to be interchangeable. Grabbing my purse, I tell Katy to cancel the cab she just ordered. I need to get out of here.

Eddie and I drive Jimmy to the airport. He's high from all the excitement of the morning, not to mention the action-packed pace of his visit. "I *like* this company," he declares, leaning forward from the backseat. "It's absolutely unpredictable. I like Los Angeles, too."

His manic grin makes me smile. I suppose people such as Jimmy, with the option of living incredible adventures inside their heads, have to love it when real life comes with the surprise factor intact. All the things that drive the rest of us bananas—vulnerability, uncertainty, chaos—he thrives on. As we let him out at the Bradley International terminal, it occurs to me that it's an illusion to see Jimmy and others like him as out of place in our mundane world. In truth, they are clearly the best equipped to deal with it.

Katy calls on the car phone to tell us we've been summoned by Lieutenant Hacket, who said they've picked up a man in connection with last night's incident at my house. We drive directly to the Santa Monica police station, but Eddie isn't able to pick Joe Miller out of a lineup. Hacket says it's not critical. Miller's already been positively identified by the man from the rental agency who supplied the blue Dodge van that nearly hit me, and by a parking attendant who saw him enter my Century City garage the day my brakes were tampered with. Apparently she remembered him because he swore at her when she wouldn't extend the grace period.

"We got a call from New York—NYPD," Hacket says. "They received an anonymous tip about Miller and another guy, this punk's cousin, some rich kid who recently paid Miller a sum of money. They think the other guy is in New York, but they haven't picked him up yet. The FBI's looking, too." I nod with what I hope is the appropriate amount of interest and awe.

Since Neil isn't speaking to me, I decide against going back to the office. Instead, I call Bennie and convince him we need a therapeutic walk on the sand; he agrees. At home, I wait for the changing of the guard: Dexter arrives, Eddie leaves, and Albie comes along with me to the beach. Especially fierce-looking, Albie hovers at the edge of my line of vision, far enough away to give us privacy, but near enough to be at my side in a few bounds. Not more than a dozen yards behind him are the two Secret Service agents Danny Court assigned to watch Bennie as soon as he learned of Hauser's interest in the late president's son.

"Dad's pretty shaken," Bennie says. "It's tough knowing he was responsible for bringing Bret Hauser into our lives—and that makes him all the more afraid that something he said or did might have contributed to Mom's death. I've finally convinced him that he can't handle it alone; he's agreed to talk to Dr. Ferris."

"If he ever needed you, Bennie, it's right now."

"Yeah, I guess. He's going to take an apartment here in LA for a while. I'm not sure I like that, but I'll work with it. You haven't asked me what I'm going to do about the fifty grand."

Now there's one thing that never occurred to me.

"At first, I was going to send it back—I don't want that asshole's money. Then, I thought, *no, why should he have it back?* I didn't want to use it for the film, though—bad vibes. This morning I wrote out a check for fifty thousand and sent it to Greenpeace. They're not my favorite charity, but if Hauser is part of some group that's against environmental reform—well, it works for me." His eyes sparkle—Melanie's eyes, a young Hank's face.

"It works for me too," I say.

"I really wanted to hand it to one of those people who ring bells on street corners—I saw that in a movie once, except I think it was a million—but this way seemed more poetic. Oh, just for the hell of it, I tried calling Hauser's number, but there was no answer."

"Both the police and the FBI are looking for him," I say.

We walk for a while longer, up the beach, down the beach, kicking sand. "How's Karen doing?" I ask finally.

A pained look crosses his face. "She's upset—she thinks we ought to cool it for a bit, not see each other. I guess she's still too fragile for the kind of stuff we put her through the other night."

"I'm sorry, Bennie."

"Yeah, me too." He smiles wistfully. "How about you and Weinhardt? You looked pretty cozy at the party."

"Well, I really like him, but sometimes it seems so impossible; there are so many obstacles."

"You mean like having to pretend you don't know about Mom's affair with the French guy?"

"Yeah, like that."

Back up on the path, we hug each other good-bye. He asks me how long I get to keep my bodyguards and I tell him that they'll probably be with me until Nathan Marks thinks I'm out of danger, until this is all over. He gets a strange, faraway look in his eyes, as if he's not sure he believes that it'll ever be really over.

Never over—my nightmares again, being caught inside an ice-cold stillness that never moves.

"Do you dream?" I ask Albie as we drive home.

"Yeah, in spurts. I dreamed about killing my mother one time; it really scared me."

"I dreamed that once, too," I confess. "I stabbed her with a knife. My shrink had a field day with it."

Albie laughs nervously. "Do you believe in that stuff? Hidden meanings and all that?"

I tell him I don't know, which is the honest-to-God truth.

TWENTY-SIX

The phone rings just as I'm heading out the door, and I rush to answer it, not sure at this point who I hope to find on the other end of the line. "I need to see you," David says, his voice scratchy as if he hasn't slept in days. "What about Saturday? We could watch Court's speech together and then have dinner or something." I refrain from asking him if he's sure he can spare the time. I haven't heard from him in days, since the birthday party, but then he warned me that the book comes first.

When I get to the office, there are two dozen long-stemmed American Beauty roses expertly arranged in a crystal vase on my desk. I reach for the tiny envelope and tear it open, wondering if David is one of those guys who sends flowers in lieu of the time he can't spare himself. My speculation evaporates into a feeling of foolishness as I read the familiar words—my roses are from an admirer.

"Happy Valentine's Day," Katy announces, poking her head through the door. "You got the first bouquet on the floor this year. I'm going to stand by the elevator until something arrives with my name on it." She twists her pretty face into a feigned pout and tosses my mail into the in-box.

Valentine's Day—I'd forgotten. Of course, Hank has this flower thing on automatic by now, with my name and address in some florist's annual tickler file so that his alter ego, the secret admirer, never fails. I close my eyes to a vivid image of fresh flowers splashing color across Melanie's grave today; a small surge of emotion washes over me, subsiding quickly in the realm of things that have been felt too much.

Katy brings in the newspaper and runs down my day's agenda, including this morning's appointment with Bennie's friend Karen Márquez, who's going to try out the math software. "Neil just got in, he's in his office," she adds meaningfully.

Through the open door, I see a delivery man with a huge floral arrangement in his arms shifting from one foot to another. Eddie, my steadfast companion, who is sitting in the reception area, looks up from the magazine he's reading and eyes the man distrustfully. "I think the first of your Valentine tributes has arrived," I tell Katy, who excuses herself to claim her prize. If this is a typical year, her desk will be overwhelmed with flowers and chocolates by the end of the day.

Neil is in his office. For two whole days, since Jimmy's demo, Neil has not been in the office and no one has been inclined to tell me where he was. Yesterday Lyle was absent also. It's corporate torture, I tell myself, leaving me in the dark like this. I've just started to sort through the memos in my in-box when Neil buzzes me on the intercom. "Got a minute, Nora? Can you come in here?"

Heart thumping, I pick up a legal pad and head down the hall. Even though I may be walking to my doom, I can't help noticing flowers on nearly every desk I pass. I realize that David, buried in his book, probably doesn't even know that it's Valentine's Day. Not that it matters, but so much for stereotypes—the absentminded professor never misses an occasion, but the detail-oriented ex-journalist doesn't even know what day it is.

Neil has the newspaper spread in front of his face when I enter; from behind it he asks me about the man the police have arrested and why I'm still bringing a bodyguard to work. I explain briefly, annoyed that I have to address my words to the back page of *The Wall Street*

Journal. Then he puts down the paper and looks at me. "I hope you feel it's all been worth it," he says in a tone I can't decipher. "I suppose we'll have to wait and see if anything comes from the fruits of your labors."

I hate the way I'm feeling—like a little girl about to get a well-deserved scolding; I just want to get it over with. "Are you talking about politics or business?" I ask, trying not to sound too defensive. When he doesn't answer I forge ahead, insisting that I didn't promise free systems to Nathan Marks because I thought he could be bought with computers or the possibility of government grants; I did it because I believe what we have here is more important than politics. All the time, I'm watching his face for signs of exasperation, disgust with my naive sappiness, but his expression doesn't change.

"I've been thinking about that," he says, leaning back in his chair and folding his hands behind his head. "If the government were to send me a big fat check to research and implement public school programs, I don't deny I'd snatch it in a minute. But in theoiy, I don't like the idea, never have liked it. Government involvement means miles of red tape and having to explain myself to people who don't have a clue what we're talking about; then there's even more government spending on bureaucrats who get to decide how to spend the money. You know I hate that." The corner of his mouth twists in a smirk. "I guess that's why I'm a Republican." He gets up, pours a cup of coffee from a pot on the adjacent table and stirs the liquid carefully even though he puts nothing else in it. "Lyle and I went to see Willis Howe yesterday."

Something akin to excitement leaps inside my stomach. Willis Howe is the CEO of a hardware components manufacturer in the Silicon Valley. I've never met him, but he's known in the industry as "Mr. Manifest," because of his uncanny ability over the last thirty years to listen to a premise and give it back to you in physical form.

"We had an extensive meeting," Neil continues, "and finally agreed that it's remotely possible to be fulfilled in what we do, make a profit and be nice guys at the same time." He pauses for a second, giving me his drum-roll look. "Willis will donate the hardware for the three systems you promised to Marks."

I open my mouth to speak, but he stops me. "After that we'll form a syndicate that will provide complete systems at fifty percent of cost—Willis is sure he can bring the hardware cost down significantly from Lyle's estimates—and raise funds to subsidize additional systems for schools in underprivileged areas. We'll lose plenty of money on every one we sell for at least the first five years and, since the whole package is ripe for a rip-off anyway, we'll open it up, let any company play as long as it's willing to take the same hit and give credit where it's due."

Too stunned to think of anything to say, I listen to Neil explain how he and Willis Howe see this as an industry-wide effort. Willis thinks the venture will be extremely profitable over the long term, but Neil isn't so sure. "Either way, we ought to be able to decrease the number of clueless kids out there, don't you think? Which is what really appeals to me, since I have no choice but to share my world with them."

I continue to stare at him wordlessly as if I suspect he's been taken over by aliens. "You don't have to look so shocked, Nora," he adds chidingly. "You're not the only one who's spent years dreaming about this—and you're not the only one with the gumption to do something about it. You can give me a little credit, you know."

"I'm more than impressed," I admit.

"Your job, which I expect to be executed flawlessly, is to convince the world that Willis Howe and I are among the planet's greatest living benefactors; to persuade dealers, educators and the consuming public to purchase great quantities of every other product Learning Parallels offers because we are such a lovely company; and to help the syndicate coax rich people into coughing up cash for additional subsidies."

"I can do that," I manage to utter. Having just had my cynicism tossed in the shredder by a couple of megamen who pray to the corporate buck, it's not surprising that I feel lightheaded. I'm genuinely touched, but he's a hard man to express it to. "Thanks, Neil."

"I'm not doing it for you, but you're welcome anyway."

We discuss strategies for a few minutes, then I attempt an exit; before I can get to the door, he clears his throat loudly, commanding me to turn around. "Forcing my hand is not usually a good idea, Nora. You'll ask next time, won't you?"

It's hard to resist the instinctive urge to hang my head and shuffle my feet; I concede that I was out of line. "Yeah, you were," he agrees.

Whew! I walk back to my office, still in a state of partial shock. On the bench beside Katy's desk, Karen Márquez is studying the top layer of an open box of chocolates, trying to guess which one has the cherry filling. I point to a piece and she slips it from its little brown paper case, takes a bite, smiles and nods. I tell her I was a chocolate expert in a former life.

We settle in my office and I give her a tissue to wipe the sticky residue from her hand; then I listen to her rave about the math program. I'm curious as to whether she thinks elementary physics could be taught the same way and her gray-green eyes flash as she tells me the technique is a natural for physical science. Then I explain to her what Neil has in mind, getting more and more excited with every word. It's just now becoming real to me. This is going to happen; we're going to do this.

"How would you like a temporary part-time job?"

"Only if you'll let me work for free." She holds up her hand before I can protest. "Like Ben, I live off a trust fund. Helping Jimmy with the physics will be fun—and I'd like the chance to do something for somebody else."

How Melanie would have liked this girl! I have to catch myself before I begin to blurt out more apologies—disclaimers that what happened last week was my fault, it had nothing to do with Bennie. I guess I know it doesn't make any difference; if Karen needs to rest in anonymity for a while, she can't be hanging around with Melanie

Lombard's son. Hopefully, when she feels stronger, she'll decide that he's definitely worth the hassle. An unspoken respect slides across the space between us, different from the one we shared when we were discussing business.

For the next couple of hours I map out details of the public relations blitz I've been carrying in my head since I first decided to—what did Neil call it?—force his hand to put this program on the street before its time. I'm adding finishing touches to the first draft when FBI Agent Williams calls. "Do you have time for a movie tonight, Ms. Whitney?" he asks.

"Excuse me?"

"Don't get excited. There's a videotape I want you to see. If you will kindly meet me at your local police station after work. We won't be serving popcorn."

TWENTY-SEVEN

The man pacing at the end of the room looks unusually large; his size probably seems exaggerated in the small, cluttered space. His right arm hangs at his side and his hand clutches an upside-down can of diet soda, apparently empty. Abruptly, he turns and throws the can at the opposite wall, a violent gesture that appears oddly calculated, as if he has done this many times before. "You worthless punk," he shouts, and leans across the wide table, planting his big hands firmly on its wooden surface. The muscles in his forearms bulge visibly beneath shirtsleeves that are rolled up to his elbows.

At first I can't make out the man who's seated at the table, except to note that he's considerably younger and seems to be expensively dressed. Then his face comes into focus and both my hands clench the arms of my chair. "I've seen him before," I say. "I ran into him, literally, on a street in London."

Bret Hauser stares up at the police detective with unnerving calm. His face is expressionless, but not really empty; he emits a maddening air of superiority, as if an invisible smirk waits just below the surface. There's an animal-like alertness, too. This is the man I considered luring back to my hotel room, I recall, horrified. He was there, in London, following me.

Agent Williams, Lieutenant Hacket and I are viewing this drama on a VCR in a back office of the Santa Monica police station. Hacket has already explained that the interrogation of Bret Hauser, taped with a hidden camera yesterday in New York, was a dead end—that Hauser refused to reveal who put him up to hiring Joe Miller.

Williams tells me that they know who his friends are, but they still can't touch them—the boy is taking the fall. He wants me to listen carefully, see if I pick up anything between the lines.

"Hauser's enjoying his position as martyr to a cause," Williams says. "He tried for about five minutes to make the detective believe the money he paid Miller was simply to help out his cousin's family, but then he gave it up in favor of making a political statement."

The detective slams a chair against the table. Like the soda can thrown at the wall, this particular ferocity also looks like an act, part of the ritual. Still, I can tell he'd love to wipe the invisible smirk off this rich kid's face. "Let's hear it one more time—just why were you trying to intimidate, then *murder* Nora Whitney?"

"Murder?" Hauser asks, examining his fingernails.

"That's what you do with a gun, isn't it, asshole?"

Hauser shrugs and shifts in his chair, crossing his legs. "She tried to stir up a subversive energy that should remain dormant," he replies, his voice even. "And she's a symbol. She's not a politician; she's a layperson. She has a different appeal when she tries to influence people. Of course, you wouldn't understand any of that."

"That's bullshit. All sorts of people try to get their way by lobbying government officials and other honchos. Do you plan to kill them all?"

"Nora Whitney targeted a very select group. We saw the unfortunate effect of that group in the last election, did we not?"

"Who's *we?*"

"I was referring to you, me and the world at large. I already told you this was my own idea."

"You belong to Le Patronage, don't you?"

"I don't speak French, Detective."

"You think you're so fucking clever, Hauser. What about Ben Cochran? What kind of slimy interest do you have in him?"

"He's a talented filmmaker. You should consider investing in his work yourself."

The detective turns his back on Hauser and paces in the narrow space between the table and the wall. "I think you were planning to use the Cochran kid against Whitney. But then you got orders to quit messing around and just take her out." He stops, turns, leans against the wall. "We know who your friends are—and we'll get them. You can count on that."

Hauser uncrosses his legs, bends forward and folds his hands on the table, the slightest hint of a smile on his face. "You don't mean my friend and mentor *Henry* Cochran, do you?"

The detective takes a step backward, as if Hauser has suddenly emitted an offensive smell. "The way you used Cochran and his professor friends makes me sick. Tell me something. Nora Whitney had already finished lobbying—already done whatever damage you thought she could do. Why kill her after the fact?"

"I told you, she's a symbol—a successful woman, a close friend of our late president. Her demise would be very depressing to those who think they've gotten over last year's little incident."

The NYPD detective's face is suddenly crimson with anger. It takes him a few seconds to get himself under control, then he spits his words through clenched teeth. "Are you implying that you—or that gang of yours—had something to do with the assassination of President Lombard?"

Hauser shakes his head slowly, maddeningly. "There was no need to get involved in that. Whenever a person as inappropriate as Ms. Lombard is elected to the highest office in the nation, you can be sure that someone will take care of it. The country is full of patriots like Miss Jennie Wheeler."

For the first time, the detective looks squarely at the camera. He knows it's there, and you can tell that he wishes it weren't, because

THE ANNIVERSARY ★ 223

he wants to hurt this man. Hauser, too, stares directly at us. The smooth, would-be handsome face makes him look even younger than his twenty-six years. The cold intelligence in his eyes is like that of a robot, tempered by nothing I think of as human. A long time ago, I studied artificial intelligence—Bret Hauser may not be made of metal, but he is surely the darkest side of brains without a conscience. He's not just my nightmare; he's everybody's nightmare.

Three thousand miles away and a day after this tape was made, I find myself hoping that the detective will go ahead and do it, brutally smash that face beyond recognition. I make a mental note to let Hank know that Hauser was not connected with Melanie's assassination; Hank can let go of that guilt, at least.

Hacket clicks off the recorder and rewinds the tape. Agent Williams explains that they are positive Hauser acted on behalf of Le Patronage, a collective of high-powered businessmen who have for years been suspected of manipulating, by whatever means necessary, the course of American business, foreign trade, the economy and the legislative process. So far they haven't made a major mistake, but they've had to sacrifice several Bret Hausers.

"Le Patronage," he says, "means just what you'd think—patronage. It also has a secondary meaning, according to the French dictionary, something like 'young men's club,' although I guarantee most of the members aren't particularly young. If President Court's environmental bill were to pass, it's safe to assume they'd be hit pretty hard on several fronts."

"Is it an international organization?" I ask warily.

"Not from what we can tell. Despite the cute French name, these guys seem to be strictly domestic."

I'm genuinely confused. The first time I ever heard of Le Patronage was when Hank rattled off the name in his list of subversive groups.

"How can a group like this exist without people knowing about it?"

"You don't want to hear how much the FBI is aware of but can't prove," Williams advises me solemnly. "Conspiracy buffs know about these things, but they mix it in with a lot of other stuff that only exists in thrillers."

"What *I* want to know," Hacket interrupts, "is whether Ms. Whitney here is safe now, or whether this elusive gang of yours is going to keep trying."

Williams looks at the police lieutenant as if he's said something absurdly naive. "This guy is just a pawn. They have a dozen like him." Then he turns to me. "Hold on to the bodyguards," he says.

Williams asks me to describe my London collision with Hauser in more detail, and I do so, skipping any elaboration on why I happened to be on that particular street corner. Le Patronage knew about Jacques, but did Jacques know about Le Patronage? Is that why he didn't show up?

I spill some of my frustration to Eddie on the way home—about Le Patronage and how Williams said the FBI has known of it for years, but can't do anything. He advises me that listening to the FBI is detrimental to your sanity. At the house, Eddie and Dexter confer in the front yard; then Eddie leaves and Dexter is joined by Albie. One of them commandeers a lawn chair in the backyard; the other guards the front.

Inside, my answering machine light flashes; I have a message that turns out to be from Nathan's assistant Jonah, who suggests that I watch *The Martin Dean Show* tonight. I'm exhausted and it's already late, but I flick on the TV to catch the show in progress. There sits Nathan in that familiar gray upholstered chair on the Channel Four set, telling Marty Dean, America's number-one talk-show host, that he's impressed by President Court's stand and looks forward to hearing his speech on Saturday. "I'm a sucker for integrity," Nathan says, "and for the second time in my memory I just might be seeing some of that in a politician. Perhaps"—he turns from Marty Dean and favors the crowd with an imperious grin—"it's a trend."

"So you support Danny Court?" Dean asks.

Nathan, of course, will never openly admit to participating in the process. Instead, he rants about a fat ineffectual political system. "I support courage and I support progress, but I don't actually support politicians."

"You do like to throw your weight around though, don't you, Nathan?" ventures Dean gamely. The two of them have been poking at each other on that same set for years.

"And there's a lot more of it lately," Nathan counters, shifting his large body in the chair and glowering at the camera.

Well, it wasn't actually an endorsement, but I'll be damned if it's not as close as an antiestablishment hero like Marks ever comes to giving his blessing. I can barely contain myself. Contrary to all the rules of logic, Nathan influences people who would never admit they even slightly admire him. First Neil and his amazing syndicate—now this! The phone rings and I grab it, expecting to hear Deena Brennan's lively "Wow!" in my ear.

"Nora?"

My jumble of emotions collide, freeze where they fall. "Jacques?"

"Yes. I'm here in Los Angeles, and I'd like to see you. To explain. Can we meet tomorrow evening? Say eight o'clock? I'm at the Beverly Hills Hotel."

TWENTY-EIGHT

Dexter and I pull up in front of the Beverly Hills Hotel at five to eight. It's Friday night and the entrance is lined with limos; we have to wait several minutes before a valet can get around to us.

The hotel, nestled midst gently waving palm trees, shimmers as if it were its own reflection; the air feels balmy here even when it isn't. I wonder why Jacques would choose this place; but then why not, if he's no longer trying to keep a low profile? And he *is* here. Unwilling to be stood up again, I phoned the hotel this afternoon to make sure he was registered. Jacques DeBrin in Beverly Hills! Don't tell me David can't find him now!

We walk around the luscious lobby until I locate a house phone. I give the operator his name and listen to the first ring and the second, reminding myself that this is not a tiny courtyard in London and, even though that was only three weeks ago, I am not the same Nora whose hand hovered nervously over the knocker of Apartment Number Four. Jacques answers on the third ring, asks if I mind coming up. I explain that I'm not alone and that Dexter will need to check out the room and probably Jacques himself. He agrees without any hesitation, almost as if he's not surprised.

Riding up in the elevator, I have this eerie sense of calm, a composure that doesn't seem to fit, considering the circumstances. It's not that I think I should be afraid of Jacques, not here in this hotel, not with Dexter by my side, but three weeks ago I was anxious about what he might tell me, how I might feel. Those things must still matter to me, somewhere inside, but they're obscured by—well, now I'm a woman who needs a bodyguard.

Jacques is standing in the hall in front of an open door. "Hello, Nora. You look wonderful," he says softly.

I introduce Dexter, who expertly frisks Jacques before shaking his hand, then disappears into the suite. I wait in the doorway with Jacques, not saying anything, just staring at him. He's still devastatingly handsome, with only a few gray strands sprinkled through his lush dark hair, only a few lines accenting his angular face. His black eyes still have that excited look; his body is still lean and firm. It's a trick, I think. My objectively watchful eye, hovering near the hallway ceiling, notes with irony that Jacques DeBrin looks even better today than he did twenty years ago.

And then for just an instant, as if that's all he can bear, he lets the shield slip, lets me look into his real eyes, and I see all the way through him. Oh yes, he's beautiful to behold. But there's something wrong with him, like he's just pretending to be alive.

Dexter gives his approval to the suite and goes into the bedroom, closing the door behind him. "Would you like a glass of wine?" Jacques asks. I start to accept, then change my mind; this isn't really a social call. I sit on the couch and watch him pour himself some wine and a glass of water for me. All the things I planned to say have flown from my mind; I'm not even certain why I'm here.

"I'm sorry about London," he begins, easing into the chair across from me with the same grace I remember. His face is solemn, like that of a public official about to announce an outbreak of plague. "I couldn't meet you. A friend warned me that my name had been leaked to an organization that wanted to destroy Melanie's reputation; also that they were following you. I couldn't chance showing up and I couldn't chance leaving a message. I had to stay out of sight until it could be taken care of."

"Taken care of?" I ask, confused.

"Sultan al Zayad threw one of his famous fits. I'm very valuable to him, you see, not just because his nephew Rashid and I are old friends, but because I handle certain business transactions for him and his associates, usually very successfully."

Jacques pauses to take a sip of wine. When he speaks again his voice is lower; I have to lean forward to hear him. "Nora, there is a network of communication in the upper echelons of global economics that neither of us wants to know about. One of the sultan's oil-cartel colleagues told him that this dissident US organization planned to make me out as a spy. They would say that I exploited a key United States senator, a presidential candidate, compromised, along with her virtue, your country's security. They could make it believable— all they had to do was find me and confirm some sort of relationship. The sultan suggested there would be dire consequences if I were to be maligned in such a way. I think your subversive US group wisely decided not to argue with the boys who have most of the oil."

I stare at him, astonished. First, it never occurred to me that Melanie's affair could be twisted like that—not *that* way. Portraying her as a lovesick dupe endangering national secrets would set the chances for another woman president back by at least a century. Second, the process he's just described is absolutely inconceivable to me. "Le Patronage—that's the group you're talking about, isn't it?"

He turns his palms up, helplessly. "I don't know anything about them. I was simply advised to disappear. Le Patronage—a French name—is that who's been after you?"

"Supposedly. Don't worry, they're not French; I'm told they're a powerful pathological element of corporate America. Their current purpose is to discourage pending legislation and, since the bill in question was originally proposed by Melanie, undermining her character and judgment is part of the plan—as is making an example of me. Unfortunately, I don't know any sultans to get them off my back."

He stares into his glass, looking both sad and embarrassed. "I told Rashid that I was worried about you, that you were my friend, but they aren't willing to interfere in what they consider an American domestic problem."

I look at him, oddly detached. I know little about his life, only that his parents owned a vineyard but he was never interested in the family business; that he was always restless, had numerous vocations, avocations. "*Are* you a spy?" I ask suddenly. I hadn't planned to say it; it just slipped out. He looks absolutely stunned. "I don't mean it like that," I add quickly. "I guess I want to know your exact relationship with Melanie for all those years. She never told me, you know."

He looks down at the thick rug and then back up at me. His eyes have a pained intensity that's almost frightening. "I wanted her to tell you. You were the only one she could have told and I wanted her to tell you because that would have forced her to admit we were real—that the time she spent with me was actually real. But she couldn't do it. To her, making it real would have destroyed that other woman your writer is writing about."

He leans forward in the chair, cradling the wineglass in both hands. "We were lovers, Nora. From that summer in Paris until she decided to seek the nomination. What happened between you and me—I never stopped feeling awful about that. I know you were hurt, and I'm sorry. I'm *still* really sorry." He says that Melanie had just broken up with him when he ran into me at the airport; she'd just met Hank. And he was so miserable . . . he couldn't tell me . . . he didn't mean for what happened to happen. I was so wonderful, he just lost control.

"I had to stop you from coming to Paris," he says. "I knew I was still in love with her. After six months she agreed it was impossible for us to let go of each other." He's quiet for a few seconds, sipping his wine.

"For me it was always that way. From the very beginning, from the first day we met, I couldn't stand to be without her—even though she made it clear that I didn't fit into her plans. Of course, I didn't believe her at first; I was sure she'd change her mind. Then I began to understand. I would have given up my citizenship, but there were other things."

He gets up and goes to the wet bar, refills his glass. As he pours, he describes how he and Melanie played their affair as if it were a game. How, when she was a student at Harvard, he'd fly to Boston and they'd meet secretly, two or three times a year. When she moved to New York, he visited her there. He says they spent a week in Bermuda. I remember that week she went to Bermuda—a legal convention, she'd said.

"By the time she and Hank were married I was already resigned to my place in her life. It was painful, but not as painful as the thought of not having her at all. I believed we would go on like that forever. We were—what is the word?—*exempt* from ordinary life."

And he never married. He just waited for those fleeting moments when she had time for him. I'm reminded suddenly of Bennie's comment about how she gave him what she could. Melanie had this unique way of convincing people that a little bit of her was worth more than all of somebody else. I look at this poor man, this handsome shell of a man; it makes me want to cry.

"Your president," he says, "the person I saw campaigning on television, was not the same Melanie Lombard I knew." He's looking at me with such misery in his eyes; I'm suddenly overcome by an urge to tell him about the stories Melanie told her son—to let him see how, in that small way, he crossed over into her other life. As he listens, his eyes grow wet and a smile plays around his lips. He knows about Melanie's ninety-ninth room.

"Nora, I wanted to contact you when it happened. I couldn't go to the funeral. I couldn't talk to anybody. You have no idea how difficult that's been."

Suddenly, we're both on our feet, looking at each other in the center of emotions that dissolve the room. Between us, there's simply too much—and too little. I watch his black eyes well up with tears. And then I'm crying too, our arms lightly around each other, my head against his shoulder. I know that he knows that I know that things will never truly be *all right.*

When the room comes back, only a minute later, Melanie no longer fills every inch of it. We sit down again.

"You did help her out, though, just a little, didn't you?" I remind him of the time Mustafa D. went to Melanie's apartment ostensibly to see the People's Hotline. He laughs and nods.

"Of course I did," he says.

I excuse myself to go to the bathroom and when I'm finished I stop, examine my face in the mirror. I feel as if I've lived for a hundred years; but I also feel as if I could live for a hundred more. I don't look so old, I don't look so young either, but I do look familiar.

Jacques and I have talked about everything now—except about David Weinhardt. How long can Jacques avoid him and what will he say to him when he's finally cornered? I ask both of these questions as soon as I emerge from the bathroom. His answer gives me a sharp jolt.

"That's why I came to LA, Nora—to see Weinhardt. I know the world isn't going to approve of my relationship with Melanie Lombard, but they're bound to find out about it someday. Weinhardt's probes have been relentless and I was afraid all his questions might tip off someone less ethical—someone who would sell the story to a tabloid. I had to stop his inquiry. I want the story that gets told to be the truth."

I feel like a salmon swimming upstream. He's absolutely right, of course. David would never give up. "I was just hoping that one generation of little girls could be allowed to grow up with its heroine intact," I say sadly. "Have you contacted David yet?"

"We spent most of yesterday together. I told him the whole story—not about you and me, of course."

No, there would be no reason to tell him that. I wonder if David will mention their meeting when I see him tomorrow night. I won't be able to stand it if he doesn't. I realize that I'm a little confused by the resentment I'm feeling. Did I think for one moment that *I* was the purpose of Jacques's trip to Los Angeles? Why would I be? He owed me an explanation, of course, but he could have given it to me over the phone any time he decided to get around to it.

I look at him as he sips his third glass of wine. I feel a fondness, a nostalgia, but mostly I just feel pity for him. He has a ghost inside him, and it's not enough to fill him up, it never has been. Suddenly I realize he's not even as handsome as I thought he was at first. It *was* a trick, after all. I stand and stretch out my hand; he stands too, puts down his glass, takes my fingers in his. Then we hold each other for a moment, his chin resting lightly against my forehead. "You're leaving tomorrow?" I ask him.

"Yes. New York for a few days; then back to Paris."

"Have a good trip." I don't know what else to say. Quickly I kiss him on the cheek; then I knock on the bedroom door, tell Dexter it's time to go home.

"Be careful, Nora—please," he says, as my bodyguard and I head down the hall to the elevator.

TWENTY-NINE

Cooking is not among my better skills, but I'm making the effort tonight because I don't feel up to dragging my entourage to a restaurant. Albie and Eddie have set up camp in the backyard, trying to afford me as much privacy as possible. David is due any minute; we'll be watching Danny's speech on TV before dinner.

I give the marinara sauce a stir, inhaling the spicy aroma that sneaks out in puffs of steam. *What do I really want from David?* I ask myself for the umpteenth time. I've been asking myself similar questions all night. How much am I willing to compromise? What makes some things worth it and other things not? When the doorbell rings, I push my hair behind my ears, take a couple of deep breaths and answer it.

"Mmmm, I could smell that sauce as soon as I got out of the car," David says, handing me a bottle of red wine. His eyes look tired from spending so many hours in front of his computer screen. He kisses me lightly on the lips. "How are you doing?"

"I'm doing okay; I'm getting used to the constant company. In fact, I'll miss them, that is if they ever go away." He follows me into the kitchen, where I hand him back the bottle along with a corkscrew. He looks preoccupied and I'm glad; I don't think I could stand any carefree joviality. I'm even gladder when he comes right out and tells me.

"I saw your friend Jacques DeBrin on Thursday, Nora; in fact—well, he first contacted me the day of your birthday party." He pauses, as if he expects a reaction, but I've already figured out that this is what he was hiding. "DeBrin told me the whole story," he says. "I was right—they were lovers. But then that's not news to you, is it?"

"No, but I didn't find out myself until quite recently." I plunk the wooden spoon around in the sauce again, afraid to look at him as I speak my piece. "I saw Jacques too, last night, and he said he told you; you didn't give him much choice. You know, I think it's ludicrous to let everything Melanie accomplished be overshadowed by a charming label like ADULTERESS—but then I'm not a reporter."

"I'm not a reporter either," he says. "I'm trying to put together a portrait of the whole woman, not just a juicy news story."

"I think you overestimate your audience." The noise I make replacing the saucepan lid is louder than I intend.

David extracts the cork from the bottle deftly and pours wine into the glasses I've set on the counter. "If I let myself be concerned with that," he says, "I'd never be able to write a word." He picks up both glasses and hands me one. "This looks like a pretty fat elephant we have stuck between us. I don't want to do anything to make you unhappy, Nora, but I have to work the way I work—that's not really negotiable."

I take a swallow of the wine; it tastes wonderful. I don't want to fight with David; it's not really his fault. It's *her* fault. And why do I have to be the goddamn keeper of the flame anyway? "It's not your fault," I say.

Melanie knew what she was doing. She *chose* to lead two lives—the one that had been programmed from childhood and the other that could be anything she wanted it to be. Now that I think about it, I can't see why any of us is surprised. She was clearly going to have it all; we were just more limited in what our version of "all" meant.

It's time for Danny's press conference. I take David's hand and lead him into the den, where we settle on the couch and turn on the TV set. A network anchorman is doing the warm-up. David grabs the remote and clicks up the volume.

"Ladies and gentlemen—the president of the United States."

Danny Court's smile fills the screen. He's always been an eloquent speaker, but now, as he describes the great honor and sense of responsibility he feels at having been elected to the office of vice president of the United States of America, an office that was only an exceedingly painful heartbeat away from the job he now holds—I sense a powerful, unspoken undercurrent: *that she shall not have lived in vain.* With no melodramatic references, no picking up of torches or finishing of races, he manages to convey a commitment once shared by the vast majority of us who now watch from our living rooms. He states that he means these words in the broadest sense, but tonight he will talk about particulars.

He lists the facts concisely, holding up two of the satellite photos that prompted the World Environmental Council to set its emissions standards. These are the photos that validated the more alarming predictions of what sort of planet may be inherited by future generations. Then, he quotes six lines from one of Melanie's campaign speeches, pledging the US as a leader in global environmental efforts. He pauses, letting us picture her in our minds, remember how convinced we once were. Finally, he outlines Senator Blackmore's bill, which proposes exactly what Melanie Lombard promised. And he stops there. He doesn't attack alternative plans; he doesn't complain about Congress. He thanks everyone for listening and opens the floor to questions.

The press goes nuts, but all the questions run along the same basic line: how does he expect this bill to pass? People don't want to make the sacrifices; it'll cost too much money, too many jobs. Again and again, Danny holds up the photos. The pictures are just blurs to most of us, but we've been told before what they mean. "The only disagreement is who really loses if we don't act now," he says. "Will it be our great-grandchildren or will it be their great-grandchildren? Is that a choice?"

David lets go of my hand and clicks off the set. "What do you think?"

"I think common sense is tough to argue with." *Bravo, Deena!*

"Well, it's a gutsy approach," David says, "treating the American public like grown-ups. The trouble is, once the set is turned off and the psychic grip is loosened, people tend to become followers again, waiting for their favorite leader to tell them what's right. Hopefully lots of them saw *The Marty Dean Show* the other night; I just caught the end of it, your buddy Nathan was terrific."

David browses through my bookshelf while I finish fixing dinner. At intervals he pokes his head into the kitchen with comments about my literary tastes. His glass is empty but he stops me before I can pour him another. "No more for me, Nora. Remember? I want to remember." I feel my body suddenly flood with warmth, but I can't be blushing. I haven't blushed in decades.

The marinara sauce is wonderful, but I can hardly taste it. We pass the garlic bread back and forth, laugh, and agree that we'll both eat it. I had planned to make a salad, but I forgot. Halfway through the meal, David stands up.

"I love the dinner, but—"

"—it tastes just as good when it's cold."

He takes my hand and leads me from the dining room into the den. "I have a bedroom," I offer, laughing.

"Right. Uh, where is it?"

I guide him back down the hall, past the guest room toward the master suite. He pauses in the doorway, pulling me to him and kissing me hungrily. Garlic and spices merge deliciously and we pass them back and forth with a passion, as if neither of us has tasted Italian in years. His hands move slowly up and down my body, under my sweater, caressing my breasts. Midst the heat, a piercing thought swoops in and collides with some tiny vestige of ego—how old, I suddenly wonder, was that artist, Gwen? David's hands work at the button on my jeans. Were her breasts young and firm? His mouth is on my throat. I'll bet her body was taut and smooth. I draw back and he looks at me with glazed eyes.

"Can we turn off the light?" I blurt.

"Oh no you don't. I'm the one who had to get past the thought that you're used to sleeping with adolescent movie stars and statuesque, hard-bodied sculptors; that I've undoubtedly got the most unremarkable male form you've ever seen. The light stays on."

He looks really angry—his curly hair is all mussed and his eyes are blazing. How is it that I never thought about this sort of insecurity from his perspective? Figuring the situation calls for something heroic, I pull my sweater over my head and throw it violently on the floor. He unbuttons his shirt, maintaining absolute eye contact, and tosses it all the way across the room. Stepping forward, I unzip his pants and gently caress him. He unbuttons mine, and we pull both pairs down in unison and kick them out the door. Then we stand there in our underwear like two wrestlers deciding where to attack.

"Well, neither one of us is terribly deformed," he says, running his eyes the length of my body and biting his lip to keep from laughing.

"I haven't counted your toes yet." Actually he has quite a nice body. No Adonis, but then the Adonises I've known could never measure up to this man. I look down at myself. There are a few areas I could work on, but we're not talking gross here.

David laughs. "How about if we just agree that we're both superb specimens of the human race?"

"Deal."

He puts his arms around me, pulling me to him and unhooking my bra. His hands run slowly up my back and over my shoulders, pushing the straps down with careful strokes as if he's memorizing the texture of my skin. We kiss again. The warmth of my breasts against his chest is intensely intimate. I'd forgotten what it's like to be this close.

We inch across the floor to the bed and I can feel something inside him begin to tremble.

David pulls off the comforter and we slide onto the sheets together, touching each other lightly, beginning our slow ritualistic exploration of each other's bodies. We move and kiss and pet, and gradually I become aware that there are other people in bed with us, several other people, everyone we've ever loved. Clutching him to me tightly, I try to push them away; I want this to be different, but I don't exactly know how to make it happen. And then the thought comes to me, like one of those guardian-angel voices you hear in your head. Do I really want there to be no one but him in my bed? Am I really willing to make love with this man for the rest of my life? Am I? I reach up and run my fingers over his face. Our eyes meet and lock—and the thought evaporates. To hell with my overactive mind. Right now all I want to do is merge with those eyes, melt my strokes into his skin. I want to touch and hold that man inside this body.

"Nora," he whispers, easing me up and pushing inside me. This is as close as we can get, I think, as we begin to move together; it's what sex is really about.

We never do finish the spaghetti. I don't remember falling asleep, I don't remember his hands ever leaving me; but when I wake up the sun is shining and he isn't here. From the den I pick up the sound of a familiar voice on the television and beyond my window, the sound of birds.

"Good morning," David booms as I make my entrance. "You missed the good part, but I got it on tape. Coffee's made."

When my eyes finally focus, I see that we're watching the Reverend Dorian Wayne, who stands before the cameras with the same humble air as when he sat across from us in his Orange County office a couple of weeks ago. His eyes are sincere. His voice is strong and moving—he's retelling one of Jesus' parables. I get a cup of coffee and return to snuggle next to David as he picks up the remote and rewinds the tape. "Wayne's talking God now, but the first part was social responsibility."

Dorian Wayne's message is about God's planet and our responsibility to care for it. He says nothing about proposed legislation, nothing about last night's speech, but he talks about accountability and not accepting compromises—Danny Court's message in a more heavenly context. David clicks off the TV. "And that's not all," he says, looking at me smugly. "Take a look at the paper."

He must've been up for a while, because the newspaper is turned inside out all over the coffee table. It takes him a second to find the right section and hold, in front of my still bleary eyes, an article about an environmental march on Washington. The event must have been planned for weeks, but it's being announced today for obvious reasons. "Wanna go?" David grins. "I haven't been to a protest march in eons."

He's probably going to think I'm a weird lady, keeping a stiff upper lip when someone threatens me, and squeezing out tears at a newspaper article, but if he's going to stick around he'd better get used to it. It's just like I told Elena Bendle—the energy Melanie stirred up has a life of its own. I think about Jimmy Barton's program and now the tears begin to pour. We're only just beginning. A faint rattling in the kitchen makes David jump. "It's Eddie—or Albie," I remind him. What I'm feeling isn't free but, for this moment anyway, it's worth it.

THIRTY

Eddie checks in with Jonah twice a day and refuses to let me relax, even though nothing scary has happened since the party. He insists I sit in the backseat of the car and I'm not supposed to lean forward to talk to someone in front; I have to shout.

Which is what I'm doing now—shouting over the seat to Hank as he drives Eddie and me down Wilshire Boulevard in the brand-new hunter green Jaguar he leased yesterday. We're on an apartment-hunting mission; I'm standing in for Bennie, who flew back to New York to pack some of his dad's things and close up the apartment there.

"I used to be quite a good driver," Hank says loudly, "but, believe it or not, I've never owned a car. I kind of wanted to buy one, but Ben's right: leasing makes more sense."

Conversation takes too much effort, so I let the two men in front talk to each other while I gaze out the window at the sun gleaming off mostly foreign automobiles. Across the street from the Federal Building on Veteran Avenue, a traditional "protest" corner, young people wave placards and shout into the passing traffic; several cars honk back in sympathy. I feel a sharp thrill when I read the placards: COURT ONE; CONGRESS ZERO—SAY *YES* TO THE WORLD COUNCIL—TELL IT LIKE IT IS, DANNY!

"I guess I'd better get used to this," Hank hollers over his shoulder, and I'm struck again by the enormity of what that means for him. Abruptly, he honks the horn loud and long. I see the face of a young woman in the crowd light up with recognition. She whispers hurriedly to a friend, who apparently isn't sure. Then the first woman waves frantically. "Mr. Cochran, Mr. Cochran." Hank honks again and smiles as traffic carries us away.

The real estate agent is waiting for us when we pull up in front of the Wilshire high-rise. It's a luxury building, all glass, marble and fountains—a bit sterile, but he could walk to UCLA, where he's already been invited to teach a seminar.

The place has every conceivable amenity and maybe its lack of individual personality is just what Hank needs right now—he'll have to make his own imprint. On our way up to the twenty-third floor, the excited, flustered manager asks Eddie if he's with the Secret Service. Hank and I trade amused glances; Eddie raises a finger to his lips and solemnly whispers, "That's a secret, ma'am."

Next we check out a charming duplex in Beverly Hills, which I nix right away because it's the kind of homey place you could curl up and die in. A refuge would be counterproductive; Hank needs to start living again.

The last place on our list is in Pacific Palisades. We're cutting back up Sunset, just about to cross over the freeway, when I notice a black Toyota that I'm almost certain I saw parked outside the Wilshire building. Breaking the rule and leaning forward, I call it to Eddie's attention. "Turn right," he instructs Hank sharply. Hank responds like a trained soldier, veering to the right, taking the street alongside the freeway; the Toyota follows. "Run the light," Eddie commands. "Step on it!"

Hank pushes the pedal to the floor and we speed past the line of cars waiting to turn left onto the freeway. Luckily, there's not much traffic past the freeway ramp. A pickup pulling out from the right swerves and screeches to a halt. Doing nearly sixty, Hank grips the wheel, his face frozen. The Toyota pulls alongside. "Get down," Eddie yells. I dive to the floor. There's a crack of gunfire. Shattering glass.

"Nora!" Hank shouts, still steering crazily up the street.

"I'm all right." But I see that Eddie isn't. He's slumped down in the seat and blood is dripping through to the back. I start to get up from the floor, but more gunfire blasts the rear window. Something grazes my shoulder, glass I think. I see my shirt is torn and there's some blood.

"Stay down," Eddie groans. "Turn the car around."

Hank obeys instantly, slamming on the brakes, wheeling dangerously around on the shoulder and speeding back in the opposite direction. The Toyota nearly runs off the road, but recovers, and through the glass web of a back window I see it gaining on us. We hit light traffic again, but Hank keeps up the pace, veering wildly and leaning on the horn as we tear through intersections, causing chaos all around us. I scream for him to take a right and head for the huge white complex across the freeway; it's a hospital. Skidding around the corner, we race over the freeway, wind around and tear into the hospital entrance. The Toyota doesn't follow.

Hank squeals up to the emergency door, jumps out of the car and starts yelling, while I climb over the seat to look at Eddie. He's unconscious, breathing unevenly. White-jacketed men pull him gingerly from the car onto a stretcher and carry him inside, while Hank talks to an intern.

In minutes, the LAPD is here, alerted by the gunfire. We all sit in the lobby of the emergency room while I try to explain. Then the overwhelmed officer excuses himself to phone his precinct, Lieutenant Hacket at the Santa Monica police department and the FBI, in that order. I try to call Nathan in New York, but Jonah tells me he's on his way to LA and I'm too much in shock to ask why.

Finally a nurse takes me firmly by the arm and leads me to an examining table, where she orders me to sit while she removes a tiny shard of glass from my shoulder and dresses my token wound. A scratch, that's all. She tears off a piece of adhesive tape and does a quick repair job on my shirt. Down the hall, the direction they took Eddie, the commotion continues.

Agent Williams and an Agent Cassidy arrive just as the doctor is telling us that the bullet nicked a lung, but that Eddie should be all right. They make us repeat the incident frame by frame, and this time an image squeezes past my shock, a blurred face in the backseat of the Toyota, a black jacket with the outline of a dragon. "I think it was the same kid who pushed me out of the way of that van at the airport," I say, stunned. Williams nods. They checked him out earlier and the information he gave at the scene didn't pan out; he was obviously working with Le Patronage; the rescue was a setup. Now I recall that Katy told me she couldn't find him when she tried to make arrangements for an appropriate reward; I thought I'd remembered the address wrong.

Williams reminds Hank that he's entitled to Secret Service protection if he wants it, that we can't be sure I was the target, but Hank declines.

"Have it your way—you end up with me instead. I have orders to keep both you and Ms. Whitney on ice until further notice."

The events of the past half hour appear in strobelike bursts before my eyes. Miraculously, we're not dead, but who's going to stop this? Can't somebody *do* something? Williams says that he and Agent Cassidy will watch over Hank and me at a "safe house"—which I guess refers to someplace obscure—for a few days.

A few days. "Maybe I'm dense, but what's the point?" I can hear the borderline hysteria in my voice. "These guys aren't in any hurry. If I'm supposed to be some sort of symbol, they won't mind waiting a week or two, then killing me."

"My orders are from the president," Williams replies.

Hank's arm, still shaking, slips around me. For a man who seemed on the edge of a nervous breakdown a few days ago, he's handling himself pretty well. In a tired voice he explains how we literally have no choice; that the system needs to feel it's done its best to protect us. I nod, too worn out to think much beyond the moment anyway. Like he says, I have no choice.

I don't want to leave until Eddie's out of surgery, but they don't give me a choice about that, either. Hank and I are smuggled out some side entrance and driven through countless winding back streets to a modest apartment building in an area I don't recognize. Inside, Agent Cassidy makes us each a tuna sandwich. Tomorrow they'll worry about things like clothes and letting friends and family know we're all right.

"That was pretty fancy driving," I remark, as Hank and I sip stale instant decaf.

He smiles. "See, you didn't believe me when I said I was a good driver. During my death-wish teenage years, I used to drive stock cars."

The TV news says nothing about our escapade. Cassidy phones the hospital and is told that Eddie is out of surgery and in fair condition; then he leaves to check the perimeter of the building. Williams peers steadily out the front window, while Hank and I huddle together in protective prison.

Naturally, Hank's a walking encyclopedia on Le Patronage. He tells me that the group is a fraternity of hard-line US profiteers, suspected, over the past few years, of manipulating the futures market, infiltrating both the Securities and Exchange Commission and the Federal Reserve Board, terminating an aggressive senior officer at a major pharmaceutical company, as well as an unfortunate junior officer at some offshore bank, and conducting ongoing heavy espionage throughout the Pacific Rim.

"I don't know why I didn't think of it before. A strict emissions control schedule will probably cost them a lot. I guess they figure that any vivid reminder of Melanie's death—such as yours, or maybe mine—would knock the spirit out of a meaningful move for change, buy them more time." He stops and sighs. "Can you ever forgive me, Nora? For Bret Hauser, I mean?"

I start to assure him that nobody thinks it's his fault—that groups like Le Patronage are insidious, they find out whatever they want to know—but isn't that what he's tried to tell me from the beginning? Hank knows that Bret Hauser and Le Patronage had nothing to do with Melanie's death, because I told him what Hauser said on the videotape; I'm glad he didn't actually see the tape though, didn't have to watch Hauser's face as he called Melanie's assassin a patriot.

Cassidy returns, tosses us each a bag of pretzels and asks if we want more coffee. When our cups are refilled, Hank tells me about his first session with Dr. Ferris and says he's aware now that his paranoia had gotten out of hand. It strikes me as funny that he's willing to admit this, at this particular moment, when everybody *is* after us.

"Conspiracy theory is addictive," he says. "You know, suddenly everything you see seems to be connected, and the import is so great you can't get your mind around it. You keep demanding patterns, forcing sense into everything even when it isn't there."

I understand. *Conspiracy* is one of those infinite words—conspiracy to create a conspiracy to create a conspiracy—but we all tried to make sense of Melanie's death, each in our own way. It's hard to accept that a president's assassination, this time anyway, was a senseless act committed by a senseless person for no real reason at all. I think of Jennie Wheeler's eyes, the way they looked in that photo; and then I remember Bret Hauser's eyes, cold and full of purpose. Different—both crazy, but different.

In a halting voice, Hank talks about seeing those placards today, realizing that what Melanie started hasn't been lost. "When I finally accepted the fact that she had an affair, it was like another knife plunged into the same raw wound, but somehow the extra pain has, well, given me a better balance."

I've already told him that I saw Jacques, and most of what was said. Unlike Jacques, who was also obsessed with Melanie, whose life was also consumed by her, Hank will survive.

The day's exertion catches up with both of us at the same time and we retire to separate bedrooms. Cassidy and Williams are playing gin rummy in the living room. Just before I fall asleep I remember being told that Nathan Marks was on his way to Los Angeles. I start to get up, thinking I'll ask one of the guys to check around, find out where he is, let me talk to him. Then I remember that Nathan and the FBI don't mix very well. I could call Jonah in New York, but I'm betting they won't let me use the phone—and, by this time, I'm too tired to care.

THIRTY-ONE

The knock on the door isn't gentle. It's a steady pounding that begins in my dream, then slips with me into the upside-down reality of a bleak bedroom I don't immediately recognize, a "safe house" bedroom. Pound, pound. And then a loud, insistent voice. "Wake up, Ms. Whitney."

Pulling on the same skirt and torn shirt I rolled all over the floor of the car in yesterday, I open the door. "I think I'd like you to call me Nora."

"We got an all clear about an hour ago," Agent Williams announces. "There's doughnuts and coffee in the kitchen; then we'll drive you home. And, you're supposed to go to your office as soon as you've had a chance to get cleaned up."

"What?"

"Which part?" he asks dryly. "The all clear came from Washington—they say you're no longer in danger. The message about getting back to work was relayed by our local bureau secretary—your boss called. Agent Cassidy brought in the doughnuts and I made the coffee. That's all I know."

I'm trying to decide if I'm still dreaming when Hank pokes his head around the kitchen door. "That's all he knows," he repeats.

Dazed, I consume a doughnut and gulp a cup of coffee, then splash some water in my face and brush my teeth with my finger. In the backseat of Williams's car, Hank mourns the bullet-ridden Jaguar and decides to rent the Wilshire high-rise apartment; he is gallantly keeping up a steady monologue, though I'm hardly listening. The FBI vehicle stops first at Hank's hotel, where he and I hug each other and I promise to call him as soon as the fog clears enough to see what's going on. Then I'm delivered to my house, where Agents Williams and Cassidy do a perfunctory check and bid me a polite good-bye. The house is empty; neither Dexter nor Albie is anywhere on the premises.

Warily, I walk through each room, peering in closets and behind drapes, feeling mentally violated. Maybe I'm a little slow adapting, but I don't feel so safe yet. How can I? One minute I'm *on ice* and the next, it's *Have a nice day.* Just because someone in Washington says so? Where are Albie and Dexter? Did that same someone in Washington give Nathan Marks the all clear too? And where the hell is Nathan?

My answering machine light flashes persistently. *Where are you? It's David. I've tried your office twice; what's going on? Call me!*

Click. *Hi, Nora, it's Katy. Call in as soon as you get back, will you? It's important.* What could be so important that Katy would track me down through the FBI? I wonder. Obviously, this message was left earlier. I try to construct a timeline, but end up chiding myself for being too cheap to buy an answering machine that gives you the time and date of your messages.

There's nothing from Nathan—not a single word to explain why I'm no longer a matter of anyone's concern.

Cursing the FBI for their stupid need-to-know hierarchy, I go into the bathroom and turn on the shower, eager to wash away the scum of the past twenty-four hours. I want to believe it's over, but the act of taking off my clothes triggers a wave of unbearable helplessness; I know that my body isn't convinced yet. Retrieving the baseball bat from under my bed, I take it into the shower with me, propping it against the opaque fiberglass door as I quickly scrub myself and wash my hair with my eyes open.

I arrive at the Century City Towers in the guise of a woman of purpose. I'm sure no one can tell that the body beneath the tailored suit is racked with nervous fury, that the head beneath its sheen of brushed hair throbs with bitter questions. But Katy isn't fooled. She intercepts me in the outer lobby, literally plants her perfect form between me and the door. "Wait a minute, Nora," she says. "Maybe you'd better sit down here for a second; you don't look right."

"I need to make a phone call," I say, stepping around her. "What was the big deal yesterday, anyway? What was so important?"

I'm striding toward my office as I talk; Katy scampers along beside me, but she doesn't answer my question. "There's somebody in there, Nora. You weren't here, so he's been using your office."

I don't have to ask who she's talking about, because the voice booming through the closed door is unmistakable. I walk in without knocking and see Nathan Marks's massive body sitting behind my desk, his broad face contorted as he growls into the phone. Dropping into one of my leather side chairs, I stare at him pointedly. After a minute, he hangs up the phone. "You're all right?" he says; it's not really a question. "Eddie's going to be all right, too."

I nod. "Someone, presumably Le Patronage, tried to shoot me," I say, "did shoot Eddie. But now everything's just fine—at least that's what the FBI tells me. What the hell does that mean? I suppose you know."

"Yes, I do. I was the one who convinced a couple of key members of Le Patronage that their obsession with you was misguided, that since it's already too late to put out the fires you started for Court, they weren't going to gain much by killing you."

His voice drops a few decibels, settles into a narrative tone as if he's telling a story or teaching a class. "This sort of thing isn't their strength really—they're far more effective with brains than brawn. At insider trading they have no match, but they should stay out of the physical-damage business. Others do it much better—*and*, I assured them, others are getting annoyed with them.

"They argued a bit at first, but let's just say I have the ability to add a great deal of misery to their collective life. In the end, I made them understand how they'd let themselves get sidetracked by clumsy prejudices and were making more of you than you really merited. These particular men, you see, don't like powerful women very much. If Court's environmental plan passes, it'll be a major blow to them, but they'll find other ways to make up for their losses.

"When I got their official word that they would leave you alone, I passed the information, through contacts, to the FBI in Washington, but it took most of the night to work its way through the channels." Shifting his bulk in my inadequate chair, he sighs deeply. "Unfortunately, I was still in the midst of these negotiations while you and Henry Cochran were dodging bullets and my loyal friend Eddie was taking one in the lung. I didn't find that out until I got to LA."

All of this would be good reading if it weren't actually happening. I stare at the floor, trying to form words around something that's been bothering me from the moment Nathan started talking. Squaring my shoulders, I address the man behind my desk.

"You *know* the men who are responsible for all this. Not some pompous name, but the people, the individual people, you know who they are."

"Some of them," he responds. "The FBI knows who they are too. They just can't prove it."

"But *you* could prove it. You talked to men who admitted they ordered someone to kill me. You could have let the FBI listen in—any number of things. Goddamnit, Nathan, you have it in your power to stop these people."

A detached expression settles over his face. "I'm going to tell you the same thing I told Melanie Lombard," he says. "I don't see good guys and bad guys the same way you do. And I operate with a certain degree of autonomy; I'm effective, in part, because my respect for privacy is *never* questioned."

I want to yell, spit, break things, but none of that will alleviate what I'm feeling. What is this bizarre outlaw code of conduct? It's like honor among thieves, but Nathan Marks is no thief. I wonder if Nathan, just as much as Bret Hauser, is also the stuff of our nation's nightmares. And yet, it's because of him, not the police or the FBI or the Secret Service, that I can go on living. Because of Nathan, Melanie and I did not fall prey to the whims of four punks in that subway station so many years ago. Because of this man and his Freedom Foundation, countless lives are more bearable, even richer.

I was wrong when I told Jacques that I didn't know any sultans. I'm grateful to Nathan, but I realize that I don't understand him and I don't like him. Melanie did—but then she had more in common with him than I do.

"Groups like Le Patronage are old school," he says, watching my face. I have the feeling he knows everything I've been thinking and that it amuses him. "They don't understand how rapidly the world is changing. They don't have a clue, for example, how valuable your *real* work is—far more important in the long run than your political dabbling. Le Patronage is part of the past, dedicated to the status quo; their heads are full of commodities like gold and oil. But here we are— looking at the future." He taps his wide fingers on the top of my desk; not one at a time, but all together, as if he's punctuating the end of his speech. "My reason for wanting you alive is vastly more interesting than their reason for wanting you dead," he says.

A rap at the door; then Neil enters. "Well, what do you think?" he asks me, smugly. Suddenly, I flash on the fact that I have no idea why Nathan is in Los Angeles, or sitting behind my desk. My revelation is obviously all over my face. "You haven't told her," he accuses Nathan, then chuckles.

"Mr. Marks and I have an agreement. I tried to reach you yester-

day, so you could help us pound it out, but you were otherwise occu-
pied." He goes on to explain how he woke up in the middle of the
night with this terrific idea about Nathan joining his new syndicate.
In typical Neil Mackey style he charges through the business techni-
calities, outlining all the gives-and-takes and wrapping up a neat little package that constitutes, from his description, the most
innovative alliance ever formed. These two men—my suave Republican boss and his new friend the oversized anarchist, both wearing
expensive suits—grin at each other. I'm simply blown away.

Nathan finally relinquishes my chair and he and Neil—strange
bedfellows, indeed—head down the hall. I'm still in a state of semi-
stun when Deena calls. "At last count, we've got a chance," she says.
"Can you believe it? This damn bill might just squeak through." I tell
her to watch the Business Section for a major announcement about
Neil's syndicate. From her response I assume that the syndicate will
probably be offered a government grant, whether they want it or not.

THIRTY-TWO

The calendar hanging above the desk in my den has a large photo of an Amazon rain forest; it also has numbers that insist only one month has passed since this all began—one month since the anniversary of Melanie's assassination. I find it hard to believe, so much has happened in a month. For one thing, I've discovered some truth in Melanie's fairy tale, that the world doesn't have to be the way you think you see it. I know that January 23rd will be forever infamous in our nation's history. But endings are also beginnings.

Ironically, I'm sitting on the couch rereading passages from David's book *Patrice* when the doorbell rings and here he is, a large yellow envelope in his hand, wearing the same olive green sweater he had on the night we got drunk on tequila shooters. His eyes are red, overworked, and he hasn't shaved; he looks terrible.

"I finished a draft of the part about Jacques DeBrin," he says. "I think it's good; I think it's very good. I want to know what you think." He walks into the den, takes a sheaf of papers from the envelope and tosses them on the coffee table; then he collapses on the couch. "Read it now, please, will you?"

I pick up the papers and sit down at my desk, my stomach queasy. I've tried to prepare myself for that distant moment when I'll have to open his published book, turn the pages, read these words, but I didn't expect to have to do it so soon. In this raw, loose-leafed form, it seems too personal somehow. No editors, designers, or giant presses between author and product. David *wrote* this. And after investing thirty years in my friendship with Melanie, I guess I still resent having to discover her in the pages of David's manuscript.

He's watching me and I know that I can't back out. I start to read and within a page he's got me, lifted me out of the mundane and immersed me in a most extraordinary love story. I read it slowly and when I'm finished I keep my eyes firmly fixed on the paper; I don't want to look at David.

He writes wonderfully; Melanie is alive on these pages, and so is her lover—but it still says that the president of the United States cheated on her husband. I can already see how that kernel of information will be distilled from the story and used; there's no way Melanie Lombard will remain the same shining symbol to America's little girls. Sadly, I realize that deep inside, beneath reason, I hoped that David would change his mind and not write about it, that he would decide the image was more important than the truth. But David is a biographer, not a storyteller. Melanie was the storyteller.

Gathering my emotions into a manageable pile, I lay the papers facedown on the desk. She won't be a shining symbol, but when the disappointment fades, maybe the rest will come back. This country can't be that tough an audience; not everything will be overshadowed by one revelation. "It's more than good, David; it couldn't be written any better."

"But you still hate it," he says, sitting up on the couch and eyeing me grimly.

"I don't hate the book, I'm just sorry about the circumstances."

"But when the book is published, when it all hits the fan, you'll hate *me*. When Henry and Ben Cochran have to suffer all over again, accompanied by pitying looks, you'll hate me. Count on it."

"I told you before, it's not your fault. Melanie knew what she was doing."

He gets up, takes a few steps in my direction, then spins around, walks to the window and stands, staring out. "Damnit, Nora, I'm not willing to feel guilty about this book; I refuse to feel rotten about what I do. I—I think I came over here to say good-bye to you." He turns slowly, as if he's forcing himself to face me. "We're stuck in a situation that won't go away—and I can't stand the thought of looking in your eyes somewhere down the road and watching the fallout from this book eat away at whatever we try to build."

"But, David, this conflict has been with us all along. You knew you were going to write about things I'd rather the world didn't know. And you have. What's different *now?*"

"What's different is the way I feel. You don't say anything, you just have that look on your face like I've smeared shit all over the sun."

My body feels heavy, worn down, worn out. He's right, this will never work; I should have known that David and I could never work. Then, in a surge of sudden energy, blood rushes to my head. I'm holding an empty coffee cup and I have to make a conscious effort not to hurl it at him.

"You son of a bitch. You have the nerve to dissect my hang-ups, tell me to give them up, then you refuse to cope with your own feelings." I hear my voice catch, but I'm determined to say this. "Isn't everybody 'stuck in a situation'? So what if your damn book keeps coming up over and over for the rest of our lives, so will a whole pile of other baggage. And as for the idea of your smearing the sun—I think that's more your problem than it is mine. Melanie is no sun to me."

The shock on his face works like a mirror, jars me out of my anger. My voice melts. "David, I need to know right now whether or not you have the courage to be my lover. If I can dig down in myself to find it, can't you?"

"Omigod," he gasps. He crosses the room and puts his arms around me, holding me tightly to his chest and burying his face in my hair.

"If I ever try to chicken out on us again—even a little bit—promise me you'll beat the hell out of me. Exactly like you just did."

After several minutes I ask him when he last slept and he shakes his head as if he can't remember. I suggest that he let me put him to bed, but he declines. "No, I'll go home. I want to finish this section, then I promise I'll sleep. I could use a cup of coffee, though."

He follows me into the kitchen and stares at me thoughtfully while I measure out the coffee. "What did you mean when you said Melanie was not a 'sun' to you?" he asks.

"I guess I meant that, for me, a lot of her shine is already gone, on a personal level. You see, she wasn't really the friend I thought she was. I used to think that she actually valued me, but I was just a useful cog in the programmed part of her life, not really important."

"I can't believe you think that," he says. "Is it because of DeBrin?" He sees my hesitation and doesn't wait for an answer. "Yeah, I know about you and Jacques—oh, he didn't tell me; he probably even forgot she mentioned it in her letters."

I turn off the water and set the glass pot on the counter. He's already out of his chair, heading for the den. When he comes back, he's clutching a packet of letters. "I wasn't sure about giving these to you," he says, "but if you're laboring under the delusion that Melanie didn't value you as a friend, as a mentor, then you'd damn well better read them."

He tosses the packet on the table, then he puts his hands on my shoulders. "She didn't tell you she was still seeing Jacques at first because she was experimenting, pretending she was someone else. But then her secrecy backfired on her. After you and he had that little fling, she thought you might hate her if you found out. Over all those years she was afraid to tell you, afraid of your disapproval. Melanie saw everything in her life as being in a state of precarious balance."

No. No, I think, looking at him. *She wasn't like that at all. She stood up to people. She wasn't afraid of me; she wasn't afraid of anyone.* Suddenly disoriented, I take a step back, lean against the counter. *That's right, isn't it? I knew her from the beginning and she was never afraid of anything.*

Or was it just that I didn't *want* her to be afraid of anything, that *I* needed her to be fearless?

Numbly I pick up the packet. It's several inches thick, lightweight blue airmail envelopes held together by a rubber band. These must be all the letters Melanie sent to Jacques over a lifetime. "Thank you," I say softly.

"Look, I should be at a natural breakpoint in a couple of weeks," David says. "What if we take a weekend and drive up the coast or something?"

"I'd really like that."

After he leaves, I wander out into the backyard; the sun has gone down and the glow of a nearly full moon washes the orchard. I want to tell her I understand that I was a lousy friend, too. That I'm sorry. I'm sorry for insisting that she always be strong, for not allowing her to seem vulnerable. But as soon as I think these things, I know that we, she and I, put it together that way. My insisting couldn't make her less vulnerable, but it did keep her strong. And in return she showed me that anything is possible.

As I gaze up at the darkened sky, I realize that Melanie Lombard is the only person besides my mother who was willing to hang around for most of my life. We took hold of each other, we didn't let go. I wonder if David and I can do that.

Inside the house, I start to remove the rubber band from Melanie's letters; then I change my mind. I carry the packet into the den and put it in a desk drawer. I'll read them someday, but not now. I don't need to read them now.

About the Author

RACHEL CANON was born on an army base in California in 1944, and grew up in Des Moines, Iowa. She has worked as an advertising writer in New York and California, and most recently directed corporate communications for an investment management firm. She now lives in Los Angeles, and writes full-time. *The Anniversary* is her first novel.

About the Type

This book was set in Photina, a typeface designed by José Mendoza in 1971. It is a very elegant design with high legibility, and its close character fit has made it a popular choice for use in quality magazines and art gallery publications.